Stark Choice

by

John Worsley Simpson

A Harry Stark Mystery

Stark Choice

Cover Art by *Debbie Taylor*

The Wild Rose Press, Inc.
PO Box 708
Adams Basin, NY 14410-0708
Visit us at www.thewildrosepress.com

Publishing History
First Edition, 2022
Trade Paperback ISBN 978-1-5092-4027-2
Digital ISBN 978-1-5092-4028-9

A Harry Stark Mystery
Previously Published 2018 MuseItUp Publishing
Published in the United States of America

"About fifteen minutes later, Stokes arrived. Ten minutes after that, I heard shots. I pulled through a gap in the trees, ran to the barn, came through that side door there with my weapon levelled, saw the woman standing there staring at Stokes's body. I shouted 'police.' Actually, I think I got to 'poli—' when the sledgehammer slammed into my head. I think the big guy just punched me."

"I hate to say this," Stark said, "but why didn't they shoot you, too?"

"I don't know. The only thing I can figure is that Beavis—"

"Who's Beavis?" Stark said.

"The policeman whose body is lying out there," Henry said angrily.

"Sorry," Stark said. "You were saying, Noel?"

"I figure Beavis must have parked on the road and then when he heard the shots, he drove in. If you drive on the gravel road that leads up here, it makes a hell of a racket. They must have heard him, thought there were a lot of us out there, and panicked. They drove straight through the barn doors, smashed them open. Beavis must have been on the radio, calling for backup from the York Regionals—"

"Which you should have done," Henry growled.

"Yeah, I know. Anyway, I guess they came out so fast, they caught him by surprise and as they drove by, they shot him."

"Through the window of the car," Henry said. "And then they opened the car door, and—poor Beavis fell out."

Praise for John Worsley Simpson

"John Worsley Simpson takes us to a hot summer in Toronto. The body of a 78-year-old jewel courier is found, stabbed, in an office building. Homicide detective Harry Stark is called in. As Stark begins to dig into the victim's life, he runs into his old nemesis, Sal Martineri, a slippery criminal Stark has never been able to pin anything on. With [Stark Choice, Simpson] proves he is a new Canadian writer worth watching."

~ *ANNA ASIMAKOPULOS, Montreal Gazette*

Preface

Saul Rabinovitch rose early, as older men do. Awake and on his feet, he knew he'd made it through another night. He performed his morning devotions, shachris, and, his soul taken care of, he did forty push-ups, keeping his lean body straight. Without a break, he rolled over and—wedging his feet beneath the dresser—completed fifty sit-ups: not the stomach crunches the kinesiologists and the physiotherapists advise for the sake of the back, but the full, floor-to-bent-knees version he had been taught in the Israeli army many years before.

There was no shower in his tiny Toronto apartment in an aged four-storey brick building on a quiet, tree-lined street off Bathurst, north of St. Clair. Rabinovitch ran six inches of moderately warm water in the tiny claw-footed tub. He was not a particularly frugal man, but electricity wasn't included in the rent, and he had to conserve what little income he had for the one vice that took most of it, a vice apparent from the copies of the *Daily Racing Form* scattered throughout the apartment. He stepped into the tub, supremely confident that his wiry, muscled legs would not let him down. There were men in his club years younger who would have taken longer to lower themselves into the bath than he took to cover himself with a film of soap, scrub his body vigorously, rinse, clamber out of the tub and dry himself with a faded rag of a towel. He lathered his face with a brush and shaved with an ancient razor, patting the result appreciatively with Aqua Velva.

He sat naked in the kitchen as he ate his breakfast of whole-wheat toast and muesli with no sugar and a little skim milk. He dumped the dishes on a pile of others in the sink and gave the drizzling tap a futile turn, thankful that the rent *did* include water. He returned to the table and drank his tea, reflecting on who he was and where he was. At seventy-three, he felt better than he had ever felt in his life, a life that had begun with more promise than had been realized. But he was certain he had many more good years left, much better years, the best years of his life. Today would be a good day, he was sure of it.

It was the middle of an oppressively hot July in 1997. The tea was making him perspire. Old people were dying in the heat, and even Rabinovitch, in his good shape, sometimes had trouble walking any distance in the hottest part of the day. The apartment had no air-conditioning, but Rabinovitch had an ancient and inadequate window air-conditioner in his bedroom that he used as little as possible. Because the apartment was in the west end of the building, if there was an evening breeze, as there had been the night before, it came through the tiny window in the living room. He slept in there on the couch for the little relief it provided. But the breeze had ended with the morning sun, and now the temperature was beginning to rise. He didn't want to be sweaty. He wanted to look cool and confident.

He hurried back to the bathroom for his morning constitutional, and hustled to the bedroom to dress, pausing for his morning ritual of the biscuit tin. As he did every morning, he retrieved it from the bottom of a drawer, removing the contents to expose a faded, worn photograph, which he held in his hand and gazed at with a longing sigh. A photograph of a young woman. He kissed it, replaced it in the tin, put back the rest of the items and returned the tin to the drawer, covering it with the other contents.

As he stood at the open apartment door, he looked around for a final time and ran through a checklist in his mind. He had left no lights on, he hadn't used the stove. The fridge door was firmly closed. He patted something in his pocket, stepped into the dimly lit hallway, closed and locked the door, checked it, and marched toward the stairway, head high, shoulders back, stomach in.

Chapter One

Detective Harry Stark swung his feet to the floor, sat for a moment on the edge of the bed, tried to shake the fog out of his head, stood up unsteadily and went looking for a cigarette. He found a blue Gauloises pack on the kitchen table. Empty. "Shit." He crumpled it and threw it in the sink. "Carol, have you got any cigarettes?"

No answer.

"Carol."

He had awakened her.

"What?" she said, groggy and irritated.

"I said, have you got any cigarettes?"

"God. There's a pack in my purse."

He opened the purse, took out a pack of ultra lights and grimaced.

"How can you smoke these things? They're like sucking hot air."

"So don't smoke them."

He sat down heavily at the table, took a cigarette out of the pack, snapped off the filter, lit the cigarette, inhaled and made a face. Carol Weems was now standing in the entrance to the kitchen, leaning against the door jamb, wearing only her panties. She stretched, rubbed her eyes, watched Stark, then went and stood behind him, combing his hair back with her fingernails. She tilted his head back against her breasts. She smelled of sleep. Stark reached up, squeezed her hand and kept hold of it.

"You want some breakfast?" she asked.

"No. I've got to go downtown."

She shook his hand from hers and pushed his head away.

"Oh, great, just bloody great. I thought you were going to be here. It's my day off, and now all of a sudden you decide to make an appearance downtown? That's just wonderful."

"Don't panic. I'll be right back. God, it's hot in here. As soon as you come out of the bedroom, you can feel it. Makes the place stink."

"Socks," Weems said, but she was on her way back to the bedroom.

"I'm going to put the air-conditioner on in the front window," Stark said. He went into the front room, raising his voice so Weems could hear him. "Come with me if you want." He turned the air-conditioner on, and had to speak even louder to be heard over its rumble. "You can turn the air-conditioner off in the bedroom now, Carol," he called out.

He heard her say something, but couldn't make it out.

"What did you say?"

Weems came to the door of the bedroom.

"I said, your landlord must be the meanest son of a bitch in the Beach¬—"

"Beaches."

"Jesus. Everybody calls it the Beach but you."

"Beaches. What were you saying about Johnny Yuma. He can't change his stripes that easily. After all, he *was* a rebel."

"One day, Jimmy Yu is going to hear you calling him that and he'll have you for racism."

"Racial insensitivity. They'd never make racism stick.

2

Speaking about stick, my God it's already, you know, like a hot, wet blanket covering everything."

"Right, so why doesn't Jimmy Yu have central air-conditioning in his building?"

"Oh, he's got it downstairs in the dental practice, all right. He just doesn't have it up here. In his defence—and by the way, you might be accused of making racially motivated assumptions yourself."

"Yeah, right."

"In his defence, Jimmy Yu had the old heating/air-conditioning system taken out when he bought the building. He had baseboard heaters put in to give the tenants closer control over things, and he put in the air-conditioner in the bedroom and the one in the living room, so the tenant could control that, too. Don't be too hard on our Johnny Yuma, the rebel of Queen Street, late of Hong Kong. In a normal summer, it's perfectly cool in here. A month like this is a once-in-a-decade thing. God. I'm already sweating. Anyway, about downtown, I'm only going to stick my head in, make an appearance. I'm *supposed* to be working on the Karen Sheltoe case." His voice suggested he wasn't pleased with the assignment.

Weems came around the corner into the kitchen, buttoning her blouse.

"Sheltoe? Isn't that the woman they found raped and murdered near the Bluffers Park Yacht Club? That must be, what, two years ago?"

"Almost exactly. Some jerk called the department yesterday and said Sheltoe's husband did it. Peters then gets the bright idea that he wants *me* to take a look at it. It wasn't my case in the first place. I haven't even looked at the file. It's just a crank call, for God's sake, guy wouldn't give his name, probably some boozy relative of the victim who took a look at the calendar and realized it's been two years since the woman died and he's got an idea about the husband in his head. We'd normally just ignore it, of course—the caller didn't talk about any new evidence or anything like that, as far as I know—but it's just the kind of opportunity Peters seizes on to pile crap on me. He's still trying to bore my bum out of there. But you know that. He's been pulling these stunts ever since the jerk got snookered when he tried to make me ride a desk. Good old Nutsy Nuttall. Helps to have friends in high places."

"Deputy Chief Stephen J. Nuttall. You went to high school or something with him, didn't you?"

"We were rookies together. Anyway, there are always silver linings. Since Peters has given me the Sheltoe case, I'll have to spend a lot of time following up leads, won't I? And I won't have to show my face downtown, will I? Today I'm just going to pop in, grunt a couple of times and leave. Did you turn off the air-conditioner in the bedroom?"

"No, I didn't."

"Jeez," Stark said, shaking his head. He went into the bedroom and switched the air-conditioner off and almost immediately the air felt heavy and dead and stifling. He retreated from the room quickly, almost shutting the door behind him, but leaving it open a little so Powder the cat could get out and prowl around after Weems left.

"I don't get it, Harry," Weems said. "How can you complain about being bored, and then just go through the motions on this Sheltoe case?"

Stark stretched and then, fearing he was making his stomach bulge, he folded his arms quickly across his chest, pulled in his gut and turned away from Weems. He was self-conscious about his shape, which was much better than he thought.

4

"It's a complex set of circumstances and thought processes, Carol, and I couldn't expect you to understand all the subtleties and nuances involved."

"Screw you."

"Anyway, the real reason I've got to go downtown is to buy some cigarettes. You *know* I can't get Gauloises in the Beaches."

"That's too bad," Weems said ironically. "I'll stay here, read my book. What time is it?"

"Ten o'clock."

"What time is your shift *supposed* to start, Harry? Or is Homicide on flex hours now?" Weems was a detective in 55 Division.

"Something like that."

"I don't know how you get away with it, great Detective Harry Stark."

"That's *how* I get away with it."

"What, because you're so good?"

"Exactly."

"God."

"Listen," he said, "if you sit on the couch, you don't need to have the air-conditioner on full blast." As he said it, a rivulet of perspiration burst from a pore beneath his right arm and ran down his side.

****

Few things could persuade Salvatore Cataldi to get up early. Early was for peasants. He did things at the right time and at the right pace. Nine o'clock, antemeridian, was the right time. Slow and steady was the right pace. He had been taught to stay in control, to consider each movement before he made it, and especially to consider each word before he uttered it. Today was no different from any other day. He had a leisurely breakfast, read the paper, spent a long and careful time at his toilet. He admired his youthful slender form, his classic good looks and his closely trimmed black hair in the full-length mirror on the back of the bathroom door. He found nothing wanting. Maybe he could have been a few inches taller.

****

Howard Stokes had not been able to sleep. The sun had just begun bleeding into the scalp of the city as he arrived at his shop. Stokes didn't function well in the heat, and a day of record highs had been threatened on the radio in his Cadillac, but Stokes had not been listening. He was worried. He owed a lot of money.

****

In the east end of the city, someone was rising who had a mission of revenge to perform. Another phone call was in order, a call to the police. A call to Homicide.

Chapter Two

Marilyn, the Homicide Unit secretary, sneaked up on Stark as he was standing at the pigeon holes, sorting through a stack of envelopes, pitching them, one after another, into the wastebasket. She pinched him on his right buttock. He jumped and spun around.

"Jesus. You know, if I did that to you—"

"Promises, promises." Marilyn was in her forties, about five-two and a good hundred-and-sixty pounds. She was in little danger of being pinched by Stark, but she wouldn't have minded. He'd hit the half-century mark in May, and his face and body betrayed years of abuse, but he was a good-looking man and he had a reputation as a lover. "Your timing is bad, big boy. Peters wants to see you."

Stark groaned. He dumped the rest of the mail into the wastebasket and shuffled with exaggerated reluctance toward the office of Inspector Wallace Peters. He stood in the doorway and waited as Peters was going through *his* mail, neatly slicing open every envelope with a long gold opener, carefully extracting the contents and examining them as if they were fragments of the Dead Sea Scrolls. After a time, Stark coughed. Peters spoke without looking up.

"Come in, Stark. Nice of you to show up. Your timing is perfect. I've got something for you. Here." He tossed a yellow rectangular sheet of notepaper across the desk. Stark picked it up. "That's an address on Eglinton, near Bathurst. It's an office building. Call just came in. Hold-up boys are already on the scene. There's a body. I don't know anything else about it. Jewel robbery or something. Get up there. Take Carter with you. He's all we've got at the moment. Sergeant Henry's on a course this morning. I'm running things—" he looked at his watch. "—until lunch. Keep me informed."

"What about Sheltoe case, Inspector? I've—"

"Just get up there."

Stark ignored the instruction to take another detective with him. He almost always ignored Peters's instructions. Grudgingly acknowledged to be the best investigator on the force, Stark could get away with being a lone wolf, except on those rare occasions when Peters actually took an interest in a case because it was high profile, or a superior had given him a nudge. Stark drove up the Bayview Extension with his flasher going, along Moore Avenue to Mount Pleasant, turned north and, to avoid the traffic on Eglinton, drove past it to Broadway, where he turned west, headed north on Yonge to Roselawn, where he deliberately switched on his siren and drove faster, crashing over the speed bumps and, at each one, cursing what he regarded as the yuppies who lived on the street and the city for acceding to their demands for the bumps. He was at the address on the notepaper in twelve minutes.

The building was a six-storey affair on the corner. Probably built in the fifties, it had a brick exterior that had been covered in recent years with alternating strips of beige and brown aluminum that were already showing signs of oxidation. The ground floor was occupied by a finance company and a dental clinic—an appropriate combination, Stark thought, running his tongue over a couple of teeth that badly needed crowns. The notepaper read Unit 501. When he emerged from the car, the heat caught him in the nostrils like two thick fingers. He hurried into the building and took the elevator to the fifth floor. When the elevator door opened, a tall, boyish-looking policeman lazily stepped away from the facing wall in the hallway. Stark flashed his ID, and the cop's back snapped straight. He gestured to his right, where three uniformed officers were standing outside an open office door, listening with wide grins to a grizzled detective telling a joke about a woman and a gorilla and affecting a caricatured woman's voice.

Stark burst the detective's balloon by delivering the punchline before he could: "He never writes, he never calls." The cop, whom Stark recognized as a stalwart of the Morality Squad, who was finishing out his time as a pencil-carrier in Hold-up, spun around, glowering. Then, recognizing Stark, he changed his expression to a weak smile.

"Good morning, Harry," he said. "This is Detective Harry Stark—the *famous* Detective Harry Stark—of the Homicide Unit." The uniformed cops nodded.

Stark grunted and stepped into the office. The Hold-up Squad detective in charge was a little fellow called Ken Coulson, whose short stature would have prevented his joining the force when Stark had become a cop. Stark liked him, which is why he remembered his name, something he didn't often do—both like people *and* remember their names. Coulson was talking to an Ident guy in white coveralls and taking notes. Apart from a cluster of people, one dead, the office was empty—no furniture, bare walls. The body was face-up, gazing at a large water stain on the acoustic-tile ceiling. The front of the man's shirt had a large, circular stain, and there was a pool of blood on the vinyl flooring extending several inches on both sides of the body.

Stark squatted to get a better look at the face. It was the face of a man in his seventies, weathered, leathery, but taut, a good-looking face that might have laughed and cried easily, a face with a story behind it, Stark thought. The stare it was giving the water stain was one of defiance. The man's long, lean body was stylishly clothed. The apparel was casual, but elegant and expensive, youthful: a pale-blue-denim, buttoned-down shirt and well-tailored, tan slacks in a lightweight material, with a perfect crease. Stark's mother would have called him an old fool, would have said he should dress his age.

"So, who was this guy?"

Coulson's head turned slowly. His expression, meant to freeze the questioner who was interrupting his own questions, brightened when he saw it was Stark.

"Harry, great to see you. I see you've brought your whole team with you, as usual."

"I would have brought them, but they've got me driving a moped now as part of the cost-cutting, and there was no room. Who was he?"

Coulson raised an eyebrow in a look of mild disbelief. "You don't know anything about it?"

"Nope."

"He was a courier for a jeweller, a dealer in estate jewellery, a few blocks from here, Howard Stokes. That's the jeweller, not the dead man. He was here for a while, Stokes, I mean, but he asked if he could go back to his shop, said he had a big customer coming in. I told him sure, because I figured you boys—well, you, I guess—could interview him there as easily as here. Stokes doesn't seem to have any connection with this place. In fact, it's a real puzzler what the courier was doing here. *His* name was Saul Rabinovitch, seventy-three years. He's some kind of friend of the jeweller's family or something. Anyway, there was no reason for the courier to be here. He was supposed to be taking a bag of diamonds to the bank, the value of which I don't know. The jewellery guy said he'd have to check his books to see what the value was. He said it's a big amount, but he wouldn't say any more."

"Insurance," Stark said knowingly.

"Yeah, exactly. He *was* shaken up. I'm going over there when we're finished here. Like I say, Rabinovitch was taking the jewels to the bank to put in the safety-deposit box. We found the key on him. The jeweller's is west of here. It's called Starflite. The bank is west of that. There was no reason for him to come east and end up here."

"Where the hell's the coroner?"

"She had to leave. Stabbing on Vaughan Road."

"She? Not Connors?" Stark made a face.

"Yeah."

"So what did *she* say? Is that a bullet wound?"

"Stabbed. This is Frank Furlong." Coulson indicated an Ident officer.

"How's it going, Sarge?" the Ident cop said, Toronto detectives having a rank equivalent to a uniformed sergeant.

"So, Ken, how long has he been dead?"

"Happened about nine o'clock."

"I thought you said he was going to the bank? Banks

don't open till ten."

Coulson smiled. "Some open at nine now. This one does."

"So he's supposed to be going to the bank. He's carrying a valuable bag of jewels. He's a courier. He must be a little nervous about the responsibility and cautious, wants to get to the bank quickly and get the diamonds out of his hands. So why does he go in a completely wrong direction? Something, somebody had to bring him here, right? Who found the guy?"

"The janitor. Listen, I haven't given you the whole picture, Harry. The guy here, Rabinovitch, he carried a gun, a .32 Browning semi-automatic, a popgun, bit of an antique. Apparently he gets the gun out and shoots the assailant. The gun's over there, against the wall. Maybe his assailant grabbed it from him and threw it there, or knocked it out of his hand, or it just flew there when he was stabbed."

"He shot the assailant?"

"Frank?"

They both looked at the Identification Unit officer. He smiled.

"Yeah. Well, the projectile hit here." He went to the wall and pointed at a hole about five feet from the floor. "See, it made a keyhole entry, so it must have been tumbling, deflected by something. The bullet didn't go very deep into the wall, just barely through the wallboard, and then fell to the floor inside the wall." There was a bigger hole at floor level they'd made to retrieve the bullet. "Even a .32 would go deeper than that from where he was standing. Probably would have gone through and into the next office. My guess is it's old ammunition. I figure he must have hit the guy, because there's nothing else in the room for him to hit. But he probably just winged him, because there's no sign of anybody else's blood besides the victim's. We'll check the bullet for traces."

Stark nodded. He pointed to a square metal plate that was leaning against the wall, having been removed from its position on the wall, where it had covered a square hole. "What's that? Did your people take that off for some reason?"

Furlong shrugged.

"Nope. It was like that. It's an access cover for a junction box. I imagine somebody must have been doing some electrical work in here, and just left it."

"Nothing inside the hole?"

"Just the junction box."

"What else do we know, Ken?"

"Well, the suspect was driving a grey van."

The word "suspect" made the same loud clunk in Stark's head it always did. He fancied himself a grammarian, and incorrect usage always bothered him. He had to fight constantly to stop himself from boorishly correcting people, and sometimes the correction just popped out. Toronto cops always used "suspect," when, Harry knew, the right word was "perpetrator," or "assailant," or "culprit." "Suspect" was somebody whose identity they already knew, or thought they knew.

"It was like a delivery van," Coulson said, "but no lettering or anything, just dull grey. One of the women in the finance company was out the back, in the alley, smoking. She said a guy rushed past her wearing one of those sweatsuit tops, with a hood."

"Did she see his face?"

"Nope. Anyway, the van was parked in the alley,

and the guy got in and peeled away. He was carrying a gym bag. She figured he'd just hit the finance company, so she got the tag number."

"You're kidding." Stark smiled in surprise.

Coulson shook his head. "Sorry, the plate comes back as belonging to a black 1987 Buick Park Avenue, owned by a little, old rich lady who lives on a street off Dunvegan. The car's parked in her side drive. She hasn't driven it in weeks. We checked it. The plates are missing."

"That was fast work. How'd you do that?"

"We've been here for an hour, Harry. And—" Coulson chuckled, "we actually have a team working on this. Takes a few seconds on the computer to find out what car the plates belong to. And five minutes for an officer to talk to the woman on Dunvegan. You do have a laptop, don't you, Harry?"

Stark made a dismissive gesture. "You've been here an hour? Why didn't Peters send somebody from Homicide right away?" He answered his own question. "I know why. He wasn't there, that's why. Ted Henry's not there this morning and Peters wanders in on banker's hours. God. Of course, if we had any budget, we wouldn't have the whole staff out on investigations. Those who aren't on vacation."

"Yeah, right."

"Okay, Dunvegan. That's not far from here. They must have stopped off on their way here, and ripped off the plates. Let's go talk to the woman."

"The car lady?" Coulson asked in surprise.

"The one who saw the perpetrator, and have your people interviewed everybody in the building?"

"Yes, they have."

"And?"

"Only the woman saw anything."

"Anybody hear the shot?"

"No, but then only the first floor is occupied. The rest of the building is vacant, except for an import-export broker at the back corner of the second floor, and he's on vacation."

"Wise man in this heat. Although it's pretty cool in this part of the building. The guy who owns it must be going nuts having to pay to keep the whole place cool when most of it is empty."

Coulson shrugged. "I guess with these old buildings, Harry, there's no way to shut off the air-conditioning in one part and leave it on in the rest."

"Mmm. Do we know who owns the building?"

"Nope. You think that's important?"

"I don't know. How does the courier end up here? Somebody had to know that the office was vacant. Got him up here where they could rob him. Something strike you about this thing?"

Coulson looked hard at Stark. He admired the old veteran, eighteen years his senior. He wanted to impress him.

"You mean, could the courier have been in on it? Came here to sell the diamonds to somebody and the guy double-crossed him, or something went sour? He pulls his gun, wings the guy and the guy shivs him?"

"Yeah, something like that." Stark smiled thinly. "Check on the building owner, will you?"

"Right."

"Okay, let's go see this woman."

They found her in the alley, smoking, standing in the shade cast by the building. There was a high board fence along the opposite side of the lane. She was leaning beside a strip of yellow police tape stretched from the fence to the wall of the building. There was another strip at the end of the lane. The woman's hand shook slightly as she put the cigarette to her lips. She was breathing in short gasps, either from too many cigarettes or from the heat, or both. She started when Coulson spoke her name.

"Mrs. Carstairs?"

"Ooh." She held a hand to her chest. She was a stout woman, in her fifties, with tightly permed hair. "I didn't see you come out."

The alley smelled and felt like damp cardboard in a boiler room. The sky was all sun, like a thick slab of yellow margarine, dripping on them. Both detectives were in suits. Stark's was linen—his summer suit, a sort of greenish tan. He'd bought it seven years earlier, at a factory outlet store in Niagara Falls, N.Y. It was not holding up well. Weems hated the suit, called it puke green and kept threatening to donate it to the Salvation Army. But Stark liked the suit because, he said, it had character. In this, as in many things, he was different from the other members of the Homicide Unit, who considered themselves the elite, wore expensive, tailored clothes, were sometimes called "the Good Suits" by other cops and wouldn't have been caught dead in something that had character. Coulson's suit was a light-chocolate. The only creases in it were the intentional ones, down the front of his trousers. He had perfectly coiffed hair, with a part that looked as if it had been made with a T-square. Stark's salt-and-pepper curls hung limp on his scalp and over his ears, like a ragged Brillo pad. Coulson managed to look cool, despite the late July temperature, which would top thirty-four that day. Stark looked as if he were about to melt into a puddle of Irish linen. But despite his sartorial preference, you'd never call Stark a slob. A cascade of perspiration streamed down his back from his hairline. He took out a handkerchief and wiped his face and neck.

"This is Detective Stark. He has some questions for you."

The woman nodded nervously.

"I told the other policemen everything I saw—everything I could remember."

Stark smiled faintly.

"Where was the van parked?"

"Just there." The woman pointed.

"The Ident boys have been over the area," Coulson said. "Just a quick once-over. They'll have a more detailed look when they're finished upstairs."

"Was the engine running? Or did he have to start the van?"

The woman looked thoughtful.

"I don't remember. I didn't notice."

"Well, when he got in, did he take a second before he pulled away, or did he drive off, right away? Which side did he get in, by the way? Driver's side?"

"No, he got in the sliding door on this side, pulled it shut, and then—when I think about it, he must have had the engine running because he was gone so fast."

"Was there anybody else in the van?"

"I couldn't see."

"But there could have been somebody else?"

"I suppose."

"You didn't happen to notice the make of the van?"

"No, I'm sorry, I was concentrating on the licence plate."

"Which way did he turn?"

She made a motion with her left hand, and then said, "Left. He turned left."

"You're checking the area?" Stark asked Coulson.

"Sure. We've got officers looking in every lane and garage in the whole district."

"Okay. Mrs.—I'm sorry—"

"Carstairs."

"Right. Tell me this, over the last few days, or weeks even, have you noticed anyone coming or going from the building, maybe going up the elevator, that you didn't recognize? Anybody behaving suspiciously? Maybe somebody hanging around in the lane, who hurried off when you came out?"

She thought for a moment, and finally said, "No. Nothing like that."

Stark patted his pockets, then remembered he was out of cigarettes and hadn't bought any downtown before he went into the office.

"Damn," he said.

"I'm sorry," the woman said, apologetically.

"No, no," Stark smiled. "I'm out of cigarettes."

"Oh, have one of mine," the woman offered, holding out a pack of the same ultra-lights that Weems smoked.

Stark sighed.

"No—that's okay. Thanks anyway. Now, tell me this, was there anything unusual about the fellow who ran past you? Did he limp? Was he holding his arm? Was he staggering, unsteady on his feet?

She shook her head slowly.

"Nothing like that."

"How was he built? A big man? Skinny?"

She shrugged. "Short, I think. Yes, short—of

course, short. I mean I noticed that he was short. I couldn't tell much else about him with that heavy sweat-suit in this weather, with the hood pulled right tight on his face. I couldn't even see his face."

"Sweatsuit, you say? He had pants to match the top?"

"That's right. Grey they were. Charcoal grey. Oh yes, and running shoes. He wore white running shoes."

"What kind of running shoes? High tops? Big, sort-of oversized ones?"

"Nope. Just ordinary, you know, like jogging shoes."

"Was he short and fat, or short and skinny? Was he light on his feet, or, you know, sort of plodding, heavy-stepping?"

"Oh, light. I mean he ran very quickly, but I don't know how he was built, or anything. The sweatsuit was so—so big."

"Big?"

"Yeah, floppy, you know. It hung—loose."

Stark rubbed his chin.

"Okay, Mrs.—Carstairs. I can't think of anything else for the moment. Listen, thanks very much. We may be in touch."

"I'll do whatever I can. This is awful. This city used to be safe—and now—"

"Thanks, Mrs. Carstairs," Coulson said.

Joe Davis, the caretaker, wasn't able to add much. Stark was struck by his composure, and commented on it. The caretaker explained that since he used to be an ambulance attendant, he'd "seen it all before." It was apparent he was making an effort to be blasé, showing off, grinning all the time. He had a face like a crumpled paper bag. He hadn't noticed anybody coming into the building that didn't belong, and he hadn't seen the van parked out back. It couldn't have been there long, he said, because he'd been out back to put some garbage in the bin no more than fifteen minutes before he went upstairs and found the body.

"Did you go up the stairs, Mr. Davis, or did you take the elevator?"

"Oh, the elevator. I can't use the stairs on account of my bum leg. That's why I had to give up the ambulances. Well, it's been twenty years or more now. I mean, I'm not a cripple, or anything," he said emphatically. "I can use the stairs if I have to, but it takes me, you know, too long, so I use the elevator."

"When you found the body, Mr. Davis, did you notice any odour in the air, like a sort of burning smell?"

"Yeah, I did. Sort of like firecrackers, like the smell of firecrackers."

"Was that office always unlocked?"

"No, that's the funny thing. I always do my rounds in the morning, check to see no kids have broken in or something. And then, when I get off the elevator, the door's wide open. so right away, I figured that kids *had* broken in. I check the door before I look inside, but the glass—it's a glass door, you know—the glass wasn't broken or nothin' and the lock wasn't jimmied—not that I could see. And those are special dead-bolt locks, with real long bolts. You gotta use a key on both sides. Even if the glass had been broken, which it wasn't, they wouldn't be able to get in. I mean that glass is really thick."

"You're saying that somebody must have had a key to the door. Is that right?"

"Far as I can see, that's the only way you'd get in like that."

"Who has a key?"

"Well, me—I've got a pass key—and the building management people and I guess the owner—maybe."

"Who owns the building?"

"I don't know."

"I'm sorry—"

"Yeah, I know. It sounds dumb, but it's owned by one of them numbered companies. The only people I see are the building-management people. They hired me. They pay my wages."

"And who are they?"

"Courtland Properties. They got an office in the east end, on Main Street."

Stark and Coulson left the caretaker in his basement office and went up to the main floor in time to see the body being carried out. Coulson's people would ask all the occupants of the building whether they'd seen anybody or anything out of the ordinary in recent days. Stark got the address of the jeweller and headed over there.

"I'm going there myself. We could go together," Coulson said, smiling.

Stark shook his head.

"No, that's all right. I'll see you there. You got somebody going with the body?"

"Couple of uniforms."

Chapter Three

Howard Stokes was a nondescript sort of man, so ordinary-looking that his ordinariness was itself remarkable. His face was disarmingly plain—disarming because the lack of distinguishing features made him *look* innocent. There was no squinty eye, or twitching cheek, or twisted mouth, no scar or blemish or hairy mole—in short, no displeasing imperfections to make you want to be suspicious of him. He was neither handsome nor ugly, neither attractive nor repulsive. Short, trim and well-built, he looked as if he might work out. He was trying too hard to appear calm, which made him seem more nervous. Stark wanted to dislike him, but he couldn't.

"Let's go through to the back," Stokes said, and led Stark into a cluttered office not much bigger than a ticket booth. The desktop was scattered with jewellers loupes. There was a scale and an assortment of weights in a wooden box, a large magnifier, books on gems, jewellery catalogues, a row of pigeon holes filled with tiny tools, little balls of crumpled paper that hadn't made it to the wastebasket, the basket itself overflowing.

Stokes took a pile of newspapers from a black vinyl-and-chrome office chair—Stark thought he saw a slight wince with the weight of the papers. Stokes dropped the pile to the floor noisily. His hands were shaking—just a little.

"Take a seat, lieutenant." Stokes pronounced it loo-tenant. Stark's face twitched.

"Detective."

Stokes sat in an ancient, wooden, armed swivel chair by the desk, leaning to one side.

"Terrible this thing, terrible. My poor wife. Take a seat."

Stark remained standing.

"I'm sorry—your wife?"

"Saul, poor Saul. He was my wife's uncle, her mother's brother-in-law, married her mother's sister. Poor Saul. It's terrible, terrible. Such a thing. Nothing like this has ever happened. Not here, not to us. This city. I ask you. It's terrible." His legs curled under the chair, one ankle on top of the other, shaking. He was wearing a cardigan, which wasn't surprising, since despite the oppressive heat outdoors, the shop felt like a cold-storage locker. The elderly female clerk at the counter was also wearing a sweater. The perspiration on Stark's body was beginning to feel like a coating of ice.

"This bag of diamonds that the old man was carrying. How much?"

Stokes hesitated, looked at Stark, then looked at the floor and said heavily, "About four-million dollars. And they weren't diamonds."

Stark stared in disbelief.

"What did you say? Four *million?*"

"I'm afraid so."

"That's—that's ridiculous."

"I know it sounds like a lot, but I'm a wholesaler, you see, as well as a retailer. I buy estate jewellery, you see. I've got a big safe in the back, a vault really, and normally I don't have that much, but I just bought from three big estates. That's not anything like what I paid for them, but that's what they're worth. It takes time to write the descriptions of all the pieces for a mailer, photograph certain pieces and so on. I make up a mailer that I send out to clients, major retailers, some individuals. It's risky to keep everything here while I'm doing that, and I was just thinking, 'Howard, you've got too much stuff here, you could be robbed, send the stuff to the bank.' I called Saul and he came down this morning early and was taking them to the bank, but I don't know why he went to that building. It makes no sense, you know. Christ, I hope to hell the insurance will pay off. But you watch, they won't even give me what I paid for the pieces. You watch."

"How much was that?"

Stokes shrugged. "About nine-hundred thousand."

"But you want four million from the insurance company?"

"No, no. That's what I would have got, I figure, from selling the pieces. The insurers will give me my nine-hundred grand back, if I'm lucky."

"You have a list of this stuff?"

"Oh yeah, your Pawn Squad insists on that. You want to see the list?"

"No, that'll be Detective Coulson from the Hold-up Squad."

"You're not in the Hold-up Squad?"

"Homicide."

"Oh, I see."

"So, tell me, Mr. Stokes, why would you send an old man out with that kind of value of jewellery, for Pete's sake?"

"Not so old." Stokes shrugged. "He's—he was

24

seventy-three. He was in the Israeli army for years, in good shape. Who would suspect a man like that would be carrying a bag of precious jewellery? I ask you? No one. The bank is two blocks away, for God's sake. Downtown, the big banks, they use couriers like that all the time, a lot of older guys. They might have a couple of million bucks' worth of bearer bonds in a briefcase. Saul has carried—well, not this much, but lots of stones before. Nobody looks sideways at the guy. Who would know?"

"Somebody did."

Stokes looked hard at Stark, then lowered his gaze and stared at the floor. He shook his head.

"Nothing like this has ever happened—to anybody in the business in this city. In New York, in the diamond district, you've got old Hassidic Jews wandering all over the place with sacks full of gems. And here, you can get robbed, all right, but in the store. I've been robbed before. But they got just a few thousand. I don't keep a lot of valuable stock out front for that very reason. And the vault? My vault? Well, Detective, even though you're a cop, I'd rather not tell you about the vault and the security in this place, but it's amazing. Even so, I don't usually keep much here. I put it in the bank, in the safety-deposit box. Listen, I know security. I know it. I never had any fear that Saul would ever get robbed." He sighed, looked at his hands. "But, my God, it happened. It happened. It did happen. It's a terrible thing. I talked to another one of your people over at the building, at that building. I guess it was that detective."

"Coulson."

"I asked him, did he know who might have done this? Maybe—I mean I know you people keep files on crooks, and this guy must have been some kind of professional criminal, I would think, isn't that right?"

"I'm sure the Hold-up Squad does, Mr. Stokes. As I said, I'm Homicide."

"Yes, of course, Homicide. Because he was killed, I guess—"

"Tell me this, Mr. Stokes, did you get along well with Mr. Rabinovitch? Did you ever argue with him? Did he owe any money? Did he owe *you* any money?"

"He's my wife's uncle. He's a nice man. I liked him. He didn't owe me anything. He was like a brother. My wife's a lot younger than I am. We never argued, Saul and I. Never. He was a nice man. But what are you saying? You're not trying to imply that Saul was involved in this? That's not possible. Not Saul. He was as straight as the day is long. He was a very religious man. Saul would never do anything wrong. Never." He rubbed his forehead, screwed his face in thought, and then said, "At least, I don't *think* he could ever do anything like this." He shook his head violently. "No, it's impossible. He couldn't have. He couldn't—but you think he might have?"

"I don't think anything at the moment, Mr. Stokes. But there is a big question about why he went to that building, don't you think?"

Stokes lifted his hands palms up and raised his shoulders in a gesture of puzzlement.

Stark said: "Who knew, besides you and he, that he was carrying that amount of jewellery?"

"No one. Absolutely no one."

"Who knew what he did for a living, that he regularly carried jewellery for you?"

"I don't know. I mean, he might have told his friends

or something. But they're all men like himself."

"Did he owe any money? Did he gamble?"

"Well, you know, he played the horses a little. Once or twice a year, maybe, he'd go to Vegas, sometimes to Atlantic City, Windsor, Niagara Falls, Casino Rama, but I mean it was all penny-ante stuff. He was no heavy gambler or anything. He didn't have that kind of money."

"Family?"

"Widowed. I guess you'd say single." Stokes had become increasingly relaxed in his demeanour, unnaturally relaxed. He sat at an angle, his body stiff, belying the appearance of calmness. The foot was still twitching. Stokes began to blather: "He was married only a short time, and she died, my wife's aunt, her mother's sister. She, uh—you don't like to speak ill of the dead, but she was a terrible person. No one liked her, not even her sister, you know. He married her late, and she, mercifully, died suddenly, burst a blood vessel in her head in the middle of a shouting fit.

"In Israel many years ago, Saul was to get married, but the young woman was killed—a terrorist bomb. Terrible. After that, he never looked at another woman for years. He stayed single until he came here twenty years ago, and met Gladys and made the mistake of marrying her. After she died, my wife's parents felt bad for him, for what he'd had to put up with, that they gave him a place to live. They're both dead now—the parents. Saul worked at odd jobs, doing this and that, I guess. And then two years ago, I hired him to be my courier. He did a lot of other things for me as well. Took the deposits to the bank, did some deliveries. That sort of thing. He was a nice man, a real nice man."

"The gun he was carrying, a .32 semi-automatic, did he have a licence for it?"

"A gun? He was carrying a gun?"

Stokes's voice trembled. His eyes darted. His surprise was forced. Stark stared at him meaningfully.

Finally Stokes sighed in submission.

"Okay, I knew about the gun. I told him not to carry it." That sounded as phoney as his surprise. "Anyway, I guess it made him feel better. I didn't see any harm in it really. I assumed it was licensed. I mean, where else would an old—would a man get a gun like that? He'd have to buy it, wouldn't he, and to buy it, he'd have to get a licence, right?"

"Why are you lying to me about this gun?"

"I'm not—" He sighed again, shook his head. "Okay, okay. I—it was my wife's father's gun. It was her stupid idea to let him have it. She thought he'd be safer with it. I know we shouldn't have. It was locked away in an old chest in the attic. The old man, her father, he had a licence for it, but I don't know where it is, or anything. I mean, I guess it was illegal for Saul to carry it, but *we* didn't really break the law—did we? I mean, *we* weren't carrying it. He was never going to use it."

Stark shook his head.

"I'm not going to bother lecturing you, Mr. Stokes. If I get angry enough, I might decide to charge you. But you should know this. He *did* use the gun, and that's probably what got him killed."

Chapter Four

Stark went downtown and picked up a couple of cartons of Gauloises before heading back to his apartment. Carol wasn't there. Both air-conditioners were going at full tilt. Stark turned the one in the front window down, switched off the one in the bedroom, felt the cooked air flood in from the baking bricks, and turned it back on—low. There was a note. *I called Homicide and they said you were on a case. I've gone to the show. Call me later. Carol*

"Shit."

Stark moved as quickly as he could down Queen Street to Sid Holtzman's deli. It was like trudging through a blizzard of hot snow. Hard to breathe. The deli was empty. That is, no customers and no Sid, either. Stark shrugged, went behind the counter, poured himself a coffee and took his usual seat in the booth at the back that was walled off into a tiny room with a sliding door. The door was open, but when it was closed it showed a sign marked "Private." He pulled Sid's copy of the *Sun* from under the *Racing Form* and flipped it open to page three, closing it quickly with an utterance of displeasure. The Sunshine Girl was skinny and wearing a full, flowered dress. She looked like a Sunday school teacher. He heard the toilet flush. The men's room door opened, and Sid emerged.

"Did you wash your hands?"

"Of course I washed my hands. What kind of a question is that?"

"Well, you can't be too careful these days, and I would say that as your best customer, I've got the right to ask that question."

"Best customer? Harry, let me tell you something. As a customer, you're not too great, you know that? First of all, you pay for one coffee, you drink four. I should thank God that at least you pay for one. Half the cops come in here don't."

"What do you mean? They walk out without paying? Homer and Joyce?"

"Oh, no, not Homer and Juicy. They always pay. Juicy's so goddamned honest. I think she'd arrest her own mother if she caught her cheatin' on a parking meter, you know that?"

"Juicy? When did you start calling Joyce, 'Juicy'?"

"I heard *you* call her that once."

"Juicy Joyce? Yeah, maybe."

"She is kind of juicy with that big bum of hers."

"Yeah, well, my advice to you, Sid, is to drop the 'Juicy' right now, because you're going to slip up and call her 'Juicy' to her face, and then your face'll be what's juicy around here."

"Anyway, about the cops not paying. They don't walk out or nothin'. They go to pay, and I tell 'em to forget it, but the thing is, you know they expect it. Some of them, anyway. It sort of bugs me."

"Did you ever think that maybe when you tell them to forget about paying, they think you're just being a grateful citizen? Costs you what? Five cents? Big deal."

"Don't get your shorts in a knot. I'm not complaining."

"Could have fooled me."

Sid made a face. "You know, some of them insist on paying. Did you know that? One guy used to come in here couple of years back. Must have transferred out, I guess. He used to have a sandwich, tomato juice, coffee. Paid every time, left a big tip, too. One time I gave him a dozen doughnuts, told him to take them home to his kids—on me, which reminds me about that business about you being my best customer."

Stark sighed affectedly.

"All right, let's hear it."

"Like I say, you drink four coffees, pay for one. You never have a sandwich or even a muffin, for God's sake. You smoke stinky Frenchie cigarettes that drive away the other customers, and you *never* leave a tip. I had to build this private room just so's you could smoke in here."

"Get outta here. You built this room so you could smoke cigars—after they passed that goddamned no-smoking bylaw. And being a good customer, you know, is not measured in just the amount of money spent. Did you know that?"

"No, actually, I didn't."

"Go ahead, raise your eyebrows, but keep this in mind: my being here adds a certain tone to the establishment."

"Tone schmone. I'd rather have hard cash. Before you light that cigarette, close the door and flip the exhaust fan switch there. Okay, changing the subject, something might interest you. A guy got killed this morning in a jewel robbery. I know the guy."

"Saul Rabinovitch? They released his name already?"

"No, but they said he was a courier for Starflite

Jewellers on Eglinton. That's Rabinovitch, the only one. I know him, and I know Stokes, too."

"You're kidding? It's my case."

"No?"

"Yeah. I just got back from interviewing Stokes."

"You'd better check you still got your wallet. The guy's a crook."

The coffee cup stopped just before it reached Stark's lips. He looked over the cup at Sid, who was shoving napkins into a chrome dispenser. The cup finished its travel. Stark took a sip.

"A crook? What kind of crook would that be, Sid?"

"I bought a ring for my ex-wife from the guy. God knows why I ever bought that woman anything, but I did. He told me the price was wholesale, rock-bottom, so to speak, for family, like."

"Family?"

"I'll tell you about it in a second. Anyway, I took the ring and got it appraised. I don't know why, but I did. Anyway, it turns out the ring was worth about twenty-five per cent of what he charged me, the putz."

"Oh, that kind of crook."

"That kind of crook, right. Ripping off family."

"What is this, family?"

"Well, not exactly. Stokes's first wife was my ex-wife's cousin's widow."

"Jeez."

"What a piece of work she was. I'm convinced he died, the brother, just to escape her. My revenge on Stokes was that when she finally divorced him, she took him to the cleaners. I think she learned a lot from my wife. What an asshole that Stokes."

Sid lit a cigar and Stark contributed to the fumes

with another Gauloise. Despite its tiny size, the booth/room was relatively free of smoke, the exhaust fan sucking it out almost as fast as it was created.

Stark said, "What else do you know about this Stokes, and what about Rabinovitch?"

"Rabinovitch. Now there's a first-class dickhead. I don't like to speak ill of the dead, but he was one of those professional Israeli Jews, a Sabra, born in Israel, Palestine, as it then was. He was in the army. Everybody was in the army there, for Christ's sake. You *had* to be in the frigging army. Anyway, he comes over here and talks down to everybody, like he's king shit, like he's a real Jew and we're all fakes. Always telling stories about what a hero he was. How he fought the British and the Arabs; how many Arabs he killed; how he got shot at; how he saw his friends get blown to pieces. Big fucking deal. Everybody over there got shot at in those days, everybody saw somebody get blown up. My old man was in the Canadian Navy. His ship got torpedoed, for God's sake. He never talked about it. It was something you did, something you had to do. But this Rabinovitch. If everything was that great in the Promised Land, why'd he leave? Jeez. Oh listen, don't get me wrong, I'm not putting down Israel. I would never do that. Never. It's just—well, anyway, Stokes got stuck with Rabinovitch."

"They didn't get along?"

Sid shrugged.

"Well, I don't know, really. But Stokes married this hot little number, twenty-five years younger. What a looker. Whoo." He fanned his face with his hand. "So, Rabinovitch is—*was* her uncle by marriage, even though she's a shiksa, a WASP. I don't know what the deal was, but she made old Howard hire him. She's got him pretty good by the knackers. They used to come to the house."

"Here?"

"No, no, not here. My old house, when I was married, my wife's house now, the bitch. I think she had a thing for Howard, or something. Anyway, she kept in touch after he split up with her sister-in-law. One thing in my wife's favour, she didn't like the sister-in-law either. But she liked Howard, and she used to invite them over for barbecues and shit. You know that woman hardly ever cooked a meal. So, if it was in-the-house cooking, she'd order in, you know, from a caterer. If it was out-of-doors cooking, the schmuck here had to stand there with a fucking apron on that said 'Chief Cook and Bottle Washer,' some goddamned thing. She bought it for me. I had to stand there flipping steaks and shishkabobs and you-frigging-name-it while she cooed at Howard over a martini or twelve. The only upside was I got to look at Barbara's tits. That's her name, Barbara. Barbara Shaw. She kept her maiden name, you know, modern-like. She used to wear these halter tops and short-shorts, strut around, bending over to smell the roses, giving me an eyeful. What a tease, I'm telling you. Whoo."

"You said Stokes ripped you off, but was he—did you ever hear about his being into anything maybe a little more seriously crooked?"

"I never heard nothing like that, but who knows?"

"And Rabinovitch? Could he have been into anything?"

"Into anything? Crooked, you mean?"

"Yeah."

Sid took a long drag on his cigar and blew a stream of smoke at the exhaust fan, watching as the smoke got sucked in. "He was a gambler. Horses, cards, Vegas. Apart from that, I don't know."

Chapter Five

Mid-afternoon, Stark attended Saul Rabinovitch's autopsy at the Centre of Forensic Sciences.

The old man had been tall and lanky. His body was firm and muscular—well-toned.

"He must have worked out," the coroner, Cheryl Connors, remarked.

The man's skin was thin, lacking the elasticity of youth, but smooth and relatively supple, wrinkled at the armpits and the crotch. There was a large, purplish bruise slightly to the left of the middle of his chest and a darker spot in the centre of the bruising. When she had completed her slicing and measuring and weighing, Connors declared that the cause of death was the penetration of the heart by a weapon with a fifteen-centimetre-long shaft, not a knife blade. The wound was cylindrical.

"An ice pick?" Stark asked.

"I don't think so—too wide for an ice pick."

"Witness said the assailant, or at least the person she saw running from the building and we assume was the assailant, was short. Could this have been done by a short person?"

Connors hesitated.

"I can't tell, really. There is a downward angle to the wound, certainly, but it could have been made by a tall person striking out with a bent elbow, starting from beside his ear." She demonstrated. "Or by a shorter person with his arm held high to put more force behind the blow. The blow was certainly extremely heavy, the bruising indicates that—a short, sharp strike by a powerfully built attacker, or a longer blow with more centrifugal force by a slighter person."

"And the weapon, what do you think?"

"Well—you know, it could have been a screwdriver, or something like that, but definitely not a knife."

Stark nodded, made a thoughtful sound, watched as Connors went about her work matter of factly. He averted his gaze from the centre of her activity, looked at the murdered man's huge, strong hands, with no sign of arthritis; his full head of hair, bone-white like his body beneath the collar line; his face with the colour and texture of an autumn leaf. Stark thought, as he often did when he looked at the face of a corpse, of all the plans that would never be realized, of what effect the removal of this factor in the human equation would have on the all the remaining parts. He shook his head.

Connors spoke into a microphone in a monotonous, rapid patter, like a bored auctioneer selling horror as ordinary fare.

Chapter Six

Courtland Properties, as the caretaker had called it, was in a two-storey, red brick blockhouse of a building just south of the Danforth on Main Street, that sat there looking uncomfortable in the heat that they were now saying had reached an "all-time record" for that date in July at about two that afternoon. Stark had automatically corrected the news reader's term, saying aloud to himself that "all time hasn't arrived yet and never will." The building sat broiling near the bridge over the Toronto-to-Montreal railway tracks, where, as a kid, Stark had sometimes come to watch the Montreal Flyer go puffing past.

The offices were as plain and old-fashioned as the building, the only concession to its being in the dwindling of the twentieth century were a couple of computers. And, thank heavens, air-conditioning. The rest of the place hadn't changed much since the Acme Building (etched in stone above the front door) had been erected (1946, according to the cornerstone). The office door was pale oak, with a pebbled-glass window, the letter "A" stencilled on the glass. A brass plate beside the door identified the premises by its full corporate name as those of Courtland Property Management Inc.

The waiting area beyond the door was separated from the rest of the space by a low rail, oak, like the door and the trim throughout. There were seven desks in the central area, only two of which were occupied, both by female clerks, one a receptionist, who sat just inside the gate in the railing. Most of the two outside walls was taken up by doorless, glass-walled offices, frosted to chest level, clear above. The corner office was much larger, with solid walls and an oak door. The receptionist looked at Stark as if he'd brought in a bad smell. He flashed his badge and identified himself. Her expression was unchanged, but he thought he saw a little twitch.

"How can I help you, Detective?" she said in a tone that belied her words. She couldn't have been more than thirty-five, but with no make-up or lipstick, she looked years older, her hair pulled severely into a roll at the back. She wore a grey suit that might have been fashionable if she had worn it to lay the cornerstone of the building.

"I'd like to speak to your manager, or president, or whatever you call the head man—or woman. If you don't mind."

"Mr. Rogers is very busy. Are you sure there isn't something—"

"Please. If you don't mind—"

She glared, eyes glazed. Stark wondered whether she'd had a liquid lunch. "One moment." She clip-clopped stiffly on sensible shoes across the black-and-white tiled floor to the corner office, somehow keeping her hips rigidly in the same plane as her upper body. Only her legs appeared to move. She walked like a drunk trying to appear sober. The other clerk, even plainer than the first, young and tiny, looked up timidly from her work, her eyes darting nervously back and forth between the receptionist and Stark. The receptionist turned her head to look at herself in the glass wall of an office. Her shoulder bumped into a pillar, and she staggered back with a little yelp.

"You okay?" Stark said. She shook herself, covering her embarrassment with haughtiness, and carried on without acknowledging him. When she reached the corner office door, she tapped and waited. It took another tapping and another wait before the door finally opened and a little round man appeared. He listened and then looked around the receptionist's thin frame, caught Stark's gaze and darted back behind her. There were a few more seconds of whispered conversation, and then she stepped aside and let him waddle past, his puffy little face taking on an artificial grin, which he wore all the way to the railing, reaching across it to shake Stark's hand.

"Detective Stark, Miss Holmes told me. What can I do for you, Detective? Not often we get the police in here."

"Mr.—"

"Rogers."

"Listen, do you mind if we go into your office?"

Rogers turned and looked in the direction of his office as if he had just been made aware of its existence. "Miss Holmes" had gone into the office after Rogers had emerged. She came out, and he turned and smiled again at Stark.

"Of course," he said. "No problem."

The furniture in the man's office was incongruously modern—and cheap. If he'd been as busy as the receptionist had said, it wasn't apparent what he'd been busy at. The plain, blond wood desk and credenza were bare, the only thing on the desktop being a gold-coloured numeral "1" curved around a golf ball. There was a trophy on the credenza topped with a golfer frozen in an exaggerated follow-through. There was a garish painting of a golfer, similarly posed, on the wall above the credenza. It looked like something you'd see for sale on the corner of a service-station lot on a hot Saturday afternoon. Two plaques on either side of it attested to the victories of Tom Rogers at golf tournaments in 1974 and 1975, as a junior.

He stuffed himself into a high-backed vinyl-covered chair behind the desk. Stark took a wobbly, black plastic secretary's chair opposite.

"So," said Rogers, "how can I help Toronto's finest today?"

Stark stared at him blankly for an instant, then said. "There's been a murder, Mr. Rogers—" The man's mouth opened, his eyes widened. "—in one of the buildings you manage, on Eglinton Avenue." Stark stuck his fingers in his jacket pocket and pulled out scraps of paper. "I've got the address somewhere. It's near Bathurst."

"I-I know the building. A murder? I don't understand."

"Someone was stabbed—in a robbery, a jewel robbery."

"A jewel robbery? There's no jewellery store in that building. In fact, there are no retailers in the building at all."

"It happened in an empty office. A courier was robbed and killed. He was carrying the jewels."

"I still don't understand. What was he doing there? What office?"

"I don't know what office. An office, an empty office—on the fifth floor. And I have no idea what he was doing there. That's why I'm here."

The little man's head bobbled nervously as if something had shaken the body beneath it and it wasn't firmly attached. "I don't see how I can help you."

"The caretaker—" Stark consulted his notebook. "Joe Davis."

"That's right. Joe."

"He said the office was locked. Had been locked. Dead-bolt lock, he said. But it was open. Not jimmied, not forced. It had been opened with a key. Now, Mr. Davis said that the only keys are his and maybe the owner of the building has one and you have one. Is that right?"

"Well, yes. I guess—yes, that would be right, but you're not surely suggesting—"

Stark raised his hands. "I'm not suggesting anything, Mr.—"

The man sighed.

"Rogers."

"Mr. Rogers, I'm not suggesting anything, but I would like to see the key."

Rogers stared at him for a moment. He shrugged and said, "Certainly. I'll just—" He picked up the phone and punched a single number. "Doreen, bring me the keys for the Eglinton building, will you please." He gave Stark an uncomfortable smile and then stared at the door. Finally, there was a tapping, and after Rogers uttered a saccharine, "Come in," in a tone that seemed to suggest he wasn't sure who was going to enter, Doreen clip-clopped to the desk and handed Rogers a large metal ring with an array of keys.

"Thank you, Doreen," Rogers said, and the woman pivoted on one heel and left with a brief, disdainful glance at Stark. He smiled at her, but her head had already snapped back upright.

"There is one problem," Rogers said after the door had closed. He smiled a little smugly.

"What's that?"

"These keys are all labelled. There's one for each office in the building, and then there's the pass key—that's this one—it opens all the other doors, including the exit doors, closets, boiler room and so on. Unless you can tell me what office it is that the—uh—this robbery took place in, I can't help you."

Stark stared at him thoughtfully, then, remembering Peters had written down the office number, he began to pull bits of paper out of his pocket and looked at them. "Damn it. I had it here," he said. Finally, he pointed at the ring of keys and said: "Those keys. How are they labelled?"

"I don't know what you mean?"

"I mean, how are they labelled?"

"Right here, on each key, there's a sticker."

"I know that," Stark said with exasperation. "What's it *say* on the label?"

"Well, this one, for instance, says four-dash-oh-one."

"And that means?"

"Well, that means it's the fourth floor, office number one."

"Right. Have you got a floor plan for the fifth floor?"

"I don't know."

"Jesus."

Rogers looked flustered.

"I'm sure we do. But—just a minute." He picked up

the phone again and pressed a button. Doreen must have been away from her desk, because it took some time for her to answer. Stark heard her clip-clop and it sounded to him as if her route began from just outside the office door and went away from it. "Ah, Doreen," the little man said at last. "Would you check the files for the Eglinton building and find me the floor plan for the fifth floor.—Yes—that's fine. Call me back.—Uh, just a minute." He held the phone away from his ear and spoke to Stark. "Do you want to see the floor plan?"

Stark nodded slowly.

"Yes, I want to see the floor plan. Are the office numbers written on the floor plan?"

"Yes, I believe so. Just a moment. Doreen, are the office numbers written—? They are? Well, yes, then bring the plans. Thank you. She'll be—she has to look it up—in the files."

"Right."

They sat in awkward silence. Finally Rogers said, "What's it like out? Hot, I bet."

Stark was saved from answering the stupid question by Doreen's tapping.

"Oh, here she is. Come in." She lugged in a huge binder, and Rogers had to move his hole-in-one trophy to the credenza in order to let her open the binder on the desk top. She flipped to the plan of the fifth floor, and stood for a moment until Rogers gave her a puzzled look. "Is there something?" he said.

"No. I just—no. That's the plan," she said.

"Well, that's fine thanks, Doreen. I'll—I'll call you." She nodded awkwardly and left.

"Well, uh, which—which office was it?"

Stark stood up and studied the floor plan. Pointing

at two small squares, he said, "Are these the elevators?"

"That's right."

"Okay, then this is the office. Right here."

"Five-oh-one. Good. That's it. Five-oh-one," Rogers said, nodding and smiling with satisfaction as if everything had been resolved.

"The key," Stark said.

"The key? Oh, yes, of course, the key. Okay, well here's the key for five-oh-six. There are six offices on the floor. You can see here on the plan—"

"Five-zero-one? The key for five-zero-one?"

"Right, the key for five-oh-one, five-oh-one, five-oh-one." He looked up at Stark with a stunned expression. "The key for five-oh-one isn't here."

Stark looked pleased with himself.

"I don't understand it," Rogers said. "That's impossible. No one has access to these keys, except. Oh—here it is." He beamed. "It was out of place. It's here among the fourth floor keys. That's funny. Anyway, problem solved."

Stark grunted.

"Who has access to those keys, Mr Rogers?"

"Well, just, uh—just the three of us—myself, Doreen and Sheila. She's the bookkeeper. You must have seen her out there."

"Just the three of you, no one else? I'm curious—what about all the empty desks and offices out there?" Stark jerked a thumb in the direction of the door.

Rogers looked embarrassed. He shrugged.

"The real estate market hasn't been good lately." He sighed. "Actually, that's not quite true. The market is picking up, but I'm afraid that our buildings are—well, they're in need of some repair, the ones we manage. We used to have some pretty good ones, but—well, anyway, we don't any more. That's why there are just the three of us."

Rogers smiled weakly, and after a few seconds, a light of realization flashed in his eyes.

"Wait a minute, wait a minute. You don't think we—Detective, we would never let any unauthorized person have one of our keys. And you can't possibly suspect one of the girls. And surely not me. Please, Mr. Stark, please. It's just not possible. Listen, let me call Doreen. I'm sure there's some explanation."

Giving him a thin smile, Stark handed Rogers one of his cards. "When you think of a good one, give me a call."

Chapter Seven

Stark's fondness for the dramatic had him leaving without asking who owned the building, and now he didn't want to spoil the effect by going back in. Besides, he thought a phone call might unsettle the little man. He pulled up in front of a doughnut shop on the Danforth, thinking he'd have a coffee while he made the call, but a big banner across the window that screamed, "Smoke-Free," annoyed him, so he stayed in the car and muttered "up yours." He called information to get the number, and had to fumble with his notebook to get the right name of the place, which, after flipping pages, discovered he hadn't written down. He wasn't speaking fast enough for Bell's computer, and a live operator came on the line, to whom he said, "Courtland Property Rentals," knowing that was wrong. The operator said: "I have a Courtland Property Management."

"That's it," he said.

Doreen answered in a voice that sounded like she'd overdosed on sweetener, but turned sour when she recognized his voice asking for Rogers.

"He's not in," she said.

"I just left him."

"He just went out."

Stark asked her for the name of the owner of the Eglinton building and she refused to give it to him, claiming at first that she didn't have authority to disclose it and then, after he pressed, protesting that she was on her lunch break. "The bastard doesn't pay me enough for this shit," she said, her language surprising Stark. Then she said that only Rogers knew the name. Finally, after Stark adopted a nasty tone and threatened to take all three of them downtown, she said, "Just a minute," curtly, and put the phone down with a clatter. Stark could hear her go away from the desk and say, "Fucking bastards," from a distance. After two minutes, she came back on the line with the name "Horace Anderton" and an address on the Bridle Path, and then she hung up.

"What the hell's eating her?" Stark said aloud. He smoked a cigarette and tried to place the name she had given him. "Bridle Path." He drew a blank on the name Anderton, and finally called an editor he knew at *Financial World Magazine,* Fred Beamish.

"Fred, what do you know about a guy called Horace Anderton?"

"Jesus, that's a blast from the past. What's he done?"

"I don't know. What can you tell me about him?"

"Must be eighty. Big stockbroker one time, retired years ago. What's the story?"

"No story, Fred. Not now, anyway."

Next, Stark called the Hold-up Squad and got Ken Coulson on the line.

"Any luck with the van?"

"Not exactly. There is something interesting, however. Howard Stokes?"

"Yeah, what about him?"

"He's reported *his* van stolen."

"You're kidding. And what does this van look like?"

"An awful lot like the one Ann Carstairs described."

"Who the hell is she?"

"The witness from the finance company."

"So when did he do this?"

"Stokes?"

"Yeah, when did he report the van stolen?"

"Fifteen minutes ago."

"You're kidding."

"No. I just got a call from the Auto Squad."

"He didn't call you direct?"

"Nope."

"That's interesting. You'd better speak to him."

"I'm just about to."

"Could Rabinovitch have taken the van, picked up the bad guys, driven to the office building? And if not, why would the robbers steal Stokes's van? If it *was* his van. Big coincidence if it wasn't, wouldn't you say? Anybody else have access to it?"

"I'm going to ask him."

"Yeah, course you are. Listen, I assume there were no reports on any gunshot wounds from the hospitals?"

"No. Oh, the forensics on the slug in the wall? It's from the .32 all right. But no trace of blood. That doesn't mean it didn't hit somebody."

"Yeah, I know about that sort of thing, Ken."

"Oh, there's one other thing."

"What's that?"

"You asked me to check on the owner of the building. It's a numbered company, but the principal is a guy called Horace Anderton."

"Yeah, I know."

"Oh."

"I went to the building-management outfit."

"Oh yeah?"

"Nothing specific, but the key was out of place."

"What key?"

"The key to the office. It was in the wrong place on the ring. And something didn't smell right about the place."

"The building-management place?"

"Yeah. Nothing hard, but—anyway, I'm going to go see this Anderton guy. I assume you've got nothing on the stolen jewels, or you'd have told me that right off."

"Nothing at all, but that's not surprising. Of course, we've alerted the Pawn Squad and we're having chats with some of our old *friends*—who've been involved in this sort of thing in the past. But I don't think we're going to have much luck in that sort of direction."

"No. That's my feeling, too. It's too messy for pros. I think we should concentrate on things closer to home, don't you?"

"Yeah, we're keeping to that line of country."

"I'll be in touch."

Chapter Eight

The home at the address Doreen had given him was unprepossessing for a Bridle Path house—a rather plain, red brick rectangle, sparsely landscaped, framed by a high hedge. Its lawn was yellowed from the unremitting solar barrage and the watering ban that had been imposed. It was six-forty-five by the time Stark got there, frazzled after fighting his way through the rush-hour traffic up Woodbine and Don Mills Road to Lawrence and west to the Bridle Path. A butler answered Stark's ring and gave him a withering stare and an icy, "Yes?"

Stark showed him his badge and asked to see Horace Anderton.

The butler looked at him as if he was a hair in the blancmange.

"Mr. Anderton is no longer with us."

"What do you mean?"

"Mr. Anderton passed away two weeks ago."

"Son of a bitch."

Chapter Nine

Carbo's Bistro is only four-hundred-and-thirty-seven walking strides along Queen Street East from Stark's building, but in the hothouse the city had become, that night, as Stark made his way there, it felt considerably longer. The thick air muffled the sounds of the street. Entering Carbo's, Stark couldn't believe what he was hearing. Morty Greenwood was playing a sugary soft-rock medley.

"What the hell are you playing?" Stark said, taking his usual stool at the piano bar on Morty's immediate left.

Morty gave him a death-ray look. Stark gestured to Sharon, the perfectly proportioned Amazonian waitress, to bring him his usual Scotch and Morty another white wine. Stark stared at Sharon as she leaned over the bar to give the order to George, the bartender. She was wearing a loose-fitting, long, flowered dress with no waistline, almost a muumuu, and yet it seemed to accentuate her curves. To give Morty his white wine, Sharon had to squeeze between Stark and a railing that divided the piano bar from the elevated dining area. She put her hand on Stark's back, coming and going. Stark gave Morty a caricatured leer of pleasure. Morty returned a dismissive look of disgust. He was not enjoying himself.

He stopped playing after the medley, and there was a round of applause from somewhere in the back. Stark wondered whether they were clapping in appreciation of the medley or because Morty had stopped playing it. He glanced in the direction of the applause, and the people at the table—three women in their forties and an effeminate-looking younger man, an office group, Stark figured—were smiling warmly. They must have requested the medley of tunes Stark recognized, but couldn't identify, probably through Ulysses, the owner of Carbo's, who was leaning against the far end of the bar with a Cheshire-cat smile. That must have been why Morty was irritated. The elegant piano player stood and acknowledged the applause with a curt nod and a thin, acerbic smile.

"Christ," Morty said between his teeth, picking up his wine and his pack of cigarettes. "C'mon, let's go have a smoke." In compliance with the city's anti-smoking by-law, Carbo's had become technically smoke-free, but while the patrons flouted the law and smoked anyway at the bar and in the actually illegal smoking area in the rear, Ulysses had ordered that none of the staff could smoke, and that included Morty. Stark and Morty went through the kitchen and into the alley. Morty gave Ulysses a withering stare as they passed, and Stark raised an eyebrow at him. Ulysses waved a hand at them as if he were flicking away an annoying bug.

Emerging from the air-conditioned interior, they hit the evening air like a plunge into a vat of warm soup. Just after nine, it was still light out. Torn rags of cloud were rosy with the fading stains from the sun's passage. The two sat on the crumpled lids of garbage cans and lit their cigarettes, blowing twin streams of smoke against the watery sky.

"Romantic, ain't it?" Stark said.

"Piss off."

"Hey, listen, I didn't ask you to play that shit. I'm the guy who asks you to play Poinciana, remember? What was that about?"

"That bastard Ulysses, what an asshole."

"I thought he was straight."

"Ha, ha. Your humour isn't appreciated."

"Speaking of your love life, how's it going?"

Morty turned his head slowly, deliberately, glowering at Stark.

Stark shrugged.

"So, why don't you get another gig? Not that I want you to go. Be a big hole in my life if you left, Mortimer. Ulysses'd probably put some nasal folksinger in there with a battered, travel-stickered guitar and big boobs." He rubbed his chin in mock contemplation. "Come to think of it—"

"What is it with you and mammaries, Stark? It's quite revolting. God. Did you say, 'get another gig?' As if I can just call my agent and bingo. The name's Mortimer Greenwood, not Harry bloody Connick. I'm a long way past being in demand, buddy. I'm a lot—older than you are." Morty sighed. He glanced at Stark. "Even though I don't look it. No, I'm afraid I'm not Flavour of the Decade, Harold. But you—God, you look terrible: I'd say you're not even Flavour of the Century."

"Drink your wine. You're depressing me."

"Good."

"Hey, watch it, or I'll tell everybody what your real name is."

"That is my real name, you jerk. You think I'd pick that for a stage name?"

"C'mon. You named yourself after an intersection

54

in East York."

"That was my mother did that, silly cow. Anyway, I was born in Winnipeg. My mother had never heard of East York."

"You're kidding. It's just a coincidence? Jeez. Did you ever *have* a stage name?"

"Yep," Morty said with a slight chuckle. "I was Lamont Lanvin."

"Jesus."

"Somebody said it sounded like a shampoo, so I dropped it. I don't mind Morty. I like it, actually. Mortimer, I hate, reminds me of Mortimer Snerd. Remember the puppet?"

Stark nodded. They smoked in silence for a time, Stark sipping his Scotch. He flicked his cigarette against a facing brick wall, creating a spray of sparks. Morty dropped his, ground it deliberately with his shoe and rose to go back inside.

"Morty." Stark put his hand on Morty's hand.

"This is so sudden. I don't know what to say."

"Listen." Stark took a gulp of his Scotch. "There's something I wanted to ask you."

"What?"

"I'm scared to death, Morty."

"Scared of what?"

"Carol."

"Well, she is a cop, but you are, too. What's the problem? Don't tell me she's pregnant."

"Don't be stupid." Stark sighed. "Ah shit, never mind. Forget it, forget it."

"Tell me."

Stark shook his head. "I don't know what to do."

"You don't know what to do about what, Harold?"

Stark sighed again.

"Don't laugh."

"I won't laugh."

"It's—I think maybe I love her." He turned to see Morty's reaction. The piano player looked back blankly. "Did you hear what I said?"

"I heard you. You think you love Carol Weems."

"But, Morty, I—don't think she feels the same way. I don't know. I just don't know, damn it."

"Have you told her this?"

"No. I can't. I—"

"How drunk are you, anyway?"

"Not much."

"So you really think you love her, do you, Harold?" Stark raised his eyebrows.

"Yeah, I think so."

"You think so? Christ, did you ever think maybe you're just desperate? Did you think about that possibility?"

Stark downed the rest of his Scotch. "Jesus. You're a big goddamned help, Morty. Let's go back in. You can play 'Lush Life' for me."

"That'll be appropriate."

Chapter Ten

In the morning, Stark put in another call to Fred Beamish at *Financial World*.

"You ever hear of Courtland Property Management Inc.?"

"Nope."

"Do you think you can find out who owns it?"

"You're a cop, you know, Stark. You can go to the Ministry of Consumer and Commercial Affairs and look it up. It's not far from headquarters."

"I'm not going near headquarters and I'm busy. I've got a big case here, Freddy."

"And I've got nothing to do?"

"Who got you the Leafs' tickets?"

"Yeah, and I didn't have to do anything for them, either, right?"

"C'mon, Freddy."

"Don't call me Freddy."

"Fred, please."

"Give me a couple of hours."

Stark called Ken Coulson.

"Anything happening?"

"Well—no hard developments. No sign of the van. No word from the street. The lads are puzzled. There's no buzz out there about the action. A couple of harebrained ideas I won't bother you with. But otherwise, nobody's got a theory."

"Which means what to you?"

"Which means either the culprits are playing it close to the vest—maybe a little freelance activity they don't want the bosses to know about—or it's an amateur job."

"And probably an inside job, and it should be easy to wrap up."

"With any luck."

"What about the old man's taking the van, or somebody having access to it? You asked Stokes?"

"I did, and he says no on both counts. There's no one else besides him who has a key. He doesn't have any delivery men or stock boys, or anything. Just six female sales clerks. There is a spare key at home."

"You check on that?"

"Stokes called his wife. She said it's still on the peg by the back door where they keep it. Course, the old man could have had one made. Easy enough for him to lift the key off the peg and put it back."

"Mmm. Yeah, I think the old man was in on it. You said 'yes and no' when I asked you whether anything was happening. What's the yes?"

"Our friend Stokes."

"What about him?"

"Well, apparently he's got some serious financial problems."

"The cheese gets more binding."

"The Pawn Squad puts Stokes down as flat broke. In hock to his eyeballs."

"Business that bad? Starflite Jewellers. I'm sure they run big newspaper ads and things, don't they? Rings a bell."

"It's not the jewellery business that went sour on him. That's apparently in good shape, at least the turnover is good and so on, but for some reason the word is out on him on the street. Nobody'll give him any credit. He's got some big loans, and he's really hurting. Howard's looking more and more like he might be in on this," Coulson said. "What do you think? Insurance scam? He gets the insurance money and still has the jewellery to unload later."

"Let's leave him alone for the moment. He certainly could have taken the old man in the van himself, which would explain why the old fellow went along. But why would he kill him? And—I can't see Stokes stabbing somebody. He's not the kind of guy who'd carry a knife, or whatever the hell it was, or know how to use it. On top of that, there's the timing. He wouldn't have had time to hide the van well enough that we can't find it and get back to his shop. So, if he *is* involved, someone else must have been in on it with him. The guy in the sweat-suit. Maybe Stokes took the old man there, to the office, and then he went out the front door of the building while the other guy went out the back. On the other hand, the sweat-suit could have been Stokes. He's the right size, and stranger things have happened. Rabinovitch shot somebody in that office. I'd like to see Stokes without his shirt on. It'd be easy if we could arrest him, but we haven't got enough to do that. The thing that really bothers me, Ken, is the key."

"You mean the van key?"

"The key to the office. Somebody had to have a key to get in there."

"What about the caretaker?"

"Check him out. If it was him, he'd be pretty stupid, though, wouldn't he? He'd have to know that we'd be looking for somebody with a key and eventually we'd get around to him. The thing is, why do it there? Unless Rabinovitch went there to meet somebody? What's the connection with that office? Except that it was empty and a place they could meet and do whatever they were going to do without being seen? They had to know about the office and they had to have a way to get in there. Anyway, check out the caretaker. I told you I went to see the building-management people and that the key to the office is there, but it was put back on the ring out of place, like somebody might have taken it off and had a copy made. But how could Stokes get hold of that key? Or Rabinovitch, for that matter? Is there some connection with the building people? I think I'm going to keep an eye on them. I've got somebody checking them out for me. I want to see who owns the place, and then we'll go from there."

"Okay. I pushed Stokes a little bit about the van," Coulson said. "I told him it sounded very much like the van in the robbery. He got shirty about it. He said the city's full of grey vans. 'It's just a coincidence,' he said."

"Well, supposing Stokes's not involved, and supposing the old man *did* take the van. Supposing he knew he'd be carrying four-million-dollars' worth of jewellery. so supposing Rabinovitch decides this is going to be his retirement package. He sets the thing up, a straight theft. It wasn't a robbery at all. He just went to the office to meet somebody he'd arranged to sell the jewellery to. Rabinovitch'd be way out of his depth on a deal like this. Who'd he be selling to? Where would he meet the guy? Well, he's been involved in the jewellery racket for a while. Maybe he knows somebody who knows somebody. But whoever it is, it's not a Sunday-school teacher. And maybe when he gets to the office and asks for the money, the other guy says, 'What money, old man?' and the old man thinks he's still a freedom-fighter, pulls his gun, and bang, bang. If that was the case, it's reasonable that Stokes would *think* the van was still parked wherever it was supposed to be parked, and wouldn't discover it was missing till later. Did you mention to him when you first interviewed him that the shooter had taken off in a van?"

"I don't think so, no. I didn't."

"So there you are. If he is innocent, he'd make no connection at all with the van. Why would he? He'd just think bad luck was coming in pairs, report it stolen."

"He would, yeah."

"Right. You carry on. I'll get back to you."

The second Stark hung up from Coulson, the phone rang.

"Stark?"

"Freddy. What've you got?"

"I've got the name of the guy who owns the property company, what's it called—Courtland Property Management Inc. It's a guy called Salvatore Cataldi."

"What?"

"You know him? He's a developer."

"A developer? Is that what he's calling himself? Yeah. Well thanks, Freddy. Thanks very much."

"Wait a second, wait a second. Cataldi's well known. What's the deal?"

"You know what I'm going to do, Freddy? I'm going to send you a bottle of single-malt Scotch. That's what I'm going to do."

"The hell with the Scotch. Give me the story."

"Story? There's no story, Freddy. If there is a story, I'll give it to you. I promise."

"Bullshit. It better be bloody good Scotch. And stop calling me Freddy." Beamish hung up.

"Cataldi," Stark said. "Well, what do you know. Can you beat that."

Chapter Eleven

Rabinovitch's body had been released for burial. Stark's visit to see Barbara, Harold's wife, was something of a courtesy, to get a feel of the world the dead man had moved in and the people who had touched his life. It was also an act of reassurance, letting those left behind know that Stark was actively involved in searching for the person who had taken their loved one from them. And, if Stokes had something to do with the crime, the reassurance would put him off his guard. Stark definitely had no intention of asking any more questions than his experience and instincts would tell him were as much as he could ask without compounding the grief.

Stark wasn't prepared for what he met late in the afternoon, when he arrived at the Stokes place, a monster home in a new development in Aurora, north of the city, a development in which every house was perched on its own bulldozer-shaped, half-acre hill lot. The windows glared at him, maliciously reflecting the merciless sun, as he slogged through the thick air, past the flick-flick of a sprinkler, futilely trying to make the brown lawn green, in flagrant contravention of the ban on watering. There was only one car in the driveway and the place appeared empty but for the woman who answered the door. She was about thirty, was wearing tight shorts and a little yellow blouse unbuttoned over a bikini top, and there wasn't even a token shiva tear anywhere in the outfit, as far as Stark could see. And, in spite of himself, he did look.

When Stark identified himself, the woman gave him a bright-eyed smile, put her hand on his arm and led him into the house as if having a cop in the place was the best thing that had happened to her all week. He thought he'd better be sure he was at the right house: "You *are* Barbara Stokes?"

"Shaw." She bubbled the correction, making it sound as if the name had two syllables.

"But you are Howard Stokes's wife?"

"Of course. You did come to see me, didn't you? Or is it Howard you want?" She pouted. "But he's not here. He went to the gym to work out. He goes every lunch hour, usually, and then he was going back to the store anyway. Of course he was late going in to work today— because of everything."

"I see." Stark nodded.

"You seem puzzled by something," Barbara Shaw said. "I'm sorry, I missed your name."

"Harry Stark."

"Are you lieutenant, or inspector, or something?" As her husband had done, she pronounced lieutenant "loo-tenant." "This is exciting. I love excitement."

Stark was stunned. This woman was either completely insensitive, or she was dealing with grief with mild hysteria—or she was a complete idiot. "It's Detective," Stark said.

"Oh." Her tone betrayed disappointment, as if "detective" was banal, not lofty enough, didn't have the right ring for a six-hundred-thousand-dollar monster home on its own half-acre hill lot. She shrugged it off and brightened as if she'd decided to make the best of it.

"Well, *Detective* Harry Stark, what can I do for you? But first, sit down." She had led him into an immense living room that stretched across most of the front of the house. Despite its size, the room felt crowded, crammed with over-sized furniture, all super-modern, including a long sectional couch in black, glove leather. Nearly everything else was in various shades of red, from pale rose through coral to the lipstick of an hourglass-shaped chair in some sort of plastic in the far corner that took Stark's attention. It looked as if it might serve for some contortionist sexual coupling well outside of his repertoire—and not much else.

"You like that?" she said, seeing his interest in the chair.

"It's—interesting."

"You *bet* it is," she said suggestively. He thought he caught a whiff of liquor on her breath when she hissed the phrase at him. "So, sit."

Stark chose the leather couch. The fingers of one hand unconsciously stroked its supple covering. She came over and trailed her fingers over the leather, grazing his hand. He moved it.

"Nice, eh? Comfortable isn't it? But not as exciting as the red chair." Her eyelids lifted.

Stark nodded awkwardly.

What is this? he thought.

She sat opposite him, on the edge of a huge, cube-shaped, dark crimson hassock in front of a massive matching chair. She sat with her legs spread wide. Her shorts, tight at the hips and buttocks, were flared at the legs. Stark had a fleeting thought about whether she was wearing the bikini bottom beneath the shorts.

"You still look confused about something,

65

Detective," she said.

Stark nodded thoughtfully.

"Yeah. Look, I'm sorry, but—in your uncle's religion—forgive my ignorance about this—but your uncle's body was released. This is none of my business, but shouldn't he be buried today?"

"He was," she said off-handedly. "Howard went to the funeral."

"Oh," he said flatly. And then again, "Oh."

"Oh. I see. I *see*." she nodded knowingly. "I see where you're coming from. You're wondering why we're not—in mourning."

"Well—" He tilted his head in a question.

"We're not religious, Detective," she said with a flip of her hand. "We're—well—" She paused and looked into space as if she were deciding what they were. "Yes. I guess you would say we're atheists." She screwed up her face in a humourless smile. "Yes, you could definitely say that. My uncle did go to temple—that's what they call it, you know, not synagogue. He always called it 'temple.' so I guess they'll be praying for him there. I imagine they will. Howard thought we should do something. But I said we'd just be hypocrites. Don't you agree?"

Stark made no acknowledgement. He sat with his arms folded, studying the woman, fascinated with how repellent she seemed to be. He was having real trouble coming to terms with it. It was surreal.

She shrugged. "I believe in life, Detective—" The line dripped with melodrama. She raised a hand as if it held the essence of this *life* she believed in. "And I don't believe in—" she sought the word and smiled with satisfaction when she found it, "in *dwelling* on death. My uncle lived his life." She shrugged. "Of course, it's a sad thing." She shrugged again. "In fact, it was a *very* sad thing that happened to him, but he's gone." Her voice on the "he's gone" went almost babyish, as if she were saying "all gone" playfully to an infant. She sighed. And then said quickly, with a firm finality, as if pronouncing her last words on the subject: "He's gone, and we have to get on with living. Maybe that doesn't make sense to you, but that's the way I feel."

Neither of them said anything for a moment, Stark's mouth hanging a little open. He didn't know whether he should laugh. Finally, he shook his head and said, "Yeah. Well, Mrs.—Ms. Shaw, it's none of my business—" He folded his arms. "You know, I have to say it's a bit surprising that you seem so—how should I put it—so *undisturbed* by what's happened." He raised his eyebrows.

"Mmm." She seemed to be thinking about something, and then her jaw went suddenly rigid and her eyes took on a hard look, and an edge of impatience came into her voice. "Well, can we get on with this? I'm sure you didn't come to pay your respects." She looked at her watch.

Stark thought about saying that that was exactly what he'd come for, but didn't. "Yeah, sure," he said, nodding. "Okay. I'd like to know some things about your uncle. What can you tell me about him?"

She made a childish puzzled face, appearing to ignore his question.

"D'you want a drink? I'm going to have something. I always drink gin and tonic in the hot weather. Isn't this weather unbearable? Will you have one?" She got up and walked to a glass-and-chrome drinks trolley. Her hips shifted from side to side in what, it was apparent, was a deliberately exaggerated motion, a sort of Mae West parody of suggestiveness.

"No, nothing. I don't want anything," he said sharply.

"Suit yourself," she said, smiling at him over her shoulder and then, seeing that he was looking at her, she bent slowly from the waist to retrieve a gin bottle from the bottom shelf.

Stark glanced briefly at her rear, gave his head shake—put off by the vulgarity of the display—and turned his attention to a garish abstract over the fireplace that reminded him of a painter's drop cloth and was probably worth a small fortune.

The woman sashayed back to the hassock, curling her legs beneath her, campfire-style. She took a long drink.

"What did you ask me? You wanted to know about my uncle?"

Stark nodded perfunctorily. "Anything you can tell me."

She pursed her lips in an expression that said she didn't think there was much to tell.

"He was a nice old man—born in Israel. He was my mother's sister's husband, came here about twenty years ago. He lived with my parents after his wife died. When they died a couple of years ago, he moved into an apartment. We hired him then to do odd jobs. That's about it." She gave her head a little shake. "I don't know what else to tell you."

"Did he have any money problems?"

"Money problems?" She made a face that said she'd never thought about it and wasn't about to begin. "I don't think so. I know he liked to gamble a little." She gave a put-upon sigh. "I don't think he owed anybody any money. I don't think he had any big debts or anything. My father left him a little money. His rent wasn't high. He didn't do much. He was an *old man*. Apart from going to the track, about the only thing I know he did was go to a social club, some kind of men's club. It was all old Jewish men. He played cards there, I guess, and, well you know what old men do. I guess he told stories. He liked to tell stories." She nodded and her upper body rocked back and forth with the nods. "Oh he liked to tell them." She tossed back the rest of her drink.

Stark was suddenly aware that all this was even more bizarre than he'd been thinking it was. He realized that he'd been so taken aback by the lack of concern the woman had displayed over her uncle's death that he'd passed over something else, something obvious, something even stranger. Over the years, he'd encountered a wide range of reactions to death: shock, tears, anger, hatred, even violence. The deaths he dealt with were violent deaths, and the people left behind were, indirectly, victims of that violence and behaved accordingly. But Shaw, he realized, was not reacting in a normal way to what was not just a death, but a violent death, and the violent death of someone in her immediate family circle. She had been speaking of her uncle's death as if he'd just passed away of old age in his bed, and she was not behaving in a way he'd ever experienced. Not the way any normal person would react to the death of someone she knew who had come to his end by being stabbed in the course of a robbery, the robbery and murder of a man who was working for her husband when he was killed. Through it all, she'd been speaking calmly, in a voice that suggested only one emotion: boredom.

She gave Stark a vacuous smile and he noticed how glassy her eyes were. That gin wasn't the first of the day for her.

"So. Is there anything else?" she said.

Stark was looking at her, straining to put together the pieces of a distorted puzzle without the benefit of the finished picture on the box lid.

She leaned toward him, returning the stare.

"So?" she said impatiently.

Stark shook his head, sighed; finally, he said, "Okay. Tell me this, then, did your uncle have a lady friend?"

"What?" She grimaced in disbelief. "Saul? A lady friend? You gotta be kidding. He was seventy-three years old." Her tone said that not only did she think Stark's question was absurd, but also that saying that her uncle had been seventy-three was like saying he'd been the village idiot.

Stark bizarrely found himself about to step in as an advocate for seniors' romantic inclinations, but quickly dismissed the idea. He was back to staring at the woman again. He felt like a skilled chess player facing a rank amateur, trying to find some point in each ridiculous move. Shaw made an inane face at him.

Finally, Stark said, "You know, Ms. Shaw, you've really knocked me for a loop here. I've got to admit I just can't quite figure you out."

"Figure *me* out?" The silly lilt had vanished from her voice.

"Look. It's just that you don't seem to be the least bit shocked by what's happened. I'm not talking about the lack of mourning. That's one thing. But if that's what you are, well, so be it But it's—well, it's almost as if you find that your uncle's being stabbed to death by a robber was nothing out of the ordinary."

"Of course it wasn't *ordinary,*" she snapped. She paused for a moment and her voice went suddenly soft. "It *was* a shock. I mean, it was—it was a terrible shock. It was an awful thing to happen to Uncle Saul. But, I mean, well, those things happen these days, don't they? I mean, you should know. You're a cop. Things like that do happen more and more."

Then the softness was swept aside as quickly as it had come and replaced by indignation.

"What am I supposed to do about it, anyway? Scream? Grind my teeth? Pull my hair out?" She got up quickly and turned as if she were going to get another drink and then seemed to change her mind. She turned slowly to face Stark again. And now when she spoke, she was back to being soft again, sounding vulnerable, less certain, defensive. "I told you. Life goes on. I think the best thing is to try to forget about it—just to get on with things. Of course I feel bad about it, what do you think?" She looked into her empty glass, and then said accusingly, "Of course, it *was* his own fault."

"How the hell do you figure that?"

She raised her eyes to the ceiling, looked agitated. "I told him not to carry that gun. I told him that if somebody wanted to rob him to just give up the money or the jewels or whatever he was carrying and forget it and not try to be a hero." Her voice changed again. In a higher pitch, quivering slightly either with tension or anger or both, she said: "But the old fool had to be a hero. Like he was still back on the kibbutz, fighting terrorists."

71

"Wait a minute. Wait a minute. Did you say you told him *not* to carry the gun?"

"Yes, I did. I told him."

"Well, you know, the only thing is, Ms. Shaw, your husband says the gun was your idea."

"What?" she hissed.

"He says the gun was your father's, and you thought your uncle would be safer if he carried it."

"That bastard. I didn't want him—Howard's forgotten, that's all. Either that or he was just blaming me because I wasn't there to defend myself. Typical." She sneered. "The gun was Saul's idea," she said adamantly. "My father showed it to him once and he remembered it. Saul insisted on it. Okay. I guess I might have got pissed off because the old—because he kept going on and on about it, and I *once might* have said, 'let him carry the damned thing,' or something. Afterwards, when I thought about it, I told him not to. I mean, I insisted. I wanted him to give it back, but he promised he wouldn't carry it. He said he wanted to keep it as a memento of my father. He promised he wouldn't take it out of his apartment." She decided she *would* have another drink and wobbled slightly as she went to refill her glass. "You sure you won't have one?"

Stark didn't answer.

"Like I say," she said, "I made him promise me he wouldn't carry it. And he said he wouldn't. He said he just going to keep it in the apartment. I believed him."

And then Stark said something he would have rejected out of hand as mean-spirited and out of place had somebody suggested earlier that he should ask on his visit to the grieving family. He said, "Well, whoever let him carry that thing was responsible for his death. And I told your husband that I just might bring charges about that gun."

She paused in the middle of pouring her drink and glared at him, then finished filling her glass.

"Do you have any more questions?" she said coldly.

"How often did your husband give your uncle a lot of money or jewels to carry?"

She shrugged. "You'd have to ask him."

"You don't know?"

"Nope."

"When was the last time you saw your uncle?"

She took a sip of her drink. She was still standing, leaning now against a tall cylindrical pedestal striped in a spiral of red and black that seemed designed to support a plant pot or a bowl or something, but wasn't. Stark wondered whether she'd stumbled against it on some other occasion and knocked the object off. "Last Sunday he was here," she said. "We had a barbecue."

"Did he behave unusually in any way? Did he seem distracted or worried about something?"

"No. He was perfectly normal."

"You say he had no money problems. Did you ever lend him any money?"

"No, I didn't lend him any money. Why do you keep asking about whether he needed money?"

Stark wondered himself why he was asking and decided to stop. Instead he asked her for the name and address of the club the uncle went to. She didn't know. Then he asked her for the address of her uncle's apartment. And she said she didn't know that either, but she'd look it up. She left the room, now walking very unsteadily, and came back with an address book opened at the page with Rabinovitch's name. Stark copied down an address on Tichester Road and handed her back the book. She flipped over a few pages and said she had found the address for the social club in the book, and gave him the book back opened to the relevant page. When Stark had finished writing down the address, and the woman got up to retrieve the address book from him, she stumbled into him, a breast pressing against his cheek.

"Sorry," she said, snickering. She pushed away from him slowly, her hands on his shoulders. She looked down at him and smiled. Stark shook his head in disbelief and looked away. She pulled herself upright quickly, snatching the address book from his hand.

"Is there anything else?" she said coldly, "because I have things to do."

"No, that'll do for now," he said, snapping his notebook closed. He sighed. There was something else he wanted to know. He forced out a thin smile and tried to sound casual. "So, your husband works out all the time, does he?" He patted his stomach. "Something I guess I should do. Where's he go, a gym or something?"

"I don't know. Some gym on Bloor Street."

"Oh, right," Stark said, nodding. "Goes every day about lunchtime, I think you said."

She made no response.

"You don't know the name of the gym?"

"What?"

"The name of the gym? Where you husband goes?"

"What do you want to know that for?"

"No reason really, except you said Bloor Street. As I said, I could use a gym myself and if it's in the right part of Bloor, it'd be handy for me."

"God, I don't know, something ridiculous." She

sighed at the strain. "Oh yeah, it was Body something—oh yeah, that's it, Bodies by Disher. The woman who owns it is called Disher, Rosemary Disher, I should have remembered." She raised her eyebrows.

"Bodies by Disher. Okay. I'll find it. Thanks," Stark said. "Oh, don't bother to see me out."

As he stepped out of that icebox of insanity, Stark found the sensation of plunging his face into hot mud a refreshing return to the real world of real feelings. What he had just endured in that red room with that mad woman had put a serious dent in his theory that he had, in one form or another, seen everything. He had encountered psychotic killers with more sympathetic personalities and more feelings for their fellow man than Barbara Shaw had manifested. He had met crack-smoking street hookers with more tenderness and certainly more class. It would take him some time to come to terms with the experience, and while he couldn't remotely imagine that airhead having anything directly to do with Saul Rabinovitch's death, he found himself half hoping that she had, because that would let him resolve the case in a way that would help balance the books for the old man.

"Jesus. I've been calling him an old man all along. He was only seventy-three. I've got a cousin who's seventy-three who's fitter than I am and looks younger."

Stark's pleasure at the cleansing heat was short lived. The interlocking bricks of the serpentine driveway were beginning to feel like hot coals through the thin soles of his tasselled loafers, he was starting to breathe through his mouth, and his underarms were melting. He looked at his car. Its grille seemed to be sneering menacingly at him. Left to bake in the afternoon sun, the vehicle looked as if it were threatening revenge, preparing to deliver a small taste of hell. He opened the door and stepped back as the car exhaled its stifling breath. He reached in and turned the key in the ignition. Then he closed the door and waited while the air-conditioner made the atmosphere liveable. There was a red sports car parked in the drive, a Miata. Stark noticed a bumper sticker. That seemed incongruous on a sport cars. It read "Remember Bill C-68," an election-time reminder to the opponents of the federal gun-registration law. Stark shook his head. His cell phone rang. Detective-Sergeant Ted Henry asked him how the case was going.

"Slowly. I'm doing some preliminary interviews. Ken Coulson in Hold-up is working with me."

"I spoke to him."

"Good."

"Listen, Stark, I'm calling about the Sheltoe murder."

"Oh yeah? Just a minute." Stark got into the car, shut the door and adjusted the louvres on the air-conditioner vents to direct the cold air to his face. "That's better."

"What the hell are you doing?"

"Eh? Nothing, nothing. What's this about the Sheltoe case?"

"We got another anonymous call, same guy as before, still saying the husband did it. As you know from the report—" Stark lifted his eyebrows. He hadn't read the report. "—his mother gave him an alibi. Anyway, the thing is, this guy doesn't really sound like a crank. He's very calm, but very insistent. He says he *knows* the son did it, that he can prove it. But when we asked him for more, he backed off. He just said we should reopen the case. 'Look harder,' the guy said. It's like he wants to tell us something, you know, but he can't bring himself to do it. Anyway, what I want to know from you is, can you handle both investigations? I really think we should move on this Sheltoe thing again. The original investigator was Dermot Kelly."

"Retired last year."

"Dropped dead six months later."

"You're kidding."

"Liver gave out. Dermot was very fond of the Bushmills. Anyway, the situation is that we don't have anybody else free at the moment. So, do you think there's any way you can handle both cases?"

"No."

"Shit, Stark, the Sheltoe case is not that—"

"Forget it. I'm not going to do both of them." Both men were silent, and then a thought struck Stark, and he said, "You know something—" He touched his lips with an index finger "There's a detective at 55 Division, Carol Weems. She's very good. I've worked with her before. She's no kid; she's experienced. Why don't you second her? Put her on the Sheltoe case?"

Henry didn't answer for a moment, then, without enthusiasm, said, "She's good, eh? Good investigator?"

"Terrific."

Henry sighed. "Shit. Okay. What's her name again?"

Chapter Twelve

Weems was bubbling when Stark saw her that night. She gave him a loud kiss on the lips, a kiss of thanks, not passion.

"This is going to get me into Homicide," she said.

"Kissing me? I don't think so. I haven't got that kind of influence."

"Thank you, Harry. You won't regret it."

"You know this isn't like investigating a break-in by some teenager at a Becker's on Kingston Road."

Weems made a face.

"No, I mean it. This is a murder."

"Wait a second. You *got* me the case. Are you suggesting I'm not up to it?"

"Well, no. But homicide is special—it's—you'll do fine." He gave her an avuncular smile.

"Gee, your confidence is overwhelming. Say, why *did* you recommend me for the Sheltoe case?"

"Because—when Ted asked me, you came immediately to mind, that's why. You're smart—you're intelligent."

"That's the same thing."

"You're a good cop. We worked together on the Andrews case, and you did great."

"I was your *messenger girl*. And that was two years ago. I notice you haven't asked me to work with you since. And you didn't run down to Homicide and tell them they should put me on the squad, did you?"

"Carol, for God's sake, you weren't the 'messenger girl.' You played a key role in solving that case. Now, if you don't want this assignment—You know, I thought you'd be delighted."

"And *grateful?* What else did you tell Henry about me—that I've got nice legs, that I'm a good lay?"

"Come off it with that feminist shit."

"Oh, that's right. I forgot about the plot, the worldwide female conspiracy to control and emasculate men."

"Oh, God."

"Yeah? So, tell me, why *did* you get Henry to give me the case?"

"All right. Okay. Because I can't do it. The other thing I'm working on is taking all my time."

"And not because the Sheltoe case is just a make-work project your inspector cooked up for you, and you figure you've got him back by handing it off to me."

"I don't get it. A minute ago, you were ecstatic about getting the case—"

"Well, am I right?"

"No, you're not right. Say, have you got both air-conditioners on full blast? Jesus, it's like a wind tunnel in here."

"Don't change the subject."

"I'm telling you. I've got a draught right down my neck—you ever hear of Bell's palsy? You can get it from sitting in a draught."

"Shut up, you hypochondriac asshole. All right, I'm going to solve this Sheltoe case, and then I'm going to rub your nose right in it."

Stark shook his head. He rose from the kitchen table

and started toward the front room.

"Where're you going?"

"I'm going to shut off that—"

"Oh, for God's sake."

Later, they made love—at first, in the wake of their spat, awkwardly, as if they felt obligated, as if her spending the night in his apartment somehow required it. But eventually, the pride that each took in his and her lovemaking skills took over, and it became a competition, as each tried to outdo the other until finally they both surrendered to the force of passion and became a frenzied tangle of legs and arms, finishing with a collapse of glistening bodies and the deep sleep of exhaustion.

About three in the morning, Stark got up to go to the bathroom. He was dripping with perspiration and realized the bedroom air-conditioner wasn't strong enough to handle the heat that had built up during the sulphurous day and was now oozing out of the bricks and plaster. He tiptoed into the front room and switched on the big air-conditioner in the window.

On his way back through the kitchen, he found Weems sitting at the table. They looked at each other and burst out laughing. Weems stood up, and they hugged. She began to pull away, but Stark held her to him.

"I have to pee," she said, extricating herself from his arms and hurrying to the bathroom. After a moment, he called out to her. "Carol?"

"What?"

"There's something—I think I should say."

"Go ahead."

Stark heard the toilet flush, the tap running. Weems came back into the kitchen. She had put on a robe.

"So?" she said.

"Mmm?"

"You said you wanted to say something."

Stark took a deep breath, changed his mind. He'd made a move toward the edge, was standing on it for an instant, and then backed away.

"Oh yeah," he said, "It's—I wanted to wish you luck on the case."

"Oh." Weems smiled, gave a little shrug. "Thanks."

Stark sighed.

"Ah, it's getting cooler," he said. "I think I'll turn the air-conditioner down a little."

Weems shook her head.

Chapter Thirteen

The next morning, Stark called a friend on the Intelligence Unit, Ernie Kowalski. They swapped gossip and told a couple of dirty jokes before Stark filled Kowalski in on the Rabinovitch killing and the apparent connection with Cataldi.

"Your old friend from that murder last winter?" Kowalski asked.

"The same. He's still counting the money from that one."

"You think he's linked to this jewellery heist because he owns the building?"

"Well, somebody had to have a key to that office. Why would the thing go down there, anyway?"

"Still carrying a torch for Cataldi? I remember you wanted him on that murder."

"Ernie, please."

"Okay. It's just I told you before about this guy. He may play a little fast and loose, but he's not a heavy hitter."

"You said that before the little hooker got offed, Ernie, and don't forget no one has seen hide nor proverbial hair of the guy who owned the mining company since that stock scam went down, have they? Nor that Bishop character, either, for that matter."

"The one you arrested by mistake for the murder?"

"Come on, Ernie. Give me a break."

"You know about the hooker, Harry. York Regionals got the guy, the hooker's ex-pimp. Cataldi admitted she'd been to see him. He never tried to hide it. He admitted he'd paid her for services rendered on the day she was seen at his place."

"Are you this guy's PR man or something, Ernie? You do remember the Mounties were watching the guy? Why *were* they watching him, anyway? Did you ever find out?"

"Nope. With them, it's always 'need to know,' and I guess they felt I didn't need to know."

"Yeah, well there had to be something. Listen, Ernie, don't think I'm out to settle a score with this guy. You'd be confusing me with somebody who gave a shit. Whether he made those guys disappear or not we'll probably never know, and frankly, I don't give a flying fuck. It could be a coincidence that he owns this building, but I think it's worth a look, don't you?"

"As long as you're not tilting at windmills."

"Ernie."

"It's just I don't think jewel robbery is this guy's style."

"Hey, I don't think he pulled the heist himself, Ernie, you know what I mean? What can you tell me about this kind of job?"

"Harry, the guy you want to talk to is Bernie Hardcastle on the Pawn Squad."

Chapter Fourteen

Weems spent the early part of the morning in the cafeteria at headquarters, looking through the Sheltoe murder file. The investigator on the case, Detective Dermot Kelly, had written a report that told her Karen Sheltoe's body had been found in her car, a white, 1990 Chevrolet Cavalier, near the Bluffers Park Yacht Club at the foot of the Scarborough Bluffs at 6:45 in the morning of July 20, two years earlier. She had been strangled with a belt. The buckle had left a clear mark. She had been found fully dressed in the back seat of the car, legs spread wide, panties hanging from her right ankle. Marks on the ground suggested she had been killed in the front seat, then dragged to the back seat. The autopsy revealed tearing that indicated she had been raped. There was no semen, suggesting that either the rapist had worn a condom, or he had not been able to ejaculate. Kelly speculated in parentheses that, "If the suspect had worn a condom—" (Weems smiled at the word "suspect." Stark, the police force's last great defender of the English language, had corrected her repeatedly on using "suspect.") Kelly's note went on: "—it might indicate that he was aware he could be identified by DNA testing, and that might suggest both intelligence and premeditation." The next part had been underlined: "It might also suggest that he had reason to fear that he would be a suspect." Weems shook her head, imagining with some annoyance she could hear the voice of Stark saying, "Now, that's the correct use of the word."

Kelly had not liked the state of the body nor the condition of the car. Apart from the ligature marks, there were no signs of violence on the body, no bruising, no skin under the fingernails to suggest scratching in self-defence. The clothing was not torn, the skirt had been lifted, but the blouse remained buttoned. Kelly had asked for a tox screen. It revealed the presence of a barbiturate, pentobarbital, and sufficient ethanol (alcohol) to indicate that the victim had consumed several drinks not long before she died.

"My God, she was drugged," Weems said aloud.

The report went on to say that all bars in a five-kilometre radius around the crime scene had been canvassed, with no success. Because the autopsy revealed that the victim had not eaten for some time before her death, restaurants that did not serve alcohol were not included in the canvass. Bartenders and servers were shown a photograph of the victim (a recent picture had been obtained from the woman's husband, Graeme Adams, 127 Fermagh Court, Scarborough) and asked whether they had seen her in the presence of a man during the pertinent time period.

Suspicion, Kelly had written, had fallen on the husband, both because his reaction to his wife's death had been unnatural, "in the opinion of myself, the lead investigator," and because the husband worked for a drug distribution company. "A discreet inquiry at the husband's place of employment, Medi-Source Inc., 678 Pharmacy Ave., Scarborough, revealed that the drug in question was in their inventory. However, during subsequent contacts with the company's president,

Harold Barnes, it was determined that no quantity of the drug could be found to be unaccounted for. Barnes told me that the husband was a reliable and highly respected employee and that he could not understand why we would be investigating him.

"Subsequently, we interviewed the husband, asking him about his whereabouts on the evening in question. He told us he had been at his mother's house all evening. We interviewed the mother, Jane Adams, 1505 Finch Ave., Apt. 1201, Scarborough. She corroborated her son's story. She said he came to her apartment at 5 p.m. and remained until 1 a.m. the following morning. According to the coroner's report, the victim's death occurred between 7 p.m. and 9:30 p.m. The body was discovered at 12:45 a.m. the following day by David McLean, a security guard employed by the Bluffers Park Yacht Club."

There was a diagram of the crime scene, including a circled area and a notation that footprints had been found. An accompanying note said the prints had no discernible tread and appeared to have been made by a man's size nine, flat-soled shoe, possibly a boat shoe, the kind worn by yacht crew.

Attached to the file folder by a paper clip was a note in handwriting that was headed by a notation in capital letters: FOR INTERNAL DEPARTMENT INFORMATION ONLY. The note, which was written by Kelly, read: "I learned that the suspect had lived in Australia and that he had had to leave that country because of some trouble he got into. Subsequently, I made inquiries with the Australian Federal Police. An Inspector Alan Forsyth in Sydney responded to my inquiries. He informed me that Graeme Adams had been the subject of an investigation involving sex with a minor, but he had no further details. He said local police in Sydney had not pursued the matter on the understanding that Adams would leave the country immediately and not return, which he apparently did. I intend to pursue this matter further with the Sydney police."

In the end, Kelly must not have pursued the matter, because there was no further reference to it. Kelly had retired shortly after the investigation had begun, and maybe he never got back to it. Adams's mother had provided Adams with a strong, albeit prejudiced, alibi. There was neither physical evidence nor witness that could put Adams at the crime scene. The case was marked "open."

Chapter Fifteen

Bernie Hardcastle looked like a man who enjoyed his beer. Stark thought he must have trouble getting his roly-poly body through the annual physical, even more trouble than *he* did. His physique was paralleled by his florid face, bulging cheeks, an extra chin and a huge, bulbous nose. He had agreed to meet Stark at Holtzman's, and Stark was glad to learn that he smoked a pipe. They had squeezed into the smoking booth, Stark sliding the door shut peremptorily after Sid had delivered them coffees.

"Nice," Sid muttered. "Now I'm running a private club for smoking cops."

Hardcastle filled his pipe from an ancient leather pouch, and went through a ritual of tamping and lighting and retamping and relighting.

"Do you know a jeweller called Howard Stokes?" Stark asked him.

"Sure, the robbery and the killing. Yeah, I know Stokes. He's been in the business all his life, inherited it from his father. Used to be, years ago, there were almost nothing but Jewish people in the jewellery racket, you know. And, no, the word doesn't come from 'Jew.'"

Interested, Stark asked,

"Where *does* it come from? Do you know?"

"Well, if you go back far enough through Old French to Latin you get 'jocale,' which meant 'plaything.'"

"You know the French word 'jouet' means 'toy'?

"Is that right?"

"Yeah."

"Mmm." Hardcastle took his pipe from his mouth and stared into the bowl as if he'd just tasted something odd in the smoke. He poked at the ashes with a tamper, gave them another press with his thumb and relit the pipe. "So," he said after a couple of puffs and another glance into the bowl, "I don't think we're here to talk about words, are we, Stark. I know about jewellery because that's my thing, but after that—"

"Well, I don't know anything about jewellery, Bernie. And the way I work, I like to get my head around the subject. I want to know a lot more than I'm ever going to need to make a case. You know what I mean?"

"Sure."

"Right. There were supposed to be three estate collections involved in the Stokes robbery. I want to know about estate jewellery. Also about insurance, about who values the pieces, who appraises them. Stokes says he paid nine-hundred-thousand for the pieces, but he aimed to sell them for four million. Now, is it likely he would send an old man out carrying so much?"

"Sure. Happens all the time. Who's going to hit the guy? He's not going to be walking around with that kind of value every time he leaves the building, is he? First, you've got know that he's a courier, and unless you know he's got a bundle with him on a particular occasion, you're liable to knock him over for a sack of sandwiches. The answer is yes, he could be carrying that amount easily." Hardcastle nodded several times, puffing on his pipe. "What it does mean, of course, is you've got to look for somebody inside, or somebody with an inside connection. Listen, why don't I give you a little primer on the whole business."

"Perfect."

"Okay. Now you asked about appraisals. The keyword here is 'reputable.' The Stokeses have been in the business long enough they qualify for that description. Now, often the dealer has an appraisal from the customer or from the estate that includes a detailed listing of the items, and using that as a guide, he can make an offer or a suggestion for dispersal. However, there are times when no paperwork is available and the dealer will make an offer, a lump sum for the lot, or there'll be a list with prices for each item and a total for the lot. The client may be given a copy, but often not. In other words, a reputable jeweller does his own appraisal, and the insurance company will accept that.

"Now jewellery stores, you know, may not have insurance. Some of them self- insure, while others have what is known as a jeweller's block policy, for a set amount—a million dollars, say—and the jeweller is mandated to keep at or near that amount in inventory. Losses over that would not be covered. In fact, they could result in voiding the policy. Now, unless a piece is *very* important, the jeweller would not specify the piece. Say he was having a special showing of, say, the jewels from that guy Mel Fisher's discovery of the ship the *Atochia.* An emerald-and-gold cross might be worth seven hundred and fifty thousand, and the jeweller would put a rider on the policy to cover himself for the event. Anyway, obviously, that's not the case here, but—" Hardcastle shrugged, removed his pipe from his mouth and looked into the bowl again. He continued to gaze intently at the ashes as if he were a shaman trying to read signs while he raised his coffee cup to his lips and took a sip. Stark watched, intrigued, as the man tamped the contents of the pipe bowl and relit it carefully with an orange lighter. In a sort of counterpoint, Stark flipped a cigarette out of his pack, stuck it in his mouth and lit it in almost one motion. They smiled at each other.

"So," said Hardcastle, pausing to fold his arms and grip the pipe bowl between thumb and forefinger, "to continue: the value of the piece is established at the time of purchase or consignment. In the event of loss, the value paid by the insurance company is based on the purchase price and not on the retail price or on anticipated profit. That's where the paper trail comes in. If the jeweller is ripped off for something he paid five hundred dollars for and he priced it at twenty-seven hundred, he would get five hundred back from the loss, based on the receipt. Incidentally, a dealer buying a very important piece or a big collection might choose to 'partner' with someone, or more than one person, to spread the risk."

Stark nodded.

"Okay. Now, we're dealing here with estate jewellery. And that often has a greater value than contemporary work because of several factors. It might have antique value. A piece from a historic era, say the French revolutionary period associated with Marie Antoinette. If that can be documented, it would be of great value. Pieces from the twenties are often worth more because the use of platinum was widespread then and it is more costly than gold. Often the older pieces are heavier."

"Is that right?" Stark said.

"Now, gems are not exactly what you'd call a rapidly renewable resource, you know, and they're getting scarcer and quality is in decline. Older pieces will often have bigger, better stones that are not treated. The technology was not as advanced as it is today. Very large, quality rubies, for example, are very rare and expensive.

"And another important factor is the name on the piece. That can add a great deal of value. I'm talking about names like Tiffany, Cartier, Bulgari, Fabergé, and Van Cleef and Arpels. These are huge firms that take their names from the owners who, at the time, did the designs for the pieces produced. They all worked at the turn of the century. Some of them had staff designers who became famous in their own right. Schlumberger at Tiffany is a good example. Cartier often used exquisite gems in finely crafted pieces that are still sought after as the finest available. Fabergé, on the other hand, often used lesser stones in quality work so his things are desired for their craftsmanship rather than the gem value."

Hardcastle took his pipe out again.

"I'm sorry," he said. "I get carried away."

"No, no, Bernie. Just carry on."

"Okay. Now if this stuff is stolen, there are places where things can be fenced in New York and L.A., to a lesser degree in Montreal and Vancouver. There is a pipeline for this stuff in Colombia."

"Would they remove the stones from their settings?"

Hardcastle gave a small shrug.

"Well, an important ring with a huge stone would be better to be taken out of the mounting even though it is signed, because the risk would be substantially less of getting caught, but there would be a loss in value, and that loss might be substantial. And don't forget, the value of many of these pieces is inherent in the settings. A historic piece would lose almost all its value if it was tampered with. You could switch stones from one mounting to another, or alter the mountings, but that would also affect the value."

"What gives a gem its value, apart from the setting?"

"Gems are sold by carat weight, but they also have components that determine value, which include cut, clarity, colour and to a lesser degree, country of origin, the name of the cutter and, again, historic association. In the Kennedy sale, for instance, some rather pedestrian pieces sold for astonishing amounts. Another example was the Duchess of Windsor's sale. But I guess we're not dealing with anything of that sort of historic association here, are we?"

Stark shook his head.

"I don't think so. What about recutting the stones?"

"I doubt it. To cut a stone would reduce the value by a factor of three or more. It's unlikely this would be done. Although to recut from a pear to a round, from an antique cut to a modern cut would lose weight but it wouldn't be as drastic."

"Naturally, *I'm* interested in the *murder* here. Hold-up is running the robbery aspect of the case. I imagine they've been in contact with you people about what's been taken?"

"They have, yes."

"So, a couple of questions: have you distributed a circular describing the stolen items? And two, is there some kind of clearinghouse for hot merchandise that a jeweller can check, to see whether a piece being offered is stolen or not?"

"To answer your second question first: no. There's no such animal. We might occasionally distribute circulars about a robbery, but that's rare, and we haven't in this case. Sometimes jewellers' associations might describe something missing."

Hardcastle went through the pipe-lighting routine again, prompting Stark to say, "I don't know how you guys put up with all that stuff."

"The Pawn Squad?"

"No, pipe smokers."

"It's more of a fetish than a habit. Years ago, before smoking became an anti-social act and the magazines were filled with tobacco ads, there was one ad in particular that I enjoyed. It showed a guy in a cardigan, and the pockets of the thing were bulging with pipes and pipe tools and pipe cleaners and a tobacco pouch, and the caption was something like: 'Anybody who'd go to this much trouble deserves the best tobacco.' Of course, I can't remember what the tobacco was. Anyway, have I given you what you want to know?"

"You've been great, Bernie."

"Listen, if you want to get any more information on estate jewellery, the outfit to contact is in the States, in Carmel, California. It's called Erickson & Erickson. They're as straight as the day is long. For instance, there's a deal in the States called the Jewelers Board of Trade, and they give them the highest rating in the States. Of course, no estate store has the stature of say Birks, or in the States, Tiffany or Shreves—"

Chapter Sixteen

Stark went to Rabinovitch's apartment on Tichester Road. The room air-conditioners protruding from a goodly number of the tiny windows in the old building were a depressing clue that the place was going to feel like a false roof in a drycleaners. The radio had said the temperature was going to be down a degree or two from the previous day, but Stark thought they must have been wrong. It didn't help that he'd had to park a block away. The superintendent, a tall, lanky, laconic man with stooped shoulders and a Newfoundland dialect, didn't want to let Stark in, and, feeling the wafts of air emanating from the interior as if the man were holding open the door to a forge, Stark had half a mind to accede to the man's objection.

"I think you're supposed to have a warrant to go searching people's apartments, aren't you? I don't think I can let you in, sir. I don't think I'd be doin' my job if I was to let you in there, sir. I don't mean to be disrespectful."

"I'm sure you don't, mister—"

"Power. John Power, sir." He extended his right hand. Stark looked at it for an instant, then took it in his. The tall man's long arm made a snaking motion, giving Stark's hand a single, slow, powerful shake. "Well, Mr Stark, I'm sure you understand—"

"He's dead."

"Who's dead?"

"Rabinovitch, the tenant in three-oh-two. He's dead."

"Oh my gosh. Oh my gosh. I'm sorry to hear that. I didn't even know 'e was sick."

Stark sighed.

"I'm afraid he was killed, Mr. Power, in a robbery."

"Oh my God. In this neighbourhood—it's so quiet around 'ere."

"No—not here. Look, I've got to get into the apartment."

"Yes—well, I guess that's different. I'll—I'll let you in."

The building was redolent of cooking odours, cabbage and onions dominating, Making his way down the hallway behind the superintendent, Stark felt as if he were wading through a pot of stew. Rabinovitch's apartment smelled old. A stifling belch of stale air even hotter than the atmosphere in the corridor hit them in the face. The place was in darkness, everything still. The venetian blinds were closed on the single narrow window in the tiny living room.

"Let me get some air in here," the superintendent said, raising the blinds and opening the window, with no discernible effect. Heavy drapes were pulled shut on the window in the tinier dining room, which connected by an opening in the wall to a kitchen not much wider than its ancient stove and fridge.

The tap was dripping. Stark gave it a futile twist.

"'E nivver told me about that," the caretaker said. "I coulda fixed it for 'im."

"What? Listen, Mr.—?"

"Power."

"Mr. Power, would you mind? I'd like to have a look around on my own. This is police business."

The old man looked concerned—Stark figured he must have been fairly deep into his seventies, but his face belied his age. The skin was smooth, pinkish, freckled, and he had a full, if wispy, head of sandy hair. "I don't know," the man said. "Don't you think I should—"

"No, I don't, Mr. Power." Stark took him by an elbow, led him to the door and eased him into the hallway. "You can wait right there, see that I don't take the TV set out with me, okay?" Stark closed the door.

Rabinovitch's apartment—scattered clothing, caked plates—looked much as Stark's had until the last few months, with Weems coming around. Stark opened the kitchen window. Car tires whooshed on the street below. He felt a whisper of cooler air on his neck. It had started to rain. In the end, it would just make it muggier.

Everything in the place seemed grey. It was hard to imagine the walls had actually been painted grey, but they looked like it in the dim light and after years of accumulated grime. Nor did the furniture actually look grey. It was more as if it felt that shade, an impression heightened by scattered newspapers and walls half-covered with old photographs, many of which displayed, among their subjects, one young man, tall and bright-eyed, with such a wide, ear-to-ear grin that the array seemed like a collage of toothpaste advertisements. In all the photos, the youthful Rabinovitch was dressed in military khakis. He was portrayed grinning from the tops of tanks; beaming with rifle in hand, guarding a group of sullen prisoners; standing—and on this occasion, many years older—with a knot of other troops around a smiling figure with a patch over one eye, Moshe Dayan. Staring at the picture, Stark wondered for a moment whether it really was Dayan. He thought of the film *I Was Monty's Double,* and pondered whether the Israelis might have used Dayan doubles for risky public appearances where he would be an easy target for Arab assassins.

The bedroom was an even bigger mess, a corner chair piled high with clothing, the bed unmade, its sheets as grey as the walls. What they used to call in the old laundry-soap ads, Stark remembered, "tattle-tale grey." The room was thick with the stink of dry sweat, drawers were open, draped with socks and underwear. Stark put on a pair of surgical gloves and began to go through the drawers, searching for he didn't know what. At the bottom of one drawer, beneath a torn, stained heating pad, he found a cookie tin, Peek Frean's biscuits. In it were Rabinovitch's Canadian citizenship certificate, dated 1984, an expired Israeli passport, a current Canadian passport, an honourable discharge from the Israeli army, dated 1968, a document signed by David Ben-Gurion, attesting to Rabinovitch's exemplary service in defence of Israel, dated 1950; a ragged, paperback copy of the *Communist Manifesto.*

Wrapped in waxy brown paper was the old man's birth certificate, in English, giving his place of birth as Haifa, in the British protectorate of Palestine, 1924. Held together with a rubber band were a number of yellowed, crumbling newspaper clippings describing various guerrilla attacks on British installations, and a committal warrant from a British military court, sentencing Saul Rabinovitch to two years' imprisonment for obstruction of justice and damaging Crown property. At the bottom of the biscuit tin, beneath the documents, was a faded photograph of a young woman in military fatigues. The age of the photo and the woman's hairstyle suggested it had been taken in the 1940s. Was this the woman Stokes had told Stark about, the one love of Rabinovitch's life, who had been killed in an Arab attack? The picture was slightly out of focus, but the woman's stunning beauty was unobscured. Stark held the picture for a moment. It reminded him of someone. He felt a tightness in his throat, felt a memory that gave him pain. He put the photo back, replaced the papers and closed the tin.

In another drawer, Stark found an assortment of travel folders from casinos in Las Vegas and Atlantic City. There were two used airline tickets for Las Vegas, one from the previous March, another for the same month a year earlier. On the floor, beside the bed, was a pile of *Racing Forms*. On a shelf in the kitchen, he discovered a stack of bills—mostly electricity and telephone, the current ones on top, both overdue. There was an overdue notice for a Visa account. Among the cancelled bills, going back at least two years, there were four warnings of imminent disconnection and three notices suspending privileges on the Visa card until the account was brought up to date.

He glanced around the tiny kitchen at the detritus of an old man living alone, a garbage can overflowing with TV-dinner packages, empty cans and pop bottles, the sink piled with dirty dishes. The fridge was littered with items all held in place by fridge magnets advertising an Eglinton Avenue travel agency. There were several newspaper clippings dealing with political and military events in or about Israel. There was a postcard from Bermuda that read, "Dear Uncle Saul: Having a wonderful time. The weather's fabulous. Hope you're looking after yourself, Barbara."

At the top left-hand corner of the fridge, there was a photograph. Stark removed it. It showed three men standing in front of Caesar's Palace in Las Vegas. The quality was poor. It had been taken facing the sun. It took Stark a moment to identify the subjects: Rabinovitch was the tall one. The slightly shorter was Howard Stokes. The third man, the shortest—"Jesus. Salvatore Cataldi."

Chapter Seventeen

At eight o'clock that night, Weems put through a call to Inspector Alan Forsyth of the Australian Federal Police. It was eleven o'clock the next morning in Canberra. Weems had called earlier and had been told the inspector would be available at that time.

"What's the weather like in Toronto?"

"Sweltering. We're in the middle of a heatwave. It was thirty-five degrees yesterday. Oh, we're in Celsius."

"Us too, been in it for years. It's bitter here. Twenty degrees."

"Inspector, I'm interested in getting some information on someone I believe lived in Australia for a time a few years back. I understand another Toronto officer contacted you two years ago concerning this person. His name is Graeme Adams."

"I do recall that, yes."

"Well, the file has been inactive for a while, but the investigation has been reopened. Unfortunately, the original investigator has since died—"

"That's a shame."

"Yes, it is. His notes are not complete. There is a mention that Adams was charged with having sex with a minor, and that the case was dropped on the condition that he left the country?"

"That's right."

"Can you tell me more about that?"

"I can, as a matter of fact."

Weems was surprised.

"You remember the case?"

The inspector chuckled.

"Oh, it's not because I have an encyclopaedic memory, or anything like that. It's only because you mentioned to my assistant what you'd be calling about, so I got the file out." He laughed again.

"Oh, I see." Weems snickered politely.

"So, what did you want to know? Of course, it wasn't actually our case. A local Sydney matter. But I pulled the information together for your late colleague. I've probably got everything you need. This fellow of yours, Adams, got involved with a minor, and the Sydney police said they wouldn't prosecute if he just quietly left the country—and didn't come back. That's about it. Of course, because they didn't prosecute, there's no actual record. For all intents and purposes, no crime took place, which means this is between you and me as a professional courtesy. But it's not information that you can release in any way, you understand that?"

"Yes, of course. In what way did he get involved with a minor?"

"Sorry, that's all I've got. If you want more, you'll have to contact the Sydney police."

Weems's chin slumped on her chest. "Okay," she said, sighing. "Can you give me the telephone number and who I would contact at the Sydney police?"

"I certainly can." He told her the number, repeating it twice, slowly. "The fellow you want to talk to is Sergeant Cowley, Ben Cowley. He'll help you out. Tell him I told you to call."

Cowley was out, wouldn't be back until two p.m.—

eleven p.m. Toronto time. Weems phoned Stark's apartment. No answer. She called Carbo's, but hung up before the phone was answered. Stark might be drunk already, and that would annoy her. She didn't want to get into a fight with him. She couldn't be bothered. She went to her car, got in the back seat, set the alarm on her watch to ten-thirty and slept.

Back in the office, she wasn't able to get Cowley on the line until eleven-thirty. Then he told her he'd have to locate the file and asked her to call back in fifteen minutes. On the second call, he said he had the information she wanted, but then he said he was reluctant to give it to her over the phone.

"You tell me you're a Toronto detective, but I don't know that that's the case, do I? I'd prefer something in writing."

Weems sighed.

"I am in the middle of an investigation, Sergeant. If I have to send you a letter—"

"A fax will do. Send me a fax on Toronto police stationery, requesting the information, then call me back."

It took her another fifteen minutes to type the request and send the fax. She waited another ten minutes before phoning again.

"Now we're in business," Cowley said. "You understand, I have to be careful—"

"Of course—"

Weems heard pages turning.

"Okay, well it seems this Adams got mixed up with a teenager. I won't give you his name—"

"His? It was a male?"

"Street kid. He was fifteen at the—" He

pronounced "fifteen" as "fifdeen." "—but he looked more like eighteen. I remember the case, and there was some question about Adams being quite blotto at the time." He chuckled. "In fact, we didn't think Adams knew the lad was a male, since the kid was dressed up as a woman. He was quite a pretty kid. He worked the streets as a male prossie. Real hard type, he was. The poor bugger's dead. I know that because I just handled the case—a few weeks back. Drug overdose. Now, when this thing happened with Adams, we were running a vice crackdown, picked up Adams in a sweep of a downtown park. He was in the bushes with the kid. I remember the case because he was a Canadian. His wife bailed him out." He gave another dry chuckle. "You know, I must say, this chappie has strange tastes in his personal relationships. His wife—she's Australian of course. I don't imagine they're still married, though, are they?"

"If it's the same wife, she's dead."

"Oh?"

"That's what the investigation is about. She was murdered—two years ago."

"Well, what do you know?"

"If it *is* the same woman."

"I've got her name here somewhere. Here it is, Sheltoe. Karen Sheltoe."

"Same woman."

"Two years ago? And you're still investigating the crime?"

"Yeah, we're a bit slow up here. It's the cold, you know. I'm sorry, Sergeant. No, the case was suspended. Now it's been reopened."

"And you suspect the husband?"

"It's always the husband."

"Spoken like a true woman."

"Mmm."

"This Sheltoe woman—you do know that she was a tart? If you'll pardon my language."

"A tart? What do you mean? She was—promiscuous?"

"No, no. I mean she was a prostitute."

"Karen Sheltoe was a hooker?"

"That's right. That's why I'm saying this Adams' taste in sexual matters was a little weird. Anyway, she, as I say, came and bailed him out. She begged us not to prosecute him, said they were leaving for Canada the next week. Under the circumstances, we thought it best to let him go, on the understanding that if they didn't leave, we'd charge him. Might have been quite serious because the boy was a minor. But then, as I say, the kid was done up like Madonna, and Adams was well under the influence."

Weems thanked Cowley for his help, offered to return the favour at any time, then had to chat with him about police work in Canada for ten minutes before she was finally able to hang up.

She looked at her notes, sitting on an otherwise bare desk, an unused desk they'd let her occupy in the back corner of the Homicide Unit. Sergeant Henry had said she could use Stark's desk. "He's never here, anyway." But she'd seen the empty desk in the corner and said she preferred it, if that was all right.

"A hooker," she said to herself. "Karen Sheltoe was an Australian prostitute. God."

Chapter Eighteen

After the search of Rabinovitch's apartment, Stark went to look for the social club Barbara Shaw had told him her uncle belonged to. According to what he copied from the address book Barbara Shaw showed him, the place should have been in a little row of shops on Bathurst, north of the 401, but there was no sign of a social club: just a travel agency, a dry cleaner's and a flower shop. He looked again at the address he'd written in his notebook and realized the squiggle after the numeral was an "a." He scanned the storefronts, and there it was: a red door, with no more identification than the street number. A car pulled carefully into a spot in the parking lot in front of the three stores. The car appeared to be driverless. A gleaming black 1986 Oldsmobile 98, it was in showroom condition. Both front doors opened and two little old men emerged, both dressed in stylish casual clothes; both smoking cigars. They shuffled toward the red door. The passenger took a key from his pocket, unlocked and held the door open for the driver. Stark could see there was a flight of stairs behind the door. The social club must be on the second floor.

Stark shut off the engine and opened the car door. Partly the wall of heat that met him and partly the germ of an idea pushed him back into the car. He closed the door and started the engine again to reactivate the air-conditioner. He thought for a moment and then nodded, deciding to pursue his idea. He picked up his cell phone, put a call through to 32 Division and finally got an Inspector Gordon on the line. He asked him about a plainclothes constable, Noel Harris.

"What do you want to know about him? He's not into something?"

"No-no. I'd like to use him on a case."

"On a case? Why do you want Noel?"

"He worked with me before, a couple of years back."

"I don't remember."

"Well, he did. He's good."

"Noel?" Stark could hear the shrug in the inspector's voice. "Well, you're welcome to him. I'll transfer you to the sergeant and he can give you Noel's cell phone number."

When Harris didn't answer the phone, Stark cursed. He left a message. He ventured into the heat again, discarding his jacket and tossing it in a heap in the corner of the front seat. He loosened his tie. The air was choking as it mixed with the fumes of the traffic on Bathurst. Stark waded through it, perspiration already streaming down his sides. He had spotted an oasis, and made his way toward it with a quick shuffle step—an ice-cream store. The frigid air practically sucked him inside. The kid at the counter had a smug grin. Stark scowled at him. The scowl grew more intense as Stark scanned the massive list of ostentatious flavours—from Apple-sin-a-mint to X-tra-atrocious-choco-licious.

"Don't you have any vanilla?" he snapped.

The kid looked at the list on the wall, then at Stark, with an expression of mild disbelief that someone could study a list of one-hundred-and-fifty of probably the most exotic and imaginative flavours of ice cream in the modern world and still be jerk enough to ask for something as boring as vanilla.

"We're out of it," he said.

"What about butterscotch?"

"Taffy-truffle is sort of like that."

"Well, give me one of those."

"Jumbo sugar cone?"

"I'll have the sugar cone, but a small."

"We only have jumbo."

"You mean, you have only jumbo," Stark corrected the kid pompously.

"That's what I said."

Stark shook his head.

"Well, give me a regular cone, small. One scoop."

"Two scoops is the smallest—"

"One scoop."

"It's no cheaper."

"Just—give—me—one—scoop."

The kid shrugged, flipped open the glass cover, dug out a chunk of coffee-coloured ice cream no bigger than a golf ball, jammed it with a crunch into the cone and handed it to Stark.

"A dollar-seventy-five," he said.

Stark came within an ace of saying, "When I was a kid, these things were a dime," but didn't. He gave a big sigh and handed the kid a five.

The kid counted thirteen quarters into Stark's hand.

"What the hell's this?" Stark said.

"I'm sorry. We've got no toonies or loonies. The boss just went to the bank. He'll be back in a few minutes if you want to wait."

Stark's cell phone rang. He had the coins in one hand and the ice cream cone in the other. He looked at each hand in turn, glared at the kid, shoved the coins into his pocket and pulled the phone out of his back pocket.

"Hot enuf fer ya?" Noel Harris asked in a feigned rustic voice.

"Who is this?"

"Noel Harris, Sarge. You called me, remember?"

Stark told Harris where his car was parked and arranged to meet him there. Harris said he was two minutes away. Stark gave the counter kid and the list of one-hundred-and-fifty exotic flavours a parting look of disgust. The kid shrugged.

Harris was already at Stark's car when Stark arrived. Stark tossed the ice cream cone, only a few licks lighter, into some weeds beside the boarded-up building.

"You didn't like it?" Harris said.

"What?"

"The ice cream cone?"

"No—it's some kind of taffy-daffy something or other. They don't even have butterscotch. And vanilla—forget it."

Harris shook his head in exaggerated commiseration.

"Gee," he said.

"God. Let's get out of this heat," Stark said, unlocking the car, reaching in and starting it to get the air-conditioner going. "Wait a second," he said.

Harris looked around.

"What are we waiting for?"

"For the air-conditioner."

"Oh." Harris raised his eyebrows.

Stark glowered. He held a hand inside the car.

"Okay," he muttered, and lowered himself gingerly into the front seat, letting out a loud "phew," and flipping the blower vents to direct the air to his face. He reached over and unlocked the passenger door. Harris got in, sitting on Stark's jacket. Stark was occupied with the business of cooling off, lifting the front of his shirt from his body. "God, it's hot," he said, and looked at Harris, who was in his early thirties, good looking, tall and gangly, long-limbed, thin fingers, fine-featured, sitting there looking through the windshield, his brow dry, not a hair out of place, wearing a light denim shirt and tight jeans. "You're sitting on my jacket," Stark growled.

"Oh, sorry. I didn't see it." He slid forward while Stark retrieved the jacket and made an absurd display of flattening its wrinkled mass and folding it carefully before flipping it on to the rear seat. Stark noticed that Harris's nostrils were flared like a puppy's, sniffing the air. He was smelling something he didn't like—the lingering odour of Stark's Gauloises.

"Inspector Gordon told me you wanted me on a case, Sarge."

"We worked together before on a case. You remember the little girl that was killed by her nanny in the mall washroom?"

"That was three years ago."

"Listen. This is a murder case. Robbery and murder. The jewel robbery on Eglinton."

"The old courier."

"Yeah. The old guy was offed in a vacant office. The whole building is practically vacant. There was no reason for him to be there. He was carrying a .32 semi-automatic. I think he may have been in on it himself, and something went sour and his accomplice wasted him. At least, that's a possibility. And I believe in running possibilities down until they either pan out, or are eliminated. Look, you see across the street there, the red door? That's a men's club, a social club or something."

Harris nodded knowingly.

"I want you to go in there and ask them about Rabinovitch."

"That's the courier's name?"

"Saul Rabinovitch. Find out whether any of them were closer to him than the others. He gambled a fair amount. Find out was he in debt? Maybe he owed a bookie. Also, I have the impression that the old man and his family didn't get along. There may have been some bitterness. His—whatever you call him—nephew-in-law owned the jewellery store. I want to know what their relationship was. And I went to see the niece, and it was like she couldn't care less that her uncle just got offed. Do you get the picture? Maybe somebody heard the old man had it in for the pair of them, which would give us another reason why he might have set up the heist. And ask them this: ask them if they ever heard the name Cataldi in connection with Rabinovitch? Salvatore Cataldi."

"Who's he?"

"That's why I'm not going in myself. Cataldi might hear that I was on his case again. He knows me. I'll tell you all about that prick—" Stark gave Harris a rundown of the robbery and the investigation. They arranged to meet in an hour at a deli on Wilson Avenue. Stark watched Harris cross Bathurst, knock on the red door and wait—and then knock again and wait. Finally the door swung open, Harris showed his badge, went inside, and Stark drove away.

Chapter Nineteen

Noel Harris had been a policeman for eight years. He was thirty-three. He had an English degree from the University of Toronto, which, he had discovered, equipped him for not much more than teaching English (to get a job at which, without moving to Kenora, in Northern Ontario, he would have had to have obtained a master's degree—and he'd had enough of analyzing the blood references in *Macbeth* and discussing the phallic symbols in *Wuthering Heights*). About the only other thing the bachelor of English degree made him a prime candidate for was selling socks in Eaton's.

It was perhaps because Stark recognized a fellow-travelling misfit that he had remembered Noel and sought his help. Had Stark not been so self-absorbed, there might not have been a three-year gap in their relationship. Like Stark, Noel had drifted into police work. It was something you could do without fear or favour (with notable exceptions): catching criminals was not a bad thing to do, whether you were a capitalist or the socialist that Noel labelled himself as. He thanked his idea of God that he had been lucky enough never to have had to part a picket line to let the scabs go through. It was the one assignment that he feared being given the most. But he had been bright enough and articulate enough to move quickly out of the uniform ranks into plainclothes. But he was stuck there, mostly by lack of ambition, but also by lack of commitment. He didn't really want to be a detective. The fact is, he didn't really want to be a cop, but he loved to read and he loved to travel, and he could put in enough overtime to give him great chunks of vacation time, in which he could journey to Thailand and India and Papua New Guinea and South America. (It was out of political and sociological awareness that he had never been to Europe, had never seen Trafalgar Square or the Louvre or Vienna or Venice.) He had, over the years, worked a number of undercover operations. They frightened him, but he was good at them. But eventually, his lack of ambition grated on his superiors, and they took to giving him office jobs, community relations, filing, that sort of thing. It annoyed them even more that he seemed to like that. So, periodically, they would give him a dangerous undercover job out of bloody-mindedness.

Noel was born in Winnipeg. His mother and father had been labour organizers, both committed Marxists. Noel's mother was university-educated, at the University of Montana; his father had barely escaped elementary school. Noel was raised as a humanist. But, in a reversal of the usual pattern of youthful rebellion, he found religion at the age of sixteen, attending a Baptist church for a couple of months until its strictures got tiresome. He tapered off into reading the bible and thought that he would study theology at university until he was captivated by the perfect placidity of a young man who joined his community-centre basketball team and he discovered Zen Buddhism, to which he remained attached until another door to enlightenment in his youthful development opened and he discovered the powerful charms of beer and marijuana and sex.

****

A heat wave is a destroyer. It crushes the mind. It kills the spirit. It sucks the life force out of the cells. It withers. It murders ambition, desires, hopes. It debilitates, defoliates and despoils. It permeates all activity. It claims the innocent young and the feeble old. It fosters violence and brings on madness. It lies on a city like the tongue of hell. The people hide in their caves. Everywhere, there is a constant, all-pervading buzz that eats away, insidiously, at the brain. Broken only by savage thunderstorms, the heatwave had smothered Toronto for twelve days. During that time, there had been six murders, seventeen stabbings and thirty-seven assaults. Countless women had been brutalized by their loved ones, and many heaving, panting, sweat-dripping young males, who would grow up to be the pillars of the community, had pulled the panties off struggling young women in cars concealed in remote corners of public parks as insects chirped in the dead-still trees.

Chapter Twenty

At the address given for Graeme Adams in Kelly's report, a black woman answered Weems's knock. There were big circles of sweat at her armpits. The place smelled of spice and floor wax. The woman was holding a baby, a little girl with the prettiest and most loving eyes Weems had ever seen. She had an urge to hold the baby and smother her with kisses. In a Jamaican accent, the woman said there was no Adams that lived there, that she and her husband had been there for a year and a half, and she couldn't remember the name of the person they'd bought the house from. She had no idea where he was living now. She did know that his wife had been killed.

"Sad ting when a young woman goes like dat."

"Yes, it is," Weems said. She smiled at the baby.

Weems drove to Medi-Source. She asked the receptionist whether Graeme Adams was at work.

"He doesn't work here anymore. Not for eighteen months at least."

"Where does he work now?"

"Just a minute," the receptionist said, and went to look in a filing cabinet.

A woman in a white smock who had been getting a coffee from a machine in the lobby approached Weems.

"You're asking about Graeme Adams?" she whispered.

"That's right."

"Meet me outside."

"Okay." Weems nodded.

"Here it is," the receptionist said, coming up to the counter with a file open in her hand. "When he left here, he went to Hermes Forwarding. Yes, of course I knew that. What am I thinking about? I'm sorry. It's just the way you asked me. It threw me off. Of course, I know where Graeme went. Anyway, here." She turned the file around and put it on the counter to let Weems could copy the name and address.

The woman in the smock was waiting at the corner of the building. She called out: "I'm over here," and led Weems to the shade of a tree on a broad lawn at the side of the building, which afforded some shelter from the unremitting onslaught of the sun. There were no windows on that side, and the woman stood behind the tree so she couldn't be seen from the front walkway.

"What's your name?" Weems asked.

The woman hesitated, then said, "Bernadette, Bernadette Truman. You're a policewoman?"

"I'm a detective. Carol Weems. You wanted to tell me something about Graeme Adams?"

"You never found who killed his wife, did you?"

"No."

"Is that what you're here about now?"

Weems shrugged.

"The papers said she was raped, but I always thought that he did it."

"Why's that?"

"A lot of things. First of all, he was weird."

"Weird how?"

"Well, he was—sex crazy, you know what I mean, always making remarks, rubbing up against you—you know, accidentally on purpose. Like, if there was something on the table in front of you that he wanted, he'd lean over you to get it, wouldn't ask you to pass it to him. And if he sat beside you in the lunchroom, his knee would always *accidentally* brush against you. I went to old man Barnes about him, but the old man thought the sun shone out of his—well, you know what I mean. And all the time, I'm sure he was having an affair with Barnes's wife. She works here, too. In the office."

"What made you think they were having an affair? Did you see them together?"

"Sure. All the time. They were always whispering and giggling. I never saw them *do* anything, but you could tell, you know what I mean. You can tell."

"Mmm. Any other reason you think Adams killed his wife? For instance, did he say anything—"

"No, that's just it. He *didn't* say anything. When his wife was killed, he took a couple of weeks off. Then he came back to work and acted as if nothing had happened. He was always clowning around, and if anything, he clowned around even more after she was dead. And when you tried to say, you know, that you were sorry to hear about his wife and that, he'd just shake his hands in front of him like to say, you know, don't say anything about it. Forget it."

"Maybe that was the way he handled it."

"Maybe. But then a couple of months go by, and he's telling everybody he's getting married again. I mean, I ask you. Your wife is hardly cold in the ground and you're getting married again? And that's another thing about Cathy Barnes. You should have seen her face when he said he was getting married. If looks could kill. She went home fifteen minutes later, said she had the flu, didn't come back for a week. They were having a thing all right. Course, she couldn't say a thing, could she? That's the thing with these rich women. They want to have their cake and eat it, too. Oh, sorry, I'm not trying to be crude, or anything."

"Does the wife still work here?"

"The wife?"

"Cathy Barnes."

"Oh, sure. She's still here. But listen. Please don't tell her that I said anything—you know, about her and Graeme, because—"

"Don't worry. I'll be very discreet. I won't mention your name. I'm sure that if you knew about the affair, lots of other people in the building knew, too, am I right?"

"Oh, sure. Everybody knew, except old Barnes, of course."

"How old is he, anyway?"

"Must be forty."

Weems smiled. "And how old is Cathy?"

"Younger. Thirty-five, maybe."

"Adams—I think he must be about thirty now?"

"About that, I guess."

"Is he—good looking?"

"Haven't you—talked to him?"

"Not yet. I'm new on the case."

"Good looking, you say? No, not really. He's all right, I guess. He has weird eyes, a bit too close together. But he's—you know—some women would like him. To me, he's like one of those lounge lizards, you know what I mean? Real sharp dresser. But phoney. All the time telling you how beautiful you are and that. Yuck. What a bullshit artist. I guess some women like that."

"I guess they must. The woman he married, do you know who she is?"

Truman made a dry laughing noise.

"Sure. I don't know her personally or anything, but her husband owned the place where Graeme works now. The husband died, and the wife inherited the business. Real convenient, eh? Graeme must have been having an affair with her at the same time he was having an affair with Cathy Barnes. What a shit."

"Is that so? How did the husband die?"

Truman shrugged. "No idea."

Chapter Twenty-One

Harris met Stark at the deli on Wilson. Harris had learned nothing of any great value at the social club. "I can tell you one thing. Nobody's going to miss the old bugger. He didn't have a friend in the place. Apparently, he was always talking about what a hero he was in Israel."

"What about Cataldi?"

"Nobody'd ever heard of him."

"Shit."

"You think he's your guy?"

"Well, it's a hell of a coincidence that he knows both Rabinovitch and Stokes and he owns the property company that manages the building where Rabinovitch was killed, don't you think?"

Harris shrugged.

"Cataldi's a goddamned crook, is what he is. I told you about the gold-mining scam."

"Oh, yeah."

"Mmm. Well, now, we've got some other possibilities we've got to eliminate."

"Like what?"

"Well, I told you that Rabinovitch got a shot off during the robbery—or whatever the hell it was?"

"Right."

"Okay. He might have winged the guy. Now, right after I was at the crime scene, I went to interview Stokes.

Anyway, I noticed that when he had to move a bundle of papers off a chair, he winced, like it hurt. so maybe—"

"Maybe he was the stabber, and he took a slug somewhere? In the arm, or something?"

"Maybe."

"So what—"

"So, he works out every day at some gym called Bodies by Disher."

"You're kidding."

"I'm not kidding. It's on Bloor Street. So, what I want you to do—I've got the number here." He handed Harris a piece of notepaper. "I called the place, and they'll give you a trial membership for twenty bucks. So, what you should do is go to the place first and pay the twenty—put the receipt in for expenses—and get signed up. Do that first. And then you should go to Stokes's jewellery store, scope the guy so you know what he looks like, then go to the gym when he's there, check him out in the locker room, whatever. See if you can spot any wound. Can you handle that?"

"Hey, that's what they pay me for. I'm even getting paid for sitting here with you eating a bagel. Where could you find a better job?"

Chapter Twenty-Two

Stark spent another night without seeing Weems, another night drinking whisky at Carbo's, alone at the piano bar.

"I don't want her to say no," he slurred at no one in particular, but the only one there to hear was Morty Greenwood, who looked up.

"What did you say? God, what's the matter with you, Harold? You look terrible. You've been drinking like a fish the last couple of nights. You have a fight with Carol?"

"That bitch."

"Oh, charming. Wised up about you, has she?"

"It's not funny, Morty. It's not funny at all."

Morty sighed.

"C'mon. Let's go out the back." They both scowled at Ulysses on their way past. He held his hands up in a gesture that asked, "What the hell am I paying you for?"

They sat on two old kitchen chairs somebody had brought in for what was now being called the staff smoking lounge. The night was nearly as hot as the day had been. The air was dead still, with the consistency of mucilage.

"So, what's your problem, big boy? Tell your father confessor."

"If you put a nun's habit on, you could be the mother superior."

"All right, Stark, if you're going to make homophobic remarks—you know that stuff only shows itself when you're pissed and feeling sorry for yourself. If I thought you meant it—you try to bring everybody else down by saying the meanest things you can think of, don't you?"

"What a stupid word, 'homophobia.' 'Phobia' means 'fear,' not 'hatred.' Therefore, homophobia would mean 'fear of something the same.' That's the trouble with words that are coined by people—"

"The hell with you. I'm going back in the bar."

"No, wait—wait. It's okay, I'm just—have a cigarette."

"One of those things? No, thank you. I have my own."

Stark shook his head.

"Damn it, Morty. I'm sorry. Jesus. Why the hell do I say crap like this?"

"I told you why. Now, do you mind letting go of my hand. I want to light my cigarette. So, what's the problem with Carol? I gather this is a follow-up to our last conversation?"

Stark looked at his hand.

"Did I bring my drink out with me?"

"No, you didn't."

"The hell with her."

"The hell with her? The other night you said you wanted to marry her. Did you ask her?"

"No."

"What are you afraid of?"

Stark stared into the darkness beyond the circle of dim light cast from the kitchen windows. He sighed. "Few people—almost nobody knows this, Morty."

"What?"

"I was married before."

"My God. You do surprise me. The eternal bachelor. You were married?"

"Years and years ago. I was a kid. A rookie cop. I met her at university. We got married while we were still at school. She was the most stunningly beautiful woman I have ever seen. When she laughed it was like—"

"A tinkling bell? A babbling brook?"

"No, really, she was—she was so gorgeous that I couldn't figure out why she was interested in me. I—I thought it was a joke."

"A joke?"

"Yeah. She had all these hunks on a string, you know. Football players. Older guys. She dated a doctor, for God's sake—and a lawyer. Sports cars and silk suits and penthouse apartments and—"

"I get the picture."

"Yeah. And then she—she asked *me* to marry *her*. *She* asked. I wouldn't have dared. I just sort of hung around her, drooling. I was kind of a nerd. I had a scrawny beard and I read poetry. I had no money, no car, and I lived in an attic. One night, we were at a party, and she asked me to walk her home. And—I don't know— we talked. We sat outside her residence on a bench. There was snow on the ground. It was freezing, but we talked for hours, didn't even notice the cold. After that, we just sort of went out together. There was nothing, you know, formal about it. We'd just arrange to meet and then when we left each other, we'd arrange to meet again the next day. I didn't even try to kiss her. Finally, after two weeks, she took me to the apartment of one of her girlfriends. I went like a puppy dog. She led me into the bedroom and we made love. It was the greatest moment of my life."

"Ah."

"Yeah, young love. But I couldn't believe it. I couldn't help thinking she was putting me on. Setting me up for something. Like it was a bet she had, or a big joke that all her friends were in on."

"My God. You had no self-esteem at all, did you?"

"I guess not. And even when she asked me to marry her, I thought I'd be waiting at the registry office and some football goon would show up with a note that said, 'Ha, ha, the joke's on you, you jerk. You really didn't seriously think someone like me would marry someone like you? What a twerp.'"

"And did he?"

"Did who?"

"Did a football goon show up with a note?"

"No, of course not. We got married. But it would have been better if it had been a joke. Because I was madly, insanely in love with her." Stark sighed. His head drooped. His eyes welled up with tears. Morty put a hand on his shoulder. After a time, Stark went on, "We were married for only a few months. When I graduated, I became a social worker. I hated it. Then I joined the force. I became a cop. At first, she seemed to like the idea. I didn't know what else to do. A teacher? Too bourgeois. Remember that word? We used it all the time. A cop was—well. The funny thing is I hated cops, too. Becoming one was some kind of antisocial act. I can't explain it. Anyway, part of it was I was afraid of people. I was afraid of being embarrassed. I was afraid of being beaten up. I figured being a cop, they'd teach me to be tough. Sort of like the army, you know. Make a man out of me. I wanted to be a man for her. A hero. You know, somebody who could protect her. Three months later, she left me. Three fucking months. And you know who she left me for?"

"A football player?"

"No, a goddamned actor. She met him in an amateur theatre thing. He had money, you know, but—I don't think that's why she went with him."

"No, of course not. She went with him because you'd taught her to like that sort of thing. The arts, poetry, philosophy. And then you went and became a bloody cop. Coming home late, smelling of beer after drinking with the other boys in blue. Telling her how you'd arrested some punk, got him in a hammerlock, wrestled him to the ground. Did you tell her about nailing queers in Allen Gardens?"

"Anyway, you see the way it was. After that, I never, ever let myself get taken in by any woman, ever. I'd love 'em and leave 'em, Morty. Mostly they were other cops, or clerks in the department. All of them bimbos you didn't have to talk to."

"Slam, bam, thank you ma'am."

"All these years. And now it's—" He shook his head. "Now it's like I can't take the risk. I've *never* taken the risk. I *won't* take the risk. I've built this shell, and it's worked. It's always worked."

"You're the tough, lone wolf. Nobody's going to break through to the soft centre."

"But, Christ, I am in love with her."

Chapter Twenty-Three

Hermes Forwarding was on Progress Avenue, west of Markham Road. Weems had no problem finding Adams. He was draped all over the receptionist in the lobby, and she was giggling as if she was enjoying it. "Silly fool," Weems thought. She cleared her throat, and Adams stood bolt upright, like a guilty schoolboy.

"I'm looking for Graeme Adams," Weems said.

"You've found him," the schoolboy said, scanning Weems's body so quickly the detective would have missed it had she not been concentrating on his eyes. The woman at Medi-Source had been wrong about Adams. He *was* good-looking, even handsome, with an oddly expressive face. With the broad grin and wide eyes he was presenting now, he looked like a country boy. His legs and arms seemed too long for his torso. His shoulders had a self-conscious droop. And then suddenly his expression changed, his eyes narrowed, his grin shrank to a thin smile, his shoulders rose, and Weems became aware that he was wearing an olive-green Armani suit and not the farmer's overalls she had dressed him in in a mental picture. He went from bumpkin to sophisticate in the lifting of an eyebrow and the way he said, "Come in to my office and I'll pour you a cooling drink," made Weems feel uncomfortable, made her check the buttons on her blouse.

His office was behind and to the left of the

receptionist. He came forward and took Weems by the elbow and directed her inside. Opposite his office, to the right of the receptionist, was another office, the door of which was lettered, "Brenda Phillips, Managing Director." Graeme's door read "Graeme Adams, Manager."

His office was spacious and expensively decorated, with a massive, glass-topped desk on a marble pedestal. Opposite it was an L-shaped, black leather sectional couch and matching armchair, surrounding a wide, square coffee table that matched the desk. The walls were hung with Bateman wildlife prints and a certificate that seemed to suggest Adams was a member of the Masonic lodge. A clock of about four feet in diameter was built into one wall. The roman numerals were affixed to the wall and the spindle to which the long, gold hands were attached came out of the wall. A slender, black sweep hand ticked off the seconds in the otherwise absolute silence there had been since Adams closed the door.

As she watched the clock, Weems became aware of the silence and realized that Adams hadn't moved from the door and was standing there studying her from behind. She felt a chill in her lower back and spun around, but Adams was quicker, and by the time she had turned to face him, he was already striding across the thick carpet toward his desk, with his head tilted upward as if he were studying a corner of the ceiling.

When he reached the desk, he looked at Weems with the disarming boyish grin back again. Weems thought she had never seen a more phoney innocent, innocuous expression.

"Take a seat." Adams gestured to the couch. "What

can I buy from you today? Oh, I promised you a drink, didn't I?" He slid open a door in a mahogany credenza on the wall behind the desk. It concealed a small refrigerator. "What'll you have? Sprite, Diet Coke, white wine?"

"Nothing, thanks. My name is Weems, Mr. Adams, Carol Weems. I'm a detective."

"A private eye?" His eyebrows lifted in an arch expression.

"No. I'm with the police."

"Oh, I see."

Weems concentrated on his eyes, trying to get a reading, but failing. He seemed distracted, almost as if he hadn't been paying attention to what she'd said. His gaze was down. Then Weems realized, with discomfort and anger, that Adams was looking at her legs. She was wearing a knee-length skirt. She cleared her throat and he raised his head.

"Police," he said, cocking his head to one side, as if the word had just registered, and this time there was a momentary look of concern. "Is there some problem? Something with one of the trucks?"

"I'm investigating your wife's murder, Mr. Adams."

He was silent for a moment, looking at her, and then he said, "That was two years ago—"

"We have some new information," Weems watched his eyes carefully. The lids fluttered.

"What sort of information?"

"I can't tell you. I'd like to go over the statement you made to the investigators at the time."

"Jesus." He shook his head, and looked at his watch. "Well—do we have to do it now? It's not really convenient."

"If you don't mind. It won't take long."

Adams sighed.

"Mr. Adams, there seems to be some discrepancy between your statement and your mother's."

"What discrepancy?" he said defiantly.

"Well, you said you were with your mother all evening—"

"That's right."

"—playing Scrabble."

"Yes. My mother likes to play Scrabble."

"Your mother said you spent the evening watching television."

He shrugged.

"That was just a matter of perception."

Weems shook her head.

"Perception?"

"Simple. There was a movie on that she wanted to watch, so she sat on the couch, facing the TV, while I sat on the hassock, facing her. The Scrabble board was on the coffee table between us. She didn't pay much attention to the game, because she doesn't have to. She's a real Scrabble wiz. She always beats me. She doesn't have to work at it, so I guess in her mind, in her recollection, we—that is, she, really—watched TV all night. In fact, when we finished the game, I did join her on the couch and watched the end of the movie with her and then the news and then I think we even watched a bit of Leno. My mother doesn't like Letterman. She says he's too much of a smart-ass." He smiled and looked boyish again.

Weems consulted the report. "Well, your mother did say, when she was questioned a second time, that you did play Scrabble *and* watched TV. However, I wonder why she—"

"That's right. This is hardly new. I mean, the other detective—we went all over this with him. Why isn't he here, if there's *new* information? I mean, why you? Why are you a woman?"

"What?"

"I'm sorry. That was a stupid way to put it. What I mean is, is there some reason they now have a woman on the case? Is it political? I hope not, because—not that there's anything wrong with you being a woman." He smiled again and his expression flashed back and forth between the good boy and the bad man, ending with a wide grin that was pure callow hayseed.

"Detective Kelly—"

"Right, that was the name."

"He's left the force. In fact, I'm afraid he died."

"You mean he was killed on the job?"

"No—he just—he died of natural causes. The case has been reassigned to me."

Adams looked thoughtful.

"When did Kelly retire?"

"I'm not sure exactly. More than a year ago, I suppose."

"Who took over the case after he retired?"

She knew what he was getting at.

"The investigation was suspended, Mr. Adams. It's now been reopened."

"Because of this new information?"

"Yes."

"Which you won't tell me about."

"No."

"Hmm. Well, I don't know what you hope to accomplish here. The fact is my poor wife was raped and murdered. I'll say the same thing now I said then. I don't know why you are questioning me," he said, touching his chest with the fingers of both hands.

"Your wife was drugged, Mr. Adams and you—"

"Yes, I know. I had access to drugs. That was all brought out before, and the firm did a complete inventory and everything was accounted for. And why in heaven's name would I kill my wife? Why? Besides, I wasn't there. I was with my mother."

"Mr. Adams, it's logical your mother would try to protect you. As for motive, you did get married again within a few months after your wife's death."

"Please. People don't kill their wives any more if they want to marry someone else. Have you never heard of divorce? I'm not Henry the eighth. What do you think, I couldn't get a papal dispensation?"

"The woman you married owns this firm."

"That's right. But what does that have to do with anything?"

"Suppose your wife wouldn't let you divorce her. Suppose she knew something about you that might— bother your prospective wife so much that she would break off the relationship?"

Adams glared, shifted in his chair.

"What are you talking about?"

Weems couldn't tell him what she'd learned from the Australian police.

"You tell me, Mr. Adams. I'm just suggesting a possibility."

Adams studied her as if he was trying to decide whether she knew anything. Finally he gave a dismissive wave of a hand and said, "That's absurd. You're making stuff up off the top of your head. It's—it's ridiculous. My wife was killed by a sick rapist, and you can't find him, so you're trying to pin the blame on whoever's handy— *me*. Now, if you have nothing else but insane accusations, I have work to do."

Weems held her hands up in a calming gesture.

"Let's assume you had nothing to do with it."

"Yes, let's."

"Okay. Your wife had a quantity of alcohol in her system, enough that she would have been intoxicated. Was she in the habit of going alone to bars?"

"The police asked me this before."

"And what was your answer?"

He stared into space for a moment.

"She wasn't in the habit of it, no. But she did go out occasionally and have a drink. I wouldn't say she had a drinking problem, but she did like a drink. If you're asking me—because this is what they asked me before— whether there was a local bar she might go to, there wasn't. I don't know of one. There's no bar in our neighbourhood—where we *used* to live. On the other hand, well, obviously, she must have gone somewhere. And she must have had a drink or two. And then—"

Weems said, "Someone might have picked her up?"

He made a face.

"What did your wife do for a living, Mr. Adams? Did she have a job?"

He shook his head.

"What about in Australia? She was Australian, wasn't she? The documents in the file say she was born in Australia. Did she have a job in Australia?"

Adams stared at her for a moment, then shook his head.

"A barmaid. She was a barmaid."

"And did you meet her there, in Australia?"

Adams nodded.

"That's where you met her? In a bar?"

"In Sydney, yes."

"What were you doing there, by the way?"

"In the bar?"

"In Australia."

"It was after school, after university. I saved up some money and took off, you know, to blow off steam. After the pressure and everything." He was thinking about something. His expression had changed. More serious. His face seemed tired, his body sagged slightly. "Pissed off my mother, I can tell you." He shook his head.

"She didn't want you to go?"

"Work, success, accomplishment. That's all my mother wants. Money. My father left us when I was a kid." He shrugged. "She had to struggle. She didn't have a good life. It was very rough for her." He shrugged again.

"Mr. Adams, I know this is a hard thing—but is it possible your wife had a boyfriend?"

He scowled.

"No, absolutely not." His head shook violently. "She had no boyfriend, for god's sake. In any case, if she did have a boyfriend, which she didn't, why would he want to kill her? If that's what you're saying. That doesn't make any sense."

"Well, supposing she was having a relationship with somebody who was obsessed with her. Supposing she told him she was going to dump him?"

Adams gave a sardonic laugh.

"You know, you've got the most crazy theories.

Where are you getting these harebrained ideas from? Why, for heaven's sake, don't you just concentrate on the most obvious thing. Some creep spiked her drink with pentobarbital, took her down the Bluffs, raped her and choked her to death. You should check your computer. See if there are any other cases like that. That would make sense to me."

"Oh, that makes perfect sense, Mr. Adams." Weems nodded. "The problem with that is that there haven't been any similar cases. None. And, you see, that is what is unusual. Because these kind of rapists almost always strike again. That's the only way they get a feeling of power. Sexual aggression. And since he succeeded in the first instance, he'd almost certainly employ the same method again."

"Did you ever think it might have been some guy just passing through from, say, Regina? Maybe he committed his next rape in Montreal and then moved on to somewhere else. Did you investigate that possibility, eh?"

"As a matter of fact, I did, Mr. Adams," Weems lied. "I couldn't find anything that matched this crime."

"Mmm. Well, I don't have any other suggestions for you."

There was a knock on the door.

"Come in," Adams said. Weems watched his face. The boyish smile burst out again. "Oh, come in, my dear. My wife," he said to Weems."

Weems was afraid her expression might betray her shock at what had come through the door. Adams's wife was one of the plainest women Weems had ever seen. In fact, plain was not the word. It would have been a euphemism to call her homely. Her hair, in a ragged part low on one side, hung limp and stringy, cut off severely just below the chin line. She had an angular face and a large, bulbous nose, with immense nostrils, which from Weems's seated angle, looked even bigger than they were. She had a jutting, cleft chin and widely spaced, frog-like eyes.

Weems stood up. It wasn't till then that she realized that the appearance of the woman's size hadn't been produced by the upward angle of view. She had a good inch on Weems, who was five-nine. The woman looked as if she were wearing shoulder pads, but the slope of the shoulders and the drape of her dress suggested otherwise. She was wearing a teal blue outfit, a Calvin Klein, although Weems didn't know who the designer was, but knew it was expensive, and it hung on her with such a tired shapelessness that Weems thought she might as well have saved her money and shopped at Zellers. Weems half stood and reached out a hand. The woman's hand squeezed hers.

"Carol Weems. I'm—"

"She's with the police, Brenda. My wife, Brenda Phillips. Ms. Weems is investigating Karen's murder—again, after all this time. They've reopened the case. She says there's *new* information. Naturally, I want them to find out who did it—"

"New information?" Brenda Phillips cut off her husband. "What? What new information?" The woman had a dry, clipped voice, with almost no modulation. It reminded Weems of something generated by a computer.

"I'm sorry, Ms. Phillips, I can't tell you that. Listen, I'm about finished here, so—Oh, by the way, did *you* know Karen Sheltoe?"

Phillips shook her head. "Never met the poor

woman. Why *are* you here? Why are you questioning Graeme? I think I have a right to know."

Adams put his hands up.

"My dear, I'll—fill you in. Let's let Miss Weems get on about her business, shall we?"

Chapter Twenty-Four

Stark trudged back and forth on Main across the street from the Acme Building. While he was waiting for Noel Harris to do his thing at Bodies by Disher, he figured he'd do a little surveillance of his own, but there was nowhere to park, and he was stuck out there squinting at the building against the beating sun. He had arrived early enough to see the three people he knew were employed there enter the Acme Building: the frumpy receptionist with her hair rolled at the back of her head, the fragile little bookkeeper, who scurried into the building as if she were frightened to be on the street, and the pudgy manager, Rogers. He had walked from The Danforth to half way across the Main Street bridge and back again, over and over, always managing to keep the entrance to the building in his sight, except when a scout car pulled up beside him, and a policewoman asked him in a nasty tone what he was doing there. He showed her his badge.

"Oh, sorry, Sarge. There was a call."

"A call?" he said, glancing anxiously at the Acme Building. "Who called?"

"A streetcar driver. He thought you looked suspicious. He was afraid you were going to jump off the bridge in front of a train."

"Jesus."

"Sorry. Anything we can help with?"

"No."

The policewoman looked at her partner and they pulled away. As they left, a black Cadillac stopped in front of the Acme Building.

"Cataldi," Stark said aloud, grinning, although with the bright sun he couldn't make out the occupants of the Caddy through its tinted windows. A woman Stark had never seen before came out of the building. "What the hell." She had long hair, down to her shoulders, and a mincing walk on stilt heels. "Who the hell is that?" She got in the car, and it drove away quickly. Stark wrote down the licence number.

That afternoon, Stark and Harris met at the deli on Wilson. Harris ordered lox and a bagel and tea. Stark, coffee.

"So, what happened?"

Harris sighed.

"You know, you'd think an assignment like this would be a snap, wouldn't you?"

"Yes, you would." Stark nodded in emphasis. "So, what happened?"

"First of all, I go this morning to this gym. The woman who runs it insists on giving me the twenty-five-cent tour. After that, she didn't want to let me have the trial membership. I had to make up a story about just moving from out of town and I didn't have a chequing account in a bank here and I only had the twenty bucks and so on. After that, I go to the jewellery store. I have to hang around in there, pretending to be interested in engagement rings. I've got this poor woman bringing out so many trays of rings, she's getting suspicious. She starts to put the tray I'm looking at away before she'll bring out the next one. I guess so if I pull a scoop-and-run, I won't get much. Stokes is there all right. I can hear him in the office. In fact, he's arguing on the phone with somebody about money."

"About money? What did he say?"

"I couldn't hear."

"You said he was arguing about money. If you couldn't hear, how do you know what he was arguing about?"

"I couldn't hear the words. I just got the impression it was about money."

"Jesus."

"Anyway, I'm there about fifteen minutes before he comes out. And then he looks straight at me."

"Jesus Christ."

"Okay, so I get out of there, and I have to catch a bus and the subway to get to the gym."

"Bus? Subway? What, d'you lose your licence or something?"

"I don't like to drive when it's not necessary. I didn't have to follow him, or anything. Transit's better for the environment."

"Oh for God's sake."

"So then, I have to wait and wait outside the gym, because the guy doesn't show up at his regular time, at least not at the time you told me he usually gets there. I'm waiting in this stinking heat. I'm practically melting before the guy finally shows. I'm so hot that when we finally go in, when I finally follow him in, I get undressed and go straight into the showers to cool off."

Stark spread his hands in a frustrated questioning gesture. "Why didn't you watch him undress?" He said it so loudly that a woman at the next table looked over. Stark scowled at her and she looked away quickly.

Harris leaned forward.

"I'll tell you why. Because when I came into the locker room, I saw him look at me as if he thought he recognized me from somewhere, but couldn't place it. so I smiled right at him. I gave him one of those 'How-do-you-do-nice-day-if-it-don't-rain-I-don't-know-you-from-Adam-I'm-just-being-polite' smiles, and I turned immediately in the other direction, down another row of lockers, stripped off and got into the shower before he had a chance to eyeball me again and maybe place me at the store. The thing is, I've got one of those kinds of faces that people always think they know from somewhere, so I figured he wouldn't make the connection, but I wanted to blend in as much as possible, not have him pay much attention to me. Okay?"

Stark groaned in exasperation.

"So I'm coming out of the shower and I'm looking for him and not where I'm going and I bang my shin on a bench—hard. Man, did that hurt. The guy is still in the locker room. Doesn't he come around and ask me if I'm okay. I nod. It hurts too much to speak. Then I *have* to speak, because the guy says, 'Don't I know you from somewhere?' and I smile inanely and explain about having one of those kinds of faces and he nods, and then he chuckles and says, 'Haven't you got the routine a little backwards. First, you're supposed to exercise and then you shower.' Schmuck. I had to explain about being so hot, etcetera."

Stark gave the ceiling a long-suffering look. He signalled the waitress for a refill on his coffee. Harris ordered another tea.

"You want just hot water for the pot?" the waitress asked.

"No, fresh tea please."

"In this weather, you should have iced tea," she said.

"I don't like iced tea."

"You're the boss."

"Where was I?" Harris asked Stark.

"Where were you? I forget where you were. What I remember is, I asked you the time, not for the history of chronometers. All I want to know is, did the guy have any kind of wound on him? Was he bandaged up somewhere?"

Harris raised his hands. "I'm coming to it. Relax. Drink your coffee."

"Jesus."

"So, finally Stokes goes into the equipment room, and I follow him in. I stay away from him. He's on the bike, and I'm on the stair climber. He's on the leg machine, and I'm on the inclined bench doing sit-ups. Like that. We go from one piece of equipment to another. Finally, the guy looks like he's ready to leave. He's got his towel, wiping off the sweat, so I hurry up out of there and into the shower again. And I'm showering and showering and showering. I'm turning into a prune. Where is the guy? I have no idea. So, I go to look. I'm just coming out of the shower and he comes in. He passes me, but too close and too fast for me to see anything. I turn around, and he's in the corner, with his back to me. What am I going to do? I can't go back in and shower again. Finally, I go and sit on a bench where I can see him coming out of the shower. In a few minutes, he comes out. Few minutes? More like ten. He showered longer than I did."

"Jeez. Will you get to the—"

"So then he comes out and he's got a big towel

draped over his shoulders and held closed over his chest. I can't see his upper body at all."

"Christ."

"So I look at his lower body, checking out his legs. Maybe he got hit in the leg."

"Christ, he didn't get hit in the—"

"As I'm looking, I glance up and he's staring at me looking at his lower body. I'm sitting on a bench conspicuous for being in a position where you can see everybody coming out of the shower, and I'm staring at his nether parts. He went past me in a hell of a hurry, let me tell you."

"Harris, please—"

"There were no wounds or bandages on his legs. Okay. I'll tell you what I did."

"I'm sure you will."

"I tied my towel around my waist, so it would look as if I was parading. There's a water fountain in the corner of the locker room, past Stokes's locker row. I go there, get a drink, take my time."

"You what?"

"I had to."

"Okay, okay, so?"

"So I turned around—and he's got his shirt on."

"Oh, for Christ's sake." Stark put his face in his hands.

"Wait. There was a stain on the shirt."

Stark brightened.

"A blood stain?"

"Not unless he's a blue blood. Ink. His pen had leaked in his breast pocket."

"Oh, for—"

"Wait. He sees the stain, and he's pissed off.

'Goddamn it,' he says, and he takes his shirt off, and he's standing there in his undershorts and he turns and lifts his arms and takes a T-shirt out of the top of his locker, and I see his entire torso."

"And?"

"Not a scratch."

"What?" Stark's exclamation was so loud, the woman looked over again.

"Nope. Nothing."

"You son of a bitch," Stark said. He got up from the table and strode out of the deli. Harris could barely restrain himself till the door closed behind Stark. At that instant, he started laughing. He laughed so loud and for so long, the people at neighbouring tables turned to watch him; some, caught up by the infectious quality of laughter, even joined in. By the time he emerged from the restaurant, he had managed to stop laughing, but when he saw Stark sitting in his car glowering, his arms folded across his chest, he started again, and had to pinch his left bicep so hard that it hurt to make himself stop again. He knew the hardest part was yet to come.

He got into the car and had to pinch his arm even harder when Stark said, "You could have told me that in two and a half seconds. If I'd wanted the Locker Room Adventures of Noel Harris I could have waited for the video."

Harris was barely able to spit out, "I like to give complete reports."

"That's not complete, that's—God." Stark sighed.

They sat in silence, and then Harris said, "So, is that it then, Sarge? Are you finished with me?"

"Being a smart-ass is not going to improve your standing with me, Harris, believe me. I'll be doing a report on you to your inspector. I think you should keep that in mind." After another short silence, Stark said, "I don't know what's next—not yet. But you're mine, so don't go taking any other assignments. Go home, or wherever. I'll call you on your mobile phone when I decide what I want you to do. Is that clear?"

"Absolutely."

Chapter Twenty-Five

"We got another phone call." Detective-Sergeant Henry loomed up beside Weems's temporary desk in Homicide. Weems had gone there to compile her notes on what she had learned so far. She was thorough and methodical. She wrote lengthy notes that included the tiniest details. Weems had also gone to Homicide because she liked being there. She could have e-mailed her report to Henry and saved the trip downtown, but she wanted to feel a link with the unit, to be a part of the team. Henry must have all his suits tailor-made, Weems thought, looking at him. He'd never find an off-the-rack jacket to fit him. His problem wouldn't be like Stark's— a little thick in the middle. His problem would be because his chest and shoulders were massive, while his waist was narrow and his abdomen flat. Stark's answer to getting a fit off the rack, she thought wryly, was to buy a jacket one size too big.

"Another call about the Sheltoe murder?" Weems said.

"This time he said, 'Somebody *knows* he's guilty. Somebody *knows* he did it'."

"That's it?"

"Yeah. Well, he started off by saying what he was calling about and repeating that Graeme Adams had done it and we had to catch him before he did it again. That's it."

"Did we get a tape of the call?"

"No." Henry glowered toward the other end of the room. "Billings took the call. He switched on his tape machine all right, but he had no cassette in it. Have you talked to Adams yet?"

Weems nodded.

"And?"

"And nothing. I talked to his new wife, too. They were a bit put off, indignant. I'm going to talk to the mother tonight. My gut instinct is that Adams did it. But with the mother's alibi and no contradictory evidence—well." Weems shrugged. "I think the key is to shake her alibi somehow, don't you?"

"It would help." Henry nodded.

"If I can put some real cracks in that—and I'm going to talk to Adams' former boss at the drug distribution company, Harold Barnes. And the boss's wife."

"Why do you want to talk to her?"

"Because Adams apparently had an affair with her."

"That's interesting." Henry shrugged. "I guess."

"Listen, our boy has quite a track record. First of all, it turns out his dead wife was an Australian hooker. And did you know Adams got into trouble in Australia? Sex with a minor, a boy."

"I didn't know it was a male."

Weems nodded.

"Yeah, and at the same time as he was having it off with Barnes's wife, he was also involved with the woman he's married to now."

"Busy boy. Sex on the brain."

"No kidding. She, the new wife, inherited the company Adams is the manager of the place now. So, supposing the Sheltoe woman knew he had marital ambitions beyond her, and supposing she threatened to tell his Australian secrets to the prospective new wife if he tried to leave her—well, it seems to me, that would give him motive up the kazoo, don't you think?

"And you know that the Sheltoe woman was drugged before she was strangled. Well, Adams had access to drugs, right?"

"I guess he did, yeah."

"Right. so if only we had some physical evidence to link him to the crime—" Weems sighed. "Anyway, I think that's going to be tough. There *was* a shoeprint, but nothing special about it. A flat-soled shoe. Man's size nine. We could see if he's a size nine, I suppose. But that's hardly enough."

Henry looked slightly concerned.

"Say, did you say you were going to interview the mother *tonight?* The overtime budget is a little stretched—"

Weems put her hands up.

"Don't worry about it, Sarge." She lowered her voice as though imparting a dark secret. "I won't put in for overtime. I'm enjoying this too much. Besides, it means I won't have to spend the whole evening with Stark."

Chapter Twenty-Six

Jane Adams lived in an apartment in the northeast corner of Scarborough, a twelve-storey building in white brick. Only a few years old, it was well appointed, brightly lit and meticulously clean, with a large, tastefully decorated foyer, the furniture in which seemed pointless, since it was sealed off by wrought-iron bars and a locked gate. Jane Adams lived on the top floor. Weems punched the numbers indicated beside "Adams, J." on the intercom list. The phone rang three times before it was answered.

"Yes."

Weems started. She was amazed that a monosyllable could carry such vitriol.

"Mrs. Adams?"

"Who is this?"

"Detective Carol Weems, Mrs. Adams. I'd like to speak to you."

"What about?"

"Well, I'd rather not discuss it over the intercom, if you don't mind."

"I do mind. You got me out of the shower. What do you want?"

"Mrs. Adams, please, would you buzz me in?"

There was silence for a moment.

"Just a minute." More silence, then, "Look up at the camera in the corner. I can see you on the TV. Okay, now hold your badge up." Weems did as she was asked. She heard the buzzer as the door lock was released.

The door to Jane Adams's apartment was flung open before Weems could knock. The woman glaring at the detective was half-a-head taller than she. The lines of a shapely figure were apparent beneath a white, terrycloth robe. Even without makeup, and with her hair hanging in wet strings, she was attractive in a shop-worn sort of way, or would have been, Weems thought, if it weren't for the scowl. There was a hardness about her face that suggested the scowl was a more-or-less constant feature.

"A phone call would have been an appropriate courtesy," Adams said icily. "You'd better come in."

"I'm sorry. I was just passing. I thought it would be an opportunity."

"An opportunity for what?" They were standing in the apartment vestibule. Adams gave no indication they were going to move from there.

"Perhaps we could—sit down?"

"Is this going to take long? I want to make my dinner, and *Jeopardy* comes on at seven-thirty. What is this about?" They still hadn't moved.

Weems motioned with her hand toward the interior of the apartment.

"Please?" she said. Adams glared, but spun around and marched into the room. Weems shook her head and followed the woman into a room of which the furnishings might charitably have been described as utilitarian. Everything was in neutral colours. Decorations were limited to a few ceramic and glass bowls on the rectangular coffee table and two square side tables, both covered in a cheap, pale-grey veneer. There were no flowers, no figurines, no knick-knacks. All the lamps were brass with unadorned, beige shades. A few unremarkable reproductions of generic country scenes hung in plain, black frames. The couch and chairs were in dark brown and of a coarse, hard-wearing material. It reminded Weems of a waiting room. Jane Adams sat on the couch. Weems took an armchair.

"Well?" Adams said.

"Mrs. Adams—"

"I prefer *Ms.* Adams, if you don't mind, even though it *is* my married name. I haven't seen the bastard in thirty years. I would have reverted to my single name, but it's 'Adams' on my son's birth certificate, so I stayed with it to avoid—complications."

"I'll get to the point. I'm here about the death of your daughter-in-law."

"That was two years ago, for God's sake. She's dead and buried, and good riddance. Do you know what she was?"

"I—yes I do." Weems nodded.

"Then, why are you still—" Adams gave a long-suffering sigh. "The investigation ended no sooner than it had begun, because they couldn't find any evidence to lead them to a killer. It was some sex maniac. There was no doubt about it. You know this makes no sense to me at all. If they couldn't find who did it back then, it's ridiculous to think *you're* going to find the killer now."

"We have some new information."

"What is this new information?" The question had no suggestion of surprise. It was asked as if she had already heard about it.

"I can't tell you that, I'm afraid. In any event, it's led us to take another look at the case."

"Well, I think it's ridiculous."

"Why should it bother you that much?"

"Because we've gotten on with our lives. We've put it behind us, the whole tawdry mess. We just want to forget the woman ever existed."

Weems shook her head. Then, with an edge in her voice, she said, "Well, she did exist, and *I* intend to find out who killed her. Now, I'd like to go over the statements you made at the time of the first investigation."

Adams gave an exaggerated sigh and affected a look of boredom.

Weems said: "You told the investigators at the time that your son arrived here on the night of the killing at six thirty p.m."

Adams shrugged.

"You said you made him dinner." Weems read from her notes: "Pork chops, green beans and mashed potatoes."

Another shrug.

Weems stared at her.

"However, your son said he got here at seven-thirty—"

"I corrected myself later," the woman said quickly.

"Yes, because Graeme couldn't have been here at six-thirty, since he didn't leave work till then."

"I told them I had made a mistake on the time, but that I knew he had been right, that it was seven-thirty, because—"

"Because *Jeopardy* was on the television when he came in."

"Yes."

Weems nodded.

"Your son said you ate Kraft Dinner and hot dogs."

"Well, he was wrong. His memory's not good about things like that. I wouldn't serve my son Kraft Dinner." Adams was looking at Weems disdainfully. "What sort of a name is Weems?" she said. "You know, people of different backgrounds—" She stopped. "*We* don't lie, you know. I wouldn't lie. And perhaps I wouldn't make a good police officer because I would tend to assume that people were telling the truth. When you come from a certain sort of background, you tend to do that. Is Weems your real family name, or—"

"You know, that's an offensive question."

"No more so than yours, because your question suggests that we're being untruthful."

"It's none of your business about my name, but we're Welsh. Our real name was Williams. My great-grandfather emigrated to the States, and when he gave his name to the immigration officer on Ellis Island, the fellow couldn't understand his accent, or couldn't spell, and wrote down Weems, and so it remained. We're of Welsh origin on my father's side, and English on my mother's."

Adams rolled her eyes.

Weems continued her questions. The woman's answers were close to those her son had given. She gave the same explanation for his having said they'd played Scrabble while she had said they had watched TV. But she made no attempt to be delicate, as her son had been, about the murdered wife.

"Graeme said she was a *barmaid?* Oh, she did that, all right, but she made most of her money as a prostitute, going out with the customers after closing time. That's how they met. She trapped the poor fool into marrying her, said she was pregnant." Adams also gave a description different from her son's about Sheltoe's habits. "She drank like a fish, and she went with other men. We saw her with one."

"Who's we?"

She hesitated.

"Mmm? Oh, somebody I used to know." She gestured dismissively.

"Do you think your son knew about all this?"

She shrugged.

"Did you tell him that you had seen his wife with somebody else?"

Adams's expression betrayed a flicker of uncertainty. After a long hesitation, she said she hadn't told him.

"Your son called you today, didn't he?"

She didn't answer for a time, then said, "What if he did? What's wrong with a son calling his mother?" The woman glowered at Weems. "What you're doing is harassment. You *want* my son to be guilty, because he's—convenient. You can put your hands on him. The only thing that makes sense is that his wife was killed by a sex pervert. But you don't know who the killer is and so you can't find him, and you're embarrassed about that. The easiest way to *solve* the case is to pin the blame on my son, isn't it? Isn't that what this is all about?"

Chapter Twenty-Seven

"So, how's the case going?"

Weems gave Stark a suspicious look. "It's going fine, but look, I'd rather not discuss it."

Stark grimaced.

"What's the problem?"

"There's no problem at all. I just don't want to talk about it. Let's talk about something else."

"That's ridiculous. Why wouldn't you—"

"See. It's starting already. We haven't even begun to discuss the case and we're arguing."

"Who's arguing? You're being ridiculous. All the experience I've got in Homicide, and you refuse to take advantage of it. This isn't an ego adventure, you know. You're not playing Nancy Drew here. The idea isn't to prove how brilliant you are. The idea is to solve the murder. And this can't be an easy thing. It's a two-year-old crime, the trail's gone cold, evidence has vanished. And if Dermot Kelly couldn't crack it, and he had twenty years' experience—Granted, he was a lush." Stark probed his ear with a pinky finger.

"Please don't do that."

"Do what?"

"Clean the wax out of your ear with your finger."

"Sorry." Stark shrugged.

"Look, if you weren't you. If we weren't—whatever we are—" Weems sighed. "But, if we start talking about this thing, it will immediately degenerate into a big fight. I know it will. There's no use thinking it won't. Because it will."

Stark shook his head.

"Have it your own way. You want something to eat?"

"I ate already."

"Oh, great. I haven't."

"So, eat."

"There isn't anything."

"So, what were you going to feed me?"

"I was going to order something in."

"So, order."

"I don't want to order something in for myself. I'm not that hungry, anyway."

"You want to go out? We could go to that place with the patio."

"It's too hot to sit outside."

"Not at night, it's not."

"It's sure as hell hot in here. God, I'm going to have to turn up that bloody air-conditioner. It's so damned muggy." Stark went and turned the air-conditioner in the front window to high. He paused, thought about it, and turned it back down two notches. Weems shook her head.

"So," Stark said, returning to the kitchen, "you want something to drink?"

"I'll have a beer."

He got her a beer from the fridge and poured himself a hefty measure of J&B. "You want a glass?"

"No, never mind. How can you drink Scotch in this weather?"

"Same way I always drink it. I open my mouth and

pour it down my throat." He demonstrated, downing half the glass.

"You're going to sulk, aren't you? You're just going to sit there and sulk all night."

"Jesus Christ. What the hell are you talking about?" She shook her head.

"You know, something I will tell you. Something I saw today made me think of you."

"What's that? No, don't tell, let me guess. Either you were in the museum and you saw a statue of a Greek god, or maybe this is an intellectual thing. You took in a lecture on nuclear physics—"

"I saw one of the ugliest people I've ever laid eyes on."

"Thank you very much."

"I thought about you because we've had arguments on the subject before, about superficiality, about women, about objectifying them—"

"Oh, yeah, here we go."

"No, listen. Normally, I don't pay any attention to that sort of thing. I look beyond the face or the shape. Hell, I got hooked up with you, didn't I?"

"Jesus."

"Lighten up. But this woman today was one of the plainest—jeez, you'd really be trying too hard if you didn't describe her as downright ugly. And it bothered me that I saw her that way. Well, you—right away you'd be saying, 'That's the ugliest cow I've ever seen.' But I found myself trying to find some redeeming features about her—maybe nice eyes, lovely hair, fine complexion, something. But this woman has nothing going for her, I'm telling you. And—here's the kicker." She paused. "She's married to a real good-looker, a guy who, by all accounts, has no problem attracting women."

"That's what reminded you of me."

"Yeah, right. Listen, the question is, how did this— *plain* woman land him?"

"Has she got money?"

"Owns a company."

"There you are, then. That's it. Simple. Mystery solved."

"Yeah, that's what I think. It adds more weight to my theory. Someone who'd marry an ugly woman for money—well, I think, anyway—is someone who'd kill his wife for the same reason. I'm talking about Karen Sheltoe's husband. He says his mother pushed him to be successful. For all I know, killing the wife might even have been her idea. She sure as hell had nothing good to say about the dead woman. Although, you'd think they'd have got the alibi down a little better."

"Money can buy you anything. You say he has no problem attracting women. Well, he probably has a little something on the side. With her, with the ugly one, he just closes his eyes and thinks about England."

"England?"

"It's an expression."

"Pour me some of that Scotch."

Stark looked at her quizzically.

"Sure." He poured a small amount for her and a stiffer measure for himself. She emptied the glass with one swallow.

"I'm going," she said.

"You're going home?"

"Yeah. I need a good night's sleep."

She got up and slung her purse over her shoulder.

Stark was staring at her. She waited.

"Let's get married," Stark said. As soon as the words left his lips, he switched on a face-saving schoolboy grin, a grin that allowed Weems to regard the suggestion as a jocular one, and him to go along with whatever her reaction was.

She screwed up her face.

"God. How much have you had to drink?"

Stark watched her leave. The instant the door closed behind her, his body was racked with sobbing. After a few moments, he raised his head, eyes closed, and shouted, "Damn it." He slammed his fist on the table. Weems's glass bounced to the floor and shattered.

Chapter Twenty-Eight

Stark sat there for a good hour, watching the billows of cigarette smoke waft up until they met the blast from the air-conditioner and shot away down the corridor toward the empty bedroom. He felt something rub against his leg. Powder, Stark's closet cat had emerged, having determined from the silence that Weems had left. At one time, briefly, Stark had introduced a dog to the household, a tiny, frenetic mutt, a homeless leftover from a murder case. The dog's arrival on the scene had been a traumatic event for Powder, who had never been particularly sociable. It was then that she took to the closet in Stark's bedroom, making a den on a pile of lost socks behind a shoe rack, and coming out only when the apartment was empty, or, when Stark was alone, to rub against him, which was a request for him to feed or water her. A mop of long, white hair, she would eat only the cheapest cat food, and, like Stark, she had a drinking problem, taking water only in one of two ways, either sucking at a thin drizzle from the bathtub faucet (the preferred method) or, if she had to, dipping a paw into a bowl and licking the water from the appendage. Stark filled her bowl with food, but she continued to rub against his legs. He started toward the bathroom and she darted past him and sat on the edge of the tub awaiting his arrival. He turned on the tap and had some trouble adjusting the flow to the thinnest stream that occurs just before the drizzle turns to drips.

Stark returned to the kitchen table, where he had been pouring small measures of Scotch in a self-deceiving gesture of temperance. The glass was merely emptied faster and refilled more frequently. He rarely displayed obvious signs of intoxication beyond a certain muddiness of speech and a tendency to tactlessness, and he would have fallen asleep at the table long before he got really drunk had the phone not rung. It was Ken Coulson.

"I've got something you'll be interested in. We recorded it earlier today."

"Today," Stark slurred. "The 'earlier' is redundant. You couldn't have recorded it later or at this moment."

"What?"

"Never mind. Play it. What is it?"

"Our friend Stokes. A phone conversation. One of our boys got naughty with a telescopic mike. I think we'll go for the okay on a proper phone tap after this. You'll see why. On this recording, naturally, we've only got Stokes's side of the chat."

"So, let's hear it."

There was a click and the whirr of the tape recorder and then Stokes's voice could be heard in a hoarse whisper:

"I haven't got it yet, for God's sake. It'll take weeks for them to pay off. You don't know the way these insurance companies work. This whole goddamned thing has gone wrong—the old man. I never should have involved the old bastard—Yes, I know it's my problem. You'll get the money." Stokes sighed. "Sure you put up half, but you—Yes, I know I owe you the money. The insurance company will pay off eventually. You knew we were going to have to wait—I can't get you the money any quicker: you know that." He sputtered several times, trying to interrupt what Stark imagined was a stream of invective from the other party.

Finally, he succeeded. "I'm sorry. Look, look, take it easy, please. Okay? It's this business with Saul, the poor old bastard—well, I know he shouldn't, but I should never have let the old fool carry that damned popgun in the first place. It was my goddamned wife. It was her idea—Yeah, yeah. Okay, she's a nice lady. Sure, yeah right. I shouldn't speak of her like that. Okay. Right, she was just trying to protect him. She has a big imagination. She lives in movies, the woman—Yeah, I *know* she likes excitement. Tried to get me to go skydiving with her once. Can you imagine? Me? I tell you what, though, I'd trade that for this right now—I can't help it. I'm scared to death—Because of the shooting. I don't know what to do. I just—No-no-no." There was a sudden edge of fear in Stokes's voice: "No-no: I won't do anything like that. Are you kidding? No-no. Don't worry about that. I'm just a little shaken, that's all. I'll hold it together—Meet? Sure, we'll meet. When?—Okay—Yeah, I remember the place. I remember how to get there. Okay, I'll see you." There was a loud click as the tape recorder was shut off.

"Well, what do you think?" Coulson said eagerly.

Stark's enthusiasm was amplified by the alcohol he had consumed:

"Good work, Kenneth, my boy. Great work, in fact. So, listen, here's what we'll do—by the way, do you know who was on the other end of that conversation?"

"No idea."

"His name is Salvatore Cataldi. Have you heard of him?"

"Nope, can't say that I have."

"Well, he's supposed to be—what he's supposed to be is a land developer, but believe me, he stinks. I've run into Mr. Cataldi before. Anyway, here's the connection. I should have told you this. Actually, I thought I had, but I guess I couldn't have, if you haven't heard of him. I'm sure I told somebody—Anyway, never mind. The connection is that the building where the whole thing went down, you know, the office building?"

"Where the heist—"

"Right. so that building is owned, no sorry—I'm rambling—anyway, he doesn't *own* the building, but he does own the management company that runs the building, Okay? Are you with me?"

"Harry, wait a second, you're running way ahead of me here. You're saying you figure the guy was in on the crime because he manages the building? That's a bit of a leap, isn't it?"

"You heard that tape."

"Well, sure, but we don't know who was on the other end."

"Oh, yes, we do. Listen, in Rabinovitch's apartment, there's a photograph of him and Stokes *and* Cataldi."

"So?"

"What do you mean, 'so'? They know each other."

"So?"

"Are you paying attention? Listen. Cataldi's a very bad dude who has never been caught. Anyway, let's not get into that. Just take my word for it, Ken, this Cataldi is a son of a bitch. Now, you've got to see that his connection with Stokes and the old man, and the fact that he manages the building where the crime went down—it all fits together."

"I mean—yeah. It makes sense. I mean, I guess it makes sense." The tone of Coulson's voice suggested he was shrugging his shoulders as he spoke.

"You're damned right it does. I mean, here we go. He manages the building with the empty office in which the courier just happens to find himself for no good goddamned reason and gets wasted, and now we've got our lad Stokes having a nice chat with him. Believe me, that was he on the other end of the line. He must be anxious, to talk on the phone like that, you know. Of course, he'd have no reason to think we'd be bugging Stokes's phone."

"We weren't. It was a telescopic mike."

"Come to think of it, why the hell *were* you watching Stokes? I mean, actually you jumped the gun on me, because I was going to talk to you tomorrow about the guy."

"Because something stinks about this robbery. I told you Stokes was in a financial jackpot."

"Right."

"And I said I figure the robbery was a set-up. He collects the insurance, unloads the jewellery offshore."

"So, why'd they kill the old man?"

"Hey, that's your territory. If you're right about this Cataldi guy, I guess you might find the answer there, eh?"

Chapter Twenty-Nine

About four hours after Stark had his conversation with Coulson, Weems found herself lying stuporously supine and flailing weakly at a jangling alarm clock with her right hand. She had gone to bed after Stark's half-baked marriage proposal with a confusion of anger and frustration and despondency, and she had been rising and falling through various levels of sleep, slipping back and forth across the ragged edge between thought and dream. Her effort to shut off the alarm was futile. The button was depressed, but the ringing continued. Finally, she realized it was the phone. She then knocked both it and the clock off the night table, and had to flop her torso halfway to the floor to retrieve the handset.

"Hello."

"Weems?"

"Who's this?"

"Ted Henry. What the hell's going on there?"

"Oh, the phone—I knocked it over."

"You haven't been drinking, have you?"

"No, no—I just—was fast asleep, that's all. What—time is it?"

"I don't know. About two o'clock, I guess. Listen, we've got another one."

"Another one? Another what?"

"We've got ourselves another body."

"Another body? I'm sorry, I'm not following you."

"Same M.O. as Sheltoe."

"What? Another rape?"

"Hardly. This time it's a male."

"A male?" Weems shook her head. "You lost me there, Sergeant. How can this be like Sheltoe—"

"Strangled with a belt, marks there just like Sheltoe, same area of Scarborough—well, a little farther east, but still by the lake. No signs of struggle. Not another mark on him. Clothes not even rumpled. Almost not a hair out of place—so to speak." Henry chuckled. "This is funny—" Weems's eyebrows lifted. "He was wearing a hairpiece, you know, a toupé, and it wasn't even knocked off his head."

"Yeah, that's funny," Weems said dryly. "You were at the scene?"

"No. Ident gave me the details over the phone. I'm at home. Duty officer called me after he got a call from one of the local boys at 42 Division. He was on the scene of the Sheltoe murder and he recognized the similarities. I've put a call in to Forensic Sciences and asked them to do a tox screen as soon as they can. I'll lay you a dollar to a doughnut we're going to find the same drug in him as was in Sheltoe. The dead guy stank of booze."

"This is bizarre," Weems said.

"How's that?"

"Well, I mean, Sheltoe *was* a rape, after all—I mean, this is a *guy*."

"I thought you were convinced that the rape business was phoney?"

"That's right. I do think it was faked, but—who *is* this guy?"

"No I.D. Pockets were emptied. Nothing, not a key chain, not a scrap of paper."

"If it was robbery, they'd just take the wallet, not everything in his pockets."

"Which means?"

"Either he didn't have anything on him when he was killed, or maybe whoever did it is trying to conceal the guy's identity."

"Exactly. You know who I think this guy is?"

"No idea."

"I've got a gut feeling this is our mystery caller."

"The guy who's been telling us Adams killed Sheltoe?"

"Right."

"Oh, my God."

"What's the matter?"

"I told Adams about the guy."

"You what?"

"Well, no, not in so many words. I said we had additional information and that's why we were reopening the case."

"So?"

"So—what was this additional information? Maybe he was blackmailing Adams, so the guy prods us to reopen the investigation to scare him, but we haven't got any more evidence to work with, so he knows Adams is *just* going to get a scare, and then he'll pay off."

"Okay," Henry said. "What are you going to do now?"

Without hesitation, Weems said, "The first place I'm going to go, and I mean tonight, is the mother's, make sure she can't provide Adams with an alibi this time. Then, I'm going to visit Adams, see what he has to say about his whereabouts tonight. Then I'll try to make the connection with this guy, and if it all comes together, bingo."

Henry's directions took Weems to a park by Lake Ontario on the edge of the bluffs in the southeast corner of Scarborough. The area, cordoned off with yellow police tape, glowed surreally in Ident's floodlights. The air was steamy, its stillness broken by occasional wafts of dead-fish-redolent breeze from the lake. The body was as Henry had described it. A man in his sixties, Weems guessed, neatly dressed, and apart from ligature marks around the throat, "no other indications of trauma were evident," she thought in the parlance. He lay on his back, arms at his sides, nothing awry except the toupee, which had shifted only slightly from its proper resting place, and the bottom of the front of the jacket, which was flipped open, revealing a triangle of gold satin lining. The jacket was caramel-coloured in a light hopsack. Beneath, over a lean, long frame, was a pale yellow, buttoned-down shirt with an open collar. The trousers were tan cotton, socks dark brown, shoes tasselled, ox-blood loafers.

"Sharp dresser," Weems said. One of two detectives present, a black man, himself sartorially well turned-out, looked in her direction with a face that took Weems's breath away.

"You must be Carol Weems." His voice was as deep and mellifluous as Stark's Johnny Hartman CDs that she had come to love. Unconsciously, she patted her hair.

"Right," she said, "Weems." She smiled.

"I'm Canton," the detective said, "Charles Canton." He smiled back at her. Weems began to feel uncomfortable. She thought she must be blushing. He kept staring. Finally he said, "You're Homicide, right?"

"Right," she said, "Homicide."

He chuckled and said, "So—have you got any questions, anything you want to know?" She *was* blushing.

"Oh, I'm sorry—Yes." She took a deep breath. "When—how long has he been dead?"

"Not long, maybe a couple of hours. Coroner's come and gone."

"I see. Who found the body?"

"Couple of teenagers—girl and a boy." He smiled. "I guess they came down here to do a little moonlight spooning." Weems smiled at the quaintness of the term. "We let them go home. I've got their addresses, if you want to speak to them."

"Did they see anybody, any vehicles, hear anything?"

"No. The girl tripped over the body. They couldn't see it in the deep grass here. I think she knocked the fellow's hairpiece askew. Vanity, eh? People are funny. Look at the guy. That thing is so unnatural. He'd look better bald. Lot of good it's doing him now. What do you think? Will they put that thing on him in the coffin, or leave him *au naturel*?"

Weems shook her head.

"Any footprints, or anything? Scraps of paper? I take it the area has been searched."

"Oh, yeah. Ident scoured it. Not a thing."

"What about labels in his clothing?"

"Nothing special. He bought the jacket at the Bay. Nothing that will help you identify the fellow."

"Okay, well—"

"Pardon me, but you haven't been doing this very long, have you?"

"What?"

"Homicide."

Weems sighed.

"It shows, does it?"

Canton nodded. He smiled warmly.

"Don't worry about it. There's nothing here that would tell you anything. Best thing is to attend the autopsy tomorrow. You can check the clothing and stuff then. If there's anything here worth finding, Ident will find it. You can get that from them tomorrow. I *can* tell you the fellow probably wasn't killed right there." He pointed to the body.

"How do you know?"

"There are drag marks in the grass from the road. I think he was pulled over here from a car. Probably killed in the car, or somewhere else, and driven here."

"Do you think it would have to be somebody strong to drag him over here?"

"Not for this guy. Look at him. His arms are like wires. I bet you he doesn't weigh a hundred-and-forty pounds. A kid could have dragged him. This guy's a real bottle baby. The coroner pointed out the blotches on his face, burst blood vessels, and all the little veins showing. He got most of his calories in liquid form. You can smell the booze on him. He's had a skinful."

"Are you the one who called and said it reminded you of the Sheltoe case?"

"Yep. I was first one on the scene at Karen Sheltoe. You see the way his arms are straight down his sides? It's as if somebody straightened him up, you know, like rearranged everything so he was neat and tidy. Karen Sheltoe was like that. There was something unnatural about the way her body was laid out. And not a bruise on her, not a hair out of place. I pointed it out to the

Homicide guy at the time. And, of course, they were both strangled with a belt."

Weems made a little grunt.

"What's that?"

"You think the killer is somebody obsessed with neatness."

"Well, obsessive, anyway. I'm no psychologist, but I know obsessive behaviour doesn't always go in sort of straight lines. I mean, the killer may not be obsessed with neatness, necessarily. Like, this could be a sort of gesture of apology, an unconscious revelation that the killing wasn't done out of anger or hate, more like it was something, you know, that had to be done, and shouldn't be taken as an act of violence."

"I thought you said you weren't a psychologist?" Weems chuckled.

Canton shrugged.

"Well—for what it's worth."

"Yes, well, you know, you could be right." She smiled warmly. "Thanks."

Chapter Thirty

Stark and Noel Harris sat in Noel's car in the parking lot of a strip plaza in Woodbridge, north of the city. Stark had visited Cataldi there two years earlier, so he knew the man's office was in the end unit, in what used to be a dry cleaner's. There was no sign identifying Cataldi Enterprises. Harris had reconnoitred, found a black Cadillac with heavily tinted windows parked by the rear entrance.

"This is going to kill me," Stark groaned, flapping the front of his shirt. "We should have brought my car."

"You should get one of those little battery-powered fans."

"Yeah, you'd get a kick out of that, wouldn't you? We *should* have brought my car."

"It would stand out like a sore thumb. This car blends in anywhere. It's unobtrusive," Harris said proudly.

"Especially if you park it beside a row of garbage cans. What year is this thing?"

"Eighty-two."

"Eighty-two?"

"Volvos last forever."

"So does herpes. Naturally, you wouldn't buy one with air-conditioning."

"Sarge, we couldn't sit here with the car running all day. Who knows how long we'll be here?"

Stark groaned.

"It's going to kill me." He looked at his watch. "Nine o'clock and it's already about a hundred degrees."

"Thirty-seven point eight."

"What?"

"Celsius."

"Put the radio on. It does work, doesn't it?"

"Sure." Harris turned a knob. CBC news came on, a report about a fishing dispute in the Pacific off British Columbia.

Stark reached out quickly and turned the volume down.

"Did you hear what he said?"

Harris scanned the parking lot, thinking he must have missed something.

"What? I don't see anybody."

"On the radio." Stark growled. "About the 'fishers.' What the hell's a 'fisher?' I know what a fissure is, but what's a 'fisher'?"

Harris gave him an incredulous look. He said slowly, "Someone who catches fish?"

"That, for God's sake, is a fisherman."

"They don't want to use sexist language."

Stark's head snapped around, his eyes ablaze, the corners of his mouth twitching. Harris had run, full speed, into his trap.

"Sexist language? There is nothing sexist about the word 'fisherman,' nor, for that matter, the word 'chairman,' nor the word 'spokesman.'"

"Of course there is—"

"The 'man' in those words doesn't mean 'male.' It means mankind, humankind—person, in other words. so all this silly destruction of the language is a product of ignorance. The whole thing is a knee-jerk—"

"Sarge."

"What?"

"You know who you're like?"

"Oh, I'm sure you're going to tell me."

"King Canute."

"What?"

"Yeah. You're sitting there on your throne, trying to hold back the sea, and the tide just keeps rolling right in."

Stark's head turned slowly. He stared at Harris.

"Uh-oh," Harris said.

"Uh-oh, what?"

"The Caddy." The black Cadillac came around the corner at some speed. Harris cranked the Volvo's starter. The engine struggled to life, chugged for a few seconds, then cut out.

"Shit," Stark said. "Why don't you get a real car, for God's sake? I'm surprised you didn't bring a tandem bicycle."

Harris spun the starter again. The engine caught with a roar. He put the car in gear and pulled out in pursuit of the Cadillac, which by this time was in the left turn lane on Highway 7, waiting for oncoming traffic to pass so it could turn down an intersecting road. The Cadillac had made the turn before the Volvo could get out of the plaza parking lot. Harris had to wait for a long stream of cars to go by.

"Shit," Stark said, slamming the dashboard.

The Cadillac made another turn, into a service station on the corner. It pulled in front of one of the bay doors, and Stark and Harris watched as a big man in a dark jacket and lime-green polo shirt emerged from the driver's side.

"Is that Cataldi?" Harris asked.

"No," Stark snapped.

The big man went into the gas-station office. Within seconds, the bay door lifted, and a mechanic came out and drove the Cadillac into the service bay.

"What now?" Harris said.

"Pull over there and park on the road, then stroll over and have a look."

Harris did as he was ordered, returning in a couple of minutes.

"What's happening?" Stark asked.

"They're giving the car an oil change."

"Shit."

"That's the problem with that tinted glass. You can't tell whether there's anybody inside. How are we ever going to know whether Cataldi's in there or not?"

"Why do you ask questions you know the answer to already?"

"To which you already know the answer," Harris said with a smug smile.

"Get in," Stark said derisively.

They drove back to the parking lot. The Cadillac returned, going behind the building again. Two hours passed. Stark slept. He woke to Harris's poking. Stark's clothes were sopping with perspiration.

"What is it?"

"The Caddy's on the move again. Here we go."

Harris had the same trouble stirring the Volvo's engine into operation, punctuated by Stark's curses. The Cadillac had headed west on Highway 7 at about thirty kilometres an hour over the limit. It didn't go far, and they managed to catch up to it in time to see it pull into the parking lot of a group of shops and draw up in front of a Chinese restaurant. Harris stopped the Volvo at the side of the highway. He and Stark both let out a groan when only the driver's door opened and the man in the dark jacket got out again. But this time, he walked around to the other side of the Cadillac and opened the rear door. A small, slender man in his early thirties, wearing a silver-grey suit, got out and stood adjusting his tie.

"That's Cataldi," Stark said. He smiled.

"Nice dresser," Harris said, and Stark glared at him.

"Yeah, for a killer. Hey, look over there. That's one of Kenny Coulson's Hold-up boys, in the black Chev." Stark recognized the grizzled detective from the jewel robbery scene. "Run over there and see what's happening."

Harris got out of the car and trotted over to the Chev, which was parked at the end of the little plaza's lot. He spoke to the Hold-up detective for a moment, then jogged back.

"The blue Cadillac at the end there is Stokes's car. I've got the plate number for future reference. He's already inside the restaurant."

"Bingo," Stark said with a wide grin.

"The cop's name is Beavis. He has a message for you. Coulson tried to call you on your cell phone, but he couldn't reach you."

"Damn it. I forgot to charge the bloody thing."

Harris rolled his eyes.

"He found out that Stokes and Cataldi are in bed together on some piece of property near Stouffville."

"I knew it. I knew it. Okay, listen. I'm going to call a cab from that pay phone. You go into the restaurant. See whether you can get a table near enough to them to hear. I've got a spare battery for my cell. I'll hook it up. You can call me on that or at my home number. Keep the tail on Cataldi. Let me know where you are later—when you get tired. I'll come up and relieve you."

Chapter Thirty-One

Jane Adams was furious at having been awakened. It was five a.m. She refused to buzz open the lobby door for Weems.

"I don't need to come in, Ms Adams. I'm sorry for waking you. I only have one question to ask."

"At this time of the bloody night? It couldn't wait till tomorrow?"

"No, it couldn't. I'm sorry. Just tell me, where you were at ten o'clock last night."

"I was working, for God's sake."

"Working? You work at night?"

"I'm a nurse, you idiot."

"Where do you work?"

"Scarborough General. I thought you said one question."

"What time did you finish work?"

"Midnight—no, eleven o'clock. I left early. I had a headache, and you've brought it back again."

"After that, you were alone the rest of the night."

"Of course I was alone, I—"

"That's fine, Ms Adams. You can go back to sleep now." Weems hung up the lobby phone.

Chapter Thirty-Two

Cataldi and Stokes were in a booth at the back of the room. The surrounding tables were empty. The arrangement looked deliberate. Harris didn't try for a seat near them. They probably wouldn't have given him one anyway, and sitting there would have been too obvious, and asking for one would have drawn attention.

The entrance to the washrooms was just beyond where the pair were sitting. Cataldi's driver (and if he wasn't also his bodyguard, Harris had never seen one) was seated at an adjacent table, his massive shoulders bent over a bowl of noodles. Harris thought he could hear him slurping them from the other side of the restaurant, but it had to be his imagination. The ambient noise was considerable. Most of the rest of the customers were business people, most of them Chinese. The din was loud and constant, the perfect place for a confidential meeting. It was all but impossible to discern what was being said at the adjoining table over the babble of the other diners.

Cataldi must have been well known there. A Chinese man in a dark suit, who appeared to be the restaurant's owner, went over at one point and shook hands with him, and Cataldi showily introduced Stokes. Stokes, appearing distracted, accorded the owner no more than a perfunctory nod. A Chinese businessman, a tall man in a slate-grey suit that would have cost the equivalent of four months' rent on Harris's flat in

Parkdale, came over from another table, and this time Cataldi stood to shake his hand, and even Stokes half rose and half smiled.

Harris's Montreal Jazz Festival T-shirt, faded jeans and the ragged Blue Jays cap he was wearing did little to inspire the staff to eagerness, and he finally had to signal a waiter to get service. After he had placed his order, he walked slowly past Cataldi and Stokes on his way to the men's room. He heard Stokes say, "Look, I'm getting the damned money together. You'll have to give me some time," and Cataldi say, "I need the fucking—" before he stopped speaking as he noticed Harris passing. Harris stopped in the entranceway to the washrooms, out of sight of the dining room. He then heard Cataldi say, "I want the money now. I've got to pay the municipal tax people by Tuesday, or they're going to seize the property. Then we'll be in a real jackpot." A chair scraped, and Harris, fearing that the goon might be coming into the washroom, hurried through the door. His fear was borne out. The door opened and the bodyguard lumbered in, his thick arm nearly touching Harris's as he occupied the other urinal. Harris's chest was firmly pressed against the ceramic. The goon, making no similar attempt at modesty, stood well back, flopped his organ out of his pants and relieved himself splashily with a loud sigh.

Harris zipped up quickly and hurried out ahead of the bodyguard. Cataldi and Stokes were standing, preparing to leave. Harris hustled ahead of them, throwing a twenty-dollar bill on the table beside an untouched plate of lemon chicken. Outside, he nodded to Beavis, who gave him a wave, and trotted to the Volvo, which he had driven into the parking lot after Stark had left. He got the car started before his quarry came out of the restaurant. Cataldi and Stokes stood speaking for a moment before parting, Cataldi giving a threatening-looking finger-point before he turned and strode quickly to the Cadillac.

Harris's effort to maintain a discreet distance between his car and Cataldi's proved fatal to the pursuit. The Cadillac pulled out and shot past a long line of traffic, ducking back into the lane just in time to avoid colliding with an oncoming truck. Harris's Volvo lacked the power for a matching move on the hilly road, and he was stuck behind a line of slower-moving vehicles. When he arrived at the strip plaza where Cataldi's office was, he found that the Cadillac wasn't there.

"Damn it," he said. He called Stark on his cell phone, and told him what had happened, endured Stark's epithets, and then got a pleased noise out of him when he related what he had heard in the restaurant. He asked Stark where Cataldi lived, and Stark gave him the address of a condo building in North York, on Bayview. Harris said he was going to head there, and Stark responded with a bitter sneer in his voice, "Yeah, well, if he's not there, hang around. He's probably stopped off for some post-prandial head."

Chapter Thirty-Three

To get to Graeme Adams, Weems had to pass Brenda Phillips's formidable frame.

"What the hell is the meaning of this? At this ungodly hour. This is taking harassment to a new low." The woman was wearing a long black satin negligée. The expression, "You can't make a silk purse out of a sow's ear" flashed into Weems's thoughts. The sleek elegance of the garment merely served to magnify Phillips's homeliness. Weems heard an echo of her father's voice, "A face that could stop a clock." The clock would have stopped at five-fifteen a.m. Weems had driven as quickly as she could from Jane Adams's apartment, but she couldn't go faster than a phone call. Brenda Phillips's hair had been brushed, and she had answered the door much more quickly than somebody who had been roused from bed. When Phillips finally moved aside and let Weems enter, Weems found Adams awake and alert, in blue silk pyjamas, hair combed, legs crossed, on an easy chair in the sunken living room that looked as if it had been brought, intact, from a display room at De Boers. Smoking a black cigarette, with a gold tip, he looked like something from much earlier in the century.

"Your mother phoned you," she said. It wasn't a question.

"His mother has his interest at heart," Phillips said.

"Why would she think I would be coming to see

you, Graeme?"

"I think you should be calling him 'Mr. Adams,' don't you?" Phillips said.

"No, no, my dear, 'Graeme's fine," he said. "Perhaps the inspector prefers to be informal at this time of the night."

"Detective," Weems said. "May I sit down?"

Adams laughed dryly.

"Isn't your politesse a bit absurd? You burst in here in your jackboots in an attempt to catch us unawares. Sit where the hell you like. I'm sure I couldn't stop you."

Weems sat on a chintz-covered loveseat that was so tightly sprung you could have used it as a trampoline. "Where were you—"

"Where was I between the hours of six p.m. and midnight? It sounds like a line from Agatha Christie. That's why I said, 'inspector.' You're as absurd as Inspector Japp."

"Where were you last night?"

Phillips started to answer: "You were at—"

Adams interrupted.

"I was at a restaurant."

Phillips looked at him sharply.

He gave her back an expression like a contrite puppy's.

"I'm sorry, my dear. I know I was supposed to be at a Lodge meeting, but—I didn't feel like going, so I just—I went to a restaurant and had a meal and then—I went to a bar. I had a couple of drinks, then came home."

"What time did you get home?" Weems asked.

Phillips and Adams both started to give the time together. Phillips shut up and let Adams say, "Midnight."

"What restaurant were you at?" Weems asked.

"Look. What is this all about? You've really got me puzzled."

"Just answer my questions, Mr. Adams."

"I think we should call our lawyer," Phillips said. "I don't think you should say a thing until our lawyer gets here, Graeme."

"What the hell for?" Adams said. "Look, I have no idea what this woman is after, but I know whatever it is ridiculous. Probably somebody double-parked on Yonge Street and she's trying to pin it on me. The hell with it. Let her do what she wants to do. I haven't done a goddamned thing. I don't need a bloody lawyer, for God's sake."

"So, you got home at midnight?"

"That's right, midnight. Is there something wrong with that? Was I out past the curfew?"

"What's the name of the restaurant you ate in, Mr. Adams?"

"Mr. Greek. On Kennedy Road."

"Did you have a reservation?"

"At Mr. Greek?" Adams's tone expressed the absurdity of the question.

"Were you alone?"

"I was."

"Would anybody there—a waiter, perhaps—be able to confirm that you ate there?"

"Christ, I have no idea what the waiter even looked like. None."

"Do you remember where you sat?"

"In the smoking section. No, I don't remember exactly. I didn't pay any attention. I didn't know I was going to be examined on it afterwards. Nobody told me there'd be a quiz." Adams sprung open a silver cigarette case. It added to the image of the nineteen-thirties. Adams took out another black-and-gold cigarette and lit it with a gold Dunhill lighter. "Would you like one?" he said, offering her the case.

"No, thanks," she said, pulling a pack of her ultra-lights out of her purse. "I'll have one of mine—if you don't mind?"

Phillips stood, walked to the buffet, and brought back a huge Waterford ashtray.

"So, Inspector Japp, anything else you'd like to know about my recent activities?" Adams said. "I can give you a progress report on my white-slave ring, if you'd like."

"What was the name of the bar you went to?"

"The bar?" He tilted his head to one side, satirizing an effort to remember. "I'm sorry. I forget."

"Look, Mr. Adams, this is not a joke."

"Well, how do I know it's not a joke? Since you won't tell me what these questions are about? I think this is illegal, isn't it? Entrapment, or something?"

"I'm going to call the lawyer," Phillips said, rising from the arm of Adams's chair, where she had perched in what seemed a display of solidarity.

He pulled her back by the elbow.

"At this time of the morning? Besides, I've decided not to answer any more questions until Japp here tells me what this is all about. So, there you are." He gave Weems a Laurel and Hardy nod, made an exaggerated circle with the hand holding the cigarette, took a long drag and started blowing smoke rings.

"There's been a murder," Weems said quietly.

"What?" Adams and Phillips said in unison. Then he said, "Who?"

"A man. We don't know who he is."

Adams held his palms up in a gesture of puzzlement.

"What's this have to do with me?" he said. "Bad enough you should be trying to nail me for taking the 'do-not-remove' tags off the mattress, but—murder? That's ridiculous."

"Look, Mr. Adams, tell me the name of the bar you were at, and if I can verify that, you'll be—well, you won't have any problems."

"Why would I have any problems?"

"Listen. I have no reason to—Why not simply clear the whole thing up right now? Give me a recent picture of you. I'll show it around the bar and the restaurant. Maybe somebody will remember you. That'll be it."

"I don't know why we're being subjected to this," Phillips said. "Who is this person who was killed? Is it somebody Graeme is supposed to know?"

Weems shrugged.

"That, I don't know, since, as I told you, we don't yet know who the person is."

"This is ridiculous," Adams said. "If you don't even know who it is, why are you coming to me?"

"There are certain similarities between this murder and the murder of Karen Sheltoe—of your wife."

"Similarities? What similarities? Was this guy brutally raped?"

"I can't tell you what similarities."

"In other words, the persecution continues," Phillips said. "Basically, you're still trying to implicate my husband in his former wife's murder, and you're clutching so wildly at straws that you get another murder—what? In the same area, or something? Whatever it is, you imagine some ridiculous connection that supports your ridiculous theory."

Weems sighed. "Please. Just tell me what bar you were at."

Adams emphasized every word: "I don't remember."

Weems shook her head.

Adams said, "Give me your card. I'll try to remember. I'll take a drive around there. When I spot the bar, I'll give you a call and tell you."

Weems glared at him. She dug a card out of her purse, tossed it on the massive glass-topped, wrought-iron coffee table and left.

Chapter Thirty-Four

Cataldi's car was nowhere in sight at the condo, and Harris concluded that if it were there, it would probably be parked in the underground garage. He could slip into the garage on foot behind a resident's car, but he might be noticed, and besides, the building was a large one, which would be reflected in the size of the garage. He might wander for hours and never find the car, and all just to determine whether Cataldi was at home. He chose a more direct approach. He would call Cataldi's apartment on his cell phone. When he dialled the number he got from information, he figured the gruff voice that answered must belong to the goon. "Oh, I'm sorry," Harris said. "I've dialled the wrong number. Sorry to—" The big man had hung up. If the monkey's home, the organ grinder must be there, too, he thought.

Harris sat in his Volvo for the rest of the afternoon and into the evening. Three times he had to duck out of sight when a security guard passed. He had to urinate into an old coffee cup he found under the seat, and fling the results out the window. He'd parked under a tree that afforded partial shade, and he had opened all the windows, but it did little to alleviate the baking of the blazing sun. Before long, his clothes were clinging to him like sodden dishcloths. The heat made him sleepy and he had a struggle to keep his eyes open. Finally, at eight-fifteen, he spoke into his cassette recorder that

Cataldi's car had pulled out of the garage. He said a little prayer and cranked the Volvo, giving a nod of thanks as the engine responded immediately.

Once again, he had difficulty keeping up with the other car. The driver weaved in and out of traffic like an impatient teenager. He followed the Cadillac north to Highway 7 and then west, marking its progress only by the taillights in the distance. The lights suddenly disappeared, and Harris panicked. If the car had turned and then turned again before he got to the intersecting road— He pushed the Volvo as fast as it would go. An approaching car swung across his lane, and he had to hit the brakes to avoid hitting it. Another time, he would have laid on the horn, but now he glared at the retreating rear of the car as it pulled into a motel parking lot. He recognized the licence plate. Stokes's Cadillac. He jammed on the brakes, swerving to the side of the road, drawing a blast from the horn of a following pick-up.

The Cadillacs were parked side by side in front of Unit 23. "Cuddling Caddies. Gives you a warm feeling," Harris said aloud. Heavy blackout curtains were drawn tightly shut on the unit. The motel was a long affair, with an interior hall. Harris listened by the window for a time, but heard nothing. He went inside and along the hallway, stopping in front of the door with "23" in gold numerals. He looked up and down the hall, then put his ear to the door. He could hear a voice, but the words were indiscernible. Then he thought he could feel pressure on the door, as if someone had pushed against it on the other side, and he ducked away and walked quickly down the hall toward the exit at the far end. He heard the door to Unit 23 open behind him, and rapid footsteps coming his way. The glass exit door opened into an alcove, at the other side of which was another glass door that led into a second line of rooms. To his right was a door to the parking lot; to his left, a cluster of coin machines. The glass door behind him was opening. Pivoting to his left would let him look as if he were going to use one of the machines and at the same time give him an opportunity to gauge the intention of the person following, while keeping the glass door between them. Salvatore Cataldi was opening the door, carrying a plastic ice bucket. They made eye contact. There was a sort of flicker in Cataldi's eyes, as if he had just snapped a picture of Harris for future reference, or to compare it with the files in his mind.

Harris nodded, got no response, pretended to be fishing for change and checking the offerings of the dispensing machine while Cataldi filled the ice bucket. Cataldi turned without paying further attention to Harris and went back through the door and down the hall. Harris went through the door to the parking lot, stood beyond the beam of the security light for some time, and seeing no sign of activity in the lot, made his way to the exterior door of Unit 23 again. He looked around once more, and then put his ear to the door. What he heard made him step back.

"What the hell?"

He heard voices, still indiscernible, and laughter. But it sounded like one of the voices and one of the laughs belonged to a woman. He put his ear back, but heard nothing for a time, and then a chair scraping on the floor and music and voices—the television had been switched on. And then a rushing sound: someone was having a shower. A beam of light swept along the wall of the motel: a car was coming into the lot. Harris ducked behind a low hedge that ran between a walkway and the parking lot pavement. The car stopped at the far end of the building, the door to a unit opened and closed, and Harris put his ear back against the door and stepped back once again.

This time, it sounded as if there was a fight going on, not an argument, but a physical battle: furniture was being moved. There was a breaking sound, as if a glass had fallen to the floor; a body landing heavily on the bed; then a squeal and a moan.

"Jesus." Harris pressed his ear harder against the door. There was no mistaking it now. He couldn't be wrong. There was a woman in the room. Harris went back to his car and waited. Two hours later, the door to Unit 23 opened and a woman emerged. She had long, blonde hair. She got into Stokes's Cadillac, and Harris watched her drive away.

Chapter Thirty-Five

The autopsy at the Centre of Forensic Sciences confirmed the man had been choked to death by what appeared to have been a belt. The coroner said the victim had had enough alcohol in his blood that "you could have made a flame-thrower with his breath." The scraps of paper and cigarette butts Ident had collected had no apparent value, although Weems thought that if it came down to it, perhaps they could get DNA from the butts. There were no black cigarettes with gold tips among them.

The toxicology results were not available till the following Monday. They revealed what Henry had suspected. The man, whoever he was, however he fit into the puzzle, had, indeed, been drugged, and with pentobarbital, the same barbiturate they'd found in Karen Sheltoe.

"So, who the hell is this guy?" Henry asked Weems.

"Nobody reported missing?"

"Nope. And this guy strikes me as somebody who could have been a loner. You know, a heavy drinker, wife probably tossed him out years ago. His landlord will miss him eventually—if he had one—but that doesn't mean the landlord's going to come to us. Probably think he's skipped. Anyway, we can't hang around waiting for somebody to come forward. Let's get a drawing of him and put it in the papers."

"We could circulate records to the dentists. What about the toupé? I could take it around to wig stores, whatever they call them, see if anybody recognizes it."

"Sure, you can try that. We'll wait a few days, hope somebody misses him. Pretty insensitive thing, putting a picture in the paper. We'll try the dentists. You try the wig people. We'll get a drawing done. Show it to stores in the neighbourhood where he was found. Then, if we have to, we'll put it in the papers. We can't leave it too long. The trail will get too cold."

Chapter Thirty-Six

"Sarge?"

"Who is this?"

"It's me, Noel."

"Noel?"

"Harris."

"You should say, 'It's I.'" Stark's words were thick and slow.

Harris nodded.

"Of course I should. How stupid of me."

"What the hell time is it? Why are you calling?"

"Cataldi? Remember?"

"That bastard. What about him?"

"I was supposed to follow him? Remember?"

"Quit saying 'remember.' Of course I remember. What about him?"

"He went to a motel."

Silence, but for Stark's wheezy breathing. Finally Stark said, "He went to a motel. What the hell are you talking about?"

"I followed him to a motel."

"God." Stark gave a long, drawn-out sigh. "What are you trying to tell me, Harris?"

"I followed Cataldi to a motel. Stokes's car came in right after him."

"Stokes? Good stuff."

"Yes, but it wasn't Stokes."

"What do you mean, it wasn't Stokes?"

"It was a blonde woman—a blonde woman was driving Stokes's car."

"A blonde woman?"

"Right. And they were doing the deed. I could hear them through the door. They were going at it."

"A blonde woman was driving Stokes's car, his Cadillac, and she and Cataldi were screwing, is that what you're saying?"

"Exactly."

"That bitch."

"Bitch?"

"Stokes's wife. I don't believe it. That was Stokes's wife you saw. Who else could it be?"

"Well, obviously it had to be somebody who had access to his Cadillac."

"Isn't that cozy, eh? There's honour among thieves for you. Stokes and his buddy Cataldi are partners in this—whatever it is— and meanwhile Cataldi's having it off with Stokes's wife. What a stinking cow."

Harris couldn't resist the temptation: "You're mixing your animal images."

Stark didn't respond.

Harris shrugged.

"So, what now?"

"What—now?" Stark said nothing for a moment, then: "Keep following him, stay on the bastard's tail."

"You want me to go there—like now? To his apartment?"

"Eh?—No.—Forget it for now. Pick up on him tomorrow. Jesus. Can you believe it? That swine Cataldi and that bitch. Women're all the same, you know, Noel. You haven't got a woman, have you? Because they'll screw you over, Noel. They'll screw you over every time. Believe me. I know. I know." Stark hung up.

"That sounded like an interesting conversation." A silver wand rattled the ice in a tall glass carafe. Ernie Kowalski fitted a strainer on the top of the carafe and poured part of the contents into two martini glasses, handing one to Harris. "Mixed animal images?"

"Three times actually, 'bitch,' 'cow' and 'swine.' Although, I suppose 'swine' doesn't count because he used it to refer to somebody else. Stokes's wife—"

"The jeweller?"

"Yeah. His wife was both a 'bitch' and a 'cow.' The 'swine' was Salvatore Cataldi."

"Cataldi. You really think he's your man?"

"Stark does."

"Oh, I know Harry does. What about you?"

"Well, there's sure as hell a connection there. I mean—"

"But what makes me doubt this is that Cataldi is not a robbery/killer kind of guy. I told Stark this. Sure, we've had our eye on him for a few years, off and on. But because we think he's into some white-collar stuff. In any case, we've never been able to persuade the Crown to proceed on anything. Cataldi buffers himself too well, or the stuff he does is right on the legal line."

"Well, maybe he strayed over it this time. There's a lot of money involved in this thing, you know?"

"So I gather. Stark was pissed, was he?"

Harris took a sip of his martini. He chuckled softly. "You mean yours and Stark's definition of 'pissed,' or the contemporary use of the word?"

Kowalski gave Harris a wry look: "I don't mean your definition, 'was he pissed off?' I mean, 'was he drunk?'"

Harris nodded.

"Mmm. I get the impression that guy's got real problems."

"Harry?" Kowalski shook his head. "Poor Harry. Yeah, he's screwed up, Harry. Nothing that a new life wouldn't cure."

"A new life?"

"You know, it makes me think there's something to Eastern philosophy."

"What do you mean?"

"Reincarnation. You know, it's as if there are certain souls that shouldn't be recycled. You know what I mean?"

"No."

"You ever read *The Outsider* by Colin Wilson?"

"I don't think so."

"You should. I'll lend it to you. Harry's like one of those guys. He doesn't fit. I don't mean he doesn't fit *in*. I mean, he's one of those people who are never going to fit any persona their souls are attached to."

"I think you're getting a bit deep here, Ernie. I think he's just a bitter old man."

Kowalski glared.

"Hey, watch the *old*. Listen, Harry hates being a cop. But I think he'd hate being anything. Call him a loner: that's inadequate. He's more like what they used to call a misfit. But by that, of course, they meant a wastrel, a bum, a do-nothing. Harry's not like that. Not at all. He's a dedicated cop. He's the best investigator—"

Harris raised a hand to stop Kowalski's tribute.

"Yeah, I know, Ernie. so people keep saying. But, you know, it seems to me—from what I've seen, not just in this case, but even the last time we worked together, which was the first time, that Stark's a bumbler. I mean, he doesn't—"

It was Kowalski's turn to lift his hand as a stop sign.

"You mean he doesn't seem to know what he's doing? It all kind of comes together by accident?"

"Well, as I said, from what I've seen—"

"What happened the last time you worked with him?"

Harris shrugged.

"We got the guy, but—"

"Never mind the but, and you haven't seen the resolution of this case, yet, have you?"

"Not yet, but—"

"Still with the but. Listen. It's just the way he works. Harry will use you. He's used me many times in the past. He uses anybody he thinks knows more than he does about something, or who can work better than he can at something. You should be flattered that he picked you. You see, he has a great instinct about people. That's how he solves his cases. If he thought the Pope could help him, he'd send him an email."

"So he doesn't use the 'little grey cells'?"

"I think he once did, you know, but most of them have probably been killed off by booze. He's an emotional wreck, you know, our Harry."

"No kidding?" Harris said knowingly.

"There's always been an enormous hole in the poor bugger's life. God knows what he missed: must have been something in his childhood. It always is, isn't it, eh? He has this self-defeating mix of searching and self-destruction. He's obsessed with women: sex and love, love and hate. Starts with sex and then he falls in love with them. Right now, he's in love with a detective, Carol Weems. Have you met her?"

"No"

"He has no trouble attracting them. With women, he's sensitive and attentive, but he's also one of those gosh, golly-gee-whiz klutzes that cries out to be mothered. At first, women are drawn to that, but then a couple of things happen. First, after a time, Stark rebels, like a kid, so the women find they can't keep the reins on him. And then they realize that they don't really want a little boy, after all, and certainly not one his age."

"I hate my mother."

"Jesus. What brought that on? That's an awful thing to say."

"You don't know her. Okay, I don't *hate* her, but she—"

"She was the dominant one, was she, the gay paradigm, is it?"

"Very funny. No. She's a mouse with my father, but passive-aggressive. She'd drive you nuts."

"Tell me. Does Stark know about you and I?"

"Are you kidding?"

Kowalski shook his head. "It wouldn't bother him."

"Stark?"

"Listen. You know what Stark would say?"

"You tell me, Ernie."

"I know he'd say it, because I've heard him say it. He'd say, 'I don't care what you do, just don't frighten the horses.'"

"What's that mean? Okay, I know what that means."

"Exactly. Anyway, now that I think of it, it might be better not to tell him. I can see how it might come in handy some time if he didn't know. So, tell me, are you enjoying the case? Better than that community-relations crap your inspector had you on, isn't it?"

"Anything's better than that. Yes, I am enjoying it."

"We're a lot like Stark, you know, you and I."

"What's that supposed to mean?"

"No, really."

Harris sighed, nodding. "We all became cops because we had something to prove, is that it?"

"Sad, isn't it?"

"But I love it, Ernie, and so do you, so we're not the same as Stark."

"Poor Harry."

Chapter Thirty-Seven

The day the drawing went in the newspapers, it produced a result.

That morning, Weems was on her way to the Right Stuff hair-replacement salon when her cell phone rang. It was Henry.

"Bingo," he said.

"Oh?"

"Woman by the name of Martha Byers just called. She saw the picture in the *Sun.* She says she's sure the guy's her brother, chap called Jim Jackson. She'll be at Forensic Sciences at eleven. I told her you'd meet her there."

Chapter Thirty-Eight

Harris was in the parking lot of Cataldi's condo at 6 a.m. He had a flask full of coffee from a Second Cup, having driven past two Starbucks, eschewing them for the Canadian company. He took a Discman portable CD player with him, and played Bartok and Débussy, and read the copy of *The Outsider* that Kowalski had lent him. He was thankful there was a nice breeze, and he'd managed to find a spot under a tree. At eleven-thirty, Cataldi's Cadillac pulled out of the underground garage. The sun was glaring, and the car's windows were so darkly tinted that Harris couldn't determine whether Cataldi was being chauffeured by the goon, or was driving the car himself.

He followed the car to the Acme Building on Main Street. He had no idea where he was. Stark hadn't told him where the property management company was located, or even the name of the place. And then he noticed the brass plate with the name Courtland Property Management Inc. He watched as a woman who looked like a caricature of a tart came out of the building, clip-clopping on high heels, and got into the car. He followed the car as far as Gerrard Street and immediately lost it when it made a couple of quick right turns.

Chapter Thirty-Nine

Weems arrived at the Centre of Forensic Sciences on Grosvenor Street sharp at eleven a.m. The woman who met her in the lobby was in her late fifties. She had tightly permed, greying hair and wore a shapeless, below-knee-length, blue print dress. She wore no make-up. She was tired-looking, with a constant expression that seemed to be an apology for taking up space in the world. Her body slouched, and her arms hung at her sides, a white cloth purse dangling from one hand.

Weems asked her whether she had been waiting long, and the woman apologized for having arrived early.

"Oh, I just hope you didn't have to wait long."

"Oh, no. It was just hard for me to time it." She spoke every word separately, as if it were an effort to drag them out. "I had to take the bus and subway from Scarborough. We live in Scarborough. West Hill?"

"You should have said. We could have had a car bring you in."

"Yes, the policeman I spoke to said that. I didn't want to cause any trouble."

"It wouldn't have been any trouble."

"Oh, well."

"Yes. Well, perhaps we should—" Weems gestured toward an interior door.

"Yes, all right."

When she was shown the body, the woman said

nothing, made no reaction. Weems gave her a questioning look and waited. Finally, she had to ask, "Is it—"

"Mmm? Oh, yes. Yes, that's Jim. I knew it was as soon as I saw the drawing. It was a very good likeness. I didn't know he'd had one done."

"One what done?"

"A drawing, a portrait of himself. It's not like him to do anything like that."

"No, no. One of our artists did the drawing."

"He did?"

"Yes."

"Well, he's very good. It was a very good likeness."

"I'll drive you home, Mrs. Byers."

"That won't be necessary. It's a long way."

"I have to go out that way, anyway. Perhaps you'll be able to answer a few questions along the way."

"I'll try."

Weems took Rosedale Valley Road to the Bayview Extension and then on to the Parkway.

"You're a very good driver," Byers said. "I'm glad you're driving and not me. We don't usually come this way. Lou and I think the Don Valley is a bit frightening. They go so fast."

"I'm used to it."

"I suppose you have to be, in your business."

"Mrs. Byers, did your brother know someone called Graeme Adams?"

"Graeme Adams?" She looked thoughtful. "I don't remember hearing the name. Is it important?"

"It might be, yes."

The woman put an index finger to her lips. Her head began to move slowly from side to side.

"No," she said, "I can't recall Jim ever mentioning the name Gray-ham." She pronounced it with two distinct syllables.

"Actually it's spelled—well, it doesn't matter."

"Oh? How *is* it spelled?"

Weems glanced at her. "It's, uh, G-r-a-e-m-e."

"Oh? That is a funny spelling, isn't it?"

Weems smiled.

"No," the woman said again, "I can't recall Jim ever mentioning the name Graym. Is that how you say it?"

"Gray-um. I have to ask you, Mrs. Byers. Forgive me, but you don't seem to be surprised that your brother was—"

"Dead?" She looked at her fingernails and sighed. "No, I'm not at all. I was expecting it."

"You were?"

"Well, he never took care of himself. He drank too much, you know."

Weems's head snapped around. She felt her stomach fall.

"Mrs. Byers, if I'm the one telling you this for the first time, I'm so sorry. God." She sighed. "Your brother didn't die of natural causes."

"What do you mean?"

"God, I'm sorry." She shook her head. "Your brother was killed. I'm afraid he was—murdered."

"My God." Byers's hands went to her cheeks. She turned and looked at Weems. "Oh, my God. Oh, that's awful. How—did he—who did it?"

Weems let her breath out in a whoosh.

"God. Detective-Sergeant Henry didn't tell you?"

"No—"

"But, you saw the picture in the paper. It must have

said—"

"It said a body had been found and the police wanted to know if anybody knew who it was, that's all. Lou cut the picture out and gave it to me. He recognized Jim, too. Anyway, it wasn't your fault. They should have said."

"Yes. I suppose they should."

They drove in silence for a time, and then Weems asked, "Do you feel up to answering some more questions, Mrs. Byers?"

"Oh, yes, sure, sure."

"Okay. Where did your brother work?"

"Jim, you mean?" Weems looked at her. The woman seemed slightly dazed. "I have another brother, Jack, but, of course, you wouldn't be asking about him, would you? No. Jack works at Canadian Tire, but Jim didn't work. Oh, he used to. He worked for forty-two years for the post office, you know, but he stopped working. He retired a couple of years ago."

"From the post office?"

"Yes, he was a clerk. You know, at the wicket? Very likeable man. Everybody liked him. He was very friendly. And a good worker. But he did drink too much. I was sure that's what must have—killed him. Who did it?"

"We don't know yet, Mrs. Byers. That's what we're trying to find out."

"Does this Graym person have something to do with it?"

"We don't know that."

"I see. Well, Jim didn't have many friends, even though he was so friendly. Not real friends, you know. Not that I'd call friends. He knew people—he used to go to a beverage room. There were people he knew there.

He'd talk about them sometimes when he'd come over for dinner. We didn't see him very often. Lou and him didn't get along so good. Lou doesn't drink. Not that we're religious or anything. He—just doesn't drink." She sighed.

"You said a 'beverage room.' Do you mean a bar?"

"Yes. I guess they don't call them 'beverage rooms' any more, do they? I'm not up on these things. My father used to go to a beverage room. It was down by the old Woodbine racetrack, what then became Greenwood and then they tore it down?"

"I see. Do you know the name of the bar?"

"Where my father used to go? No, I don't remember, I'm sorry."

"The bar your brother went to."

"Oh. No, I don't think so. Lou might know. I'll ask him."

"It would be helpful if you could remember. I'm sorry. I should have asked you this before—but are you in a hurry to get home?"

"Oh no. I told Lou I didn't know how long I would be, so he's not expecting me."

"Well, I'm wondering whether we can go to your brother's place. I'd like to have a look around there, if you don't mind. I hope we're going in the right direction."

"Well, I don't know. I think we're pretty far north now. It's actually down by the lake, at Midland and Kingston Road. His apartment is down there."

"Oh, that won't be a problem. We're going the right way."

"It's nice they give you air-conditioning in these cars. This heat is terrible."

Chapter Forty

Harris called Stark and reluctantly told him he'd watched Cataldi's car pick up a woman at the Acme Building, but had lost them.

"Jesus."

"I'm sorry. They just—"

"Never mind. When was this, this morning?"

"Just about noon, a little after. He was probably taking her to lunch."

"Yeah right, lunch. You say this broad looked like a hooker?"

"Well. I mean, gaudy makeup and stilt heels."

"Yeah, I saw that woman come out of there myself. God, this Cataldi, he's doing everything in skirts. Jesus. Okay, listen. Go back to the apartment, and keep an eye out. I've got to think. This isn't getting us anywhere. I think we're going to have to tap a few phones."

Chapter Forty-One

On the way to Martha Byers's brother's apartment, Weems had learned that the woman had a key, so when they arrived, they didn't have to go through the hassle of looking for the superintendent. Weems was surprised that opening the apartment door released a rush of cool air. She had braced herself for a hot box. The streets were shimmering with the heat. In the short walk from the car, Weems had already begun to perspire, and the waddling Mrs. Byers seemed to be having trouble breathing. The relative coolness of the apartment was a relief. Mrs. Byers found it puzzling.

    "That's funny," she said. "Jim must have left his air-conditioner on."

Weems made a knowing sound.

Byers nodded.

"You think it's funny, too."

"No, I was just thinking about someone I know who has a thing against leaving air-conditioners on."

Byers said, "I suppose that when you're drinking, you forget things." She looked meaningfully at a half-empty bottle of Glenlivet on the counter that divided the kitchen area from the rest of the bachelor apartment. There were two glasses beside the bottle.

Weems cast her eyes around the apartment. Every surface, every edge, every protrusion that could support something seemed to have an object on it—glasses, empty bottles, crumpled potato-chip packages, scraps of paper. There was an open pizza box, containing all but two pieces of a small pepperoni and mushrooms, the shrivelled slices suggesting it might have been sitting there for days. Socks hung from lampshades. A pair of red bikini briefs was draped over the arm of an open sofa bed, the mattress of which was topped by an unzipped, crumpled sleeping bag, on which was balled a cotton sheet. Jackson must have slept on the sleeping bag and covered himself with the sheet. In winter, he probably inverted the layers, Weems thought. The impression of coolness was wearing off. The air-conditioner was cheap and underpowered, inadequate for the heat wave. A chromed clothing rack, the kind used in retail stores, stood in one corner. The pressed neatness of the jackets and trousers and shirts hanging there, some still in polyethylene dry-cleaning bags, seemed incongruous in the littered surroundings.

Byers saw Weems staring at the rack.

"Jim was always a natty dresser," she said. She went over and began ruffling through the clothes. "I'll have to find a suit to bury him in," she said.

Weems reached out a hand to stop her.

"Mrs. Byers, please don't touch anything. In fact, I'm beginning to think we shouldn't even be in here." She was looking at the two glasses beside a bottle of Scotch the high price of which didn't fit the surroundings.

"But I'll have to take some clothes for him."

"You'll have to come back later to do that. You see, some of our people will be coming here to examine things. It's part of the investigation."

"Oh, my goodness." She recoiled. "You didn't find

Jim's body here, did you?"

"No, we didn't. Your brother's body was found a few miles from here, in a park above the Bluffs."

"That *is* odd. What would he have been doing there? He doesn't have a car, you know."

"I see," Weems said. "So the bar he drank in is probably somewhere in the neighbourhood?"

"I believe it's somewhere on Kingston Road."

"Mmm. All right, well—I think we should leave now, and, you know, not touch anything."

"If you say so. Miss Weems, you haven't told me— can you tell me, unless it's not allowed, why was Jim killed? Was it a robbery? He has no money. There was a watch they gave him when he left the post office—"

"No, he was still wearing his watch. I'll see to it that all his personal effects are returned to you in due course. As to why he was killed, we don't know that yet. But it wasn't a robbery. That much I can tell you."

"How was he—"

Weems sighed. "I'm afraid he was strangled."

"Oh, my Lord."

Weems thought for a moment, decided it wouldn't hurt to tell the woman, and it might make it easier for her: "He didn't—feel anything. You see, he was already unconscious. He'd been drugged."

"Drugged?"

"Yes, he—"

"Jim didn't take drugs. I can tell you that for sure. For heaven's sake."

"We think someone slipped him the drug, put it in his drink."

"Who would want to kill poor Jim?"

"That's what we're trying to find out."

The woman stood there shaking her head

Weems's gaze ran around the apartment. It stopped on something. "What's that, beside the bed there?"

"Where?"

Weems pointed. The woman started to walk toward the spot.

"Don't move," Weems said sharply.

The woman looked puzzled. "All right," she said a little put out. "It's Jim's diary box. He was always writing things down. I think he got into the habit all those years in the post office. He's been keeping a diary for— as long as I can remember. See, there's a whole row of them on that shelf there, beside that picture. Oh my Lord, he's still got her picture up."

"Whose picture?"

"His girlfriend. *Ex*-girlfriend, actually. That woman. She had him on a string, I'll tell you. She bossed him around. They split up about three months ago."

"Split up? Did she live here?"

"Oh, no." The expression on Byers's face suggested the idea was preposterous. "She lives miles away, almost in Markham. And she made him take the bus to her place, even though she has a car. We only met her with him once, at Scarborough Town Centre. Snooty woman, hardly said two words to us."

Weems went to the low bookshelf, bent down and looked at the framed photograph.

"My God," she said.

"What is it?" Byers asked.

Staring back at Weems, over a tight, mirthless smile, were the piercing eyes of the woman Weems was convinced was lying to keep her son from being charged with his wife's murder.

Byers looked back and forth between the picture and Weems.

"Do you know her? Jane Adams?"

Weems nodded.

"I do, yes. How long was your brother going out with her?"

"Oh—five years, I would say. At least. They met in the post office. She was a customer, I mean. That's what I understand. How do you know her?"

"At the moment, I'd rather not say." Weems took out her notebook and wrote a reference to the diary box.

"Listen, Mrs. Byers, I'm going to have to stay here for a while. I'll call for a car to take you home." She took out her cell phone.

"Don't be silly. I won't hear of it. I'll take the bus. It's just straight out Kingston Road."

"No—please, let me call you a car."

"No," Byers said adamantly, waddling quickly toward the door. "I'm going right now, so put that phone away. Just tell me when I can come back and get his clothes."

Weems shook her head. "I'll have to call you."

"That's fine. I hope you find whoever did this to Jim."

"Oh, we will. Don't you worry."

Chapter Forty-Two

"We've got some interesting stuff for you."

Ken Coulson had reached Stark on his cell phone.

"And what might that be, Kenneth?"

"Cataldi has a boat, at the RCYC—on the Island?"

"Yeah, I know where the Royal Canadian Yacht Club is, Ken."

"He took Stokes there, this morning."

"This morning?"

"Yep."

"What time was this?"

"Eleven-fifteen."

"Eleven-fifteen?"

"Yeah."

"That's impossible. You sure your guys didn't screw up on the time?"

"Harry."

"Eleven-fifteen? And they're sure it was Cataldi?"

"We're following Stokes, right?"

"Yeah."

"Well, my guy talked with your guy at that Chinese restaurant, right?"

"Yeah."

"Well, your guy identified Cataldi, all right? So, we knew who he was, and we knew when we saw him that he was the guy, all right?"

"All right, all right. There's something here that

doesn't make sense. You saw Stokes get on to Cataldi's yacht. What then?"

"Then nothing. They were on there for a couple of hours, and Stokes left. We're still on his tail. That's it. I just thought—"

"Good, good, good. Okay, Ken. That's good. Stokes and Cataldi. Good."

Chapter Forty-Three

Weems called the Identification Unit and explained the situation. Frank Furlong took the call. He asked her whether she had touched anything, and when she explained what she had done and the care she had taken, he responded with such a long, frustrated sigh, she thought it better not to ask him what the problem was. Furlong said they'd be there in an hour, told her not to touch another thing, put tape on the door and stay out of the apartment until he told her she could go back in. Weems then called Ted Henry, told him she thought Jackson might have been killed in the apartment, or perhaps drugged there, led out while he could still walk, driven to the park where the body was found, and killed there. She said she'd called Ident and had put tape over the door. Henry said they'd better canvass the neighbourhood, see whether anybody had seen anything. He'd send some uniforms over. "We've had quite a few calls on the picture in the papers," he said. "This Jackson used to work as a clerk in the post office, apparently."

"That's right."

"He was quite well liked. Even some of his old customers called to identify his picture."

Weems found the superintendent, a fat woman with thin, stringy hair and teeth missing. Her arms bulged out of a tent-like house dress that was covered with big sunflowers. She smelled of ammonia. She said her name was Cora Cripps.

"Jeeziz. It *was* Jim?"

"What was Jim?"

"The picture in the paper. I said, 'Jeeziz, that looks like Jim Jackson.' But Otto said, 'Naw, doesn't look a bit like him. Keep your nose out,' he said. Asshole. Anyways, I went up to Jim's apartment this morning, but then I heard the air-conditioner running, so I figured Otto was right. So, what happened? Some nut, or something? Did he get into a fight?"

"Why? Did he get into fights?"

"Who, Jim Jackson? Little skinny Jim? Never. Nice fellow, he was. Real nice fellow. Give you the shirt off his back, he would. Not that that would do me any good." She chortled and her body shook.

"Did you see anybody around here last night that you didn't recognize?"

"Last night I was asleep before eight o'clock. In this terrible heat, I don't go out, even at night. The air-conditioner's in the bedroom, so I get in there early, watch the *Wheel* and *Jeopardy.* And I usually drop off before Final Jeopardy. The hum of the air-conditioner usually lulls me off to sleep—like a baby."

Some baby, Weems thought.

"So obviously, you didn't see Jim Jackson leave with anybody? Maybe about eleven o'clock?"

"No, like I said, I was asleep. Sorry."

Cripps said she had never known Jackson to have visitors. Most nights he went out about eight o'clock and staggered back a few hours later. She did know the name of the bar he frequented, Ed's Grill, on Kingston Road, about halfway between Stop 13 and Stop 12, she said. These were bus stop designations.

The uniformed officers arrived, Weems filled them in, and they began their canvass. When Ident showed up, she brought them up to speed and gave them the objects she had packaged as evidence, apologizing for having moved them, but explaining again that she had been particularly careful in handling them. They weren't impressed. She told them she'd be back shortly, and went off to find Ed's Grill, which turned out to be a formica-and-chrome souvlaki joint, with a tiny bar you entered through swinging doors, like a western saloon. The bar was dark and cool, and occupied by three old men drinking draft beer, who looked at her suspiciously. The barmaid was a buxom woman in her mid-twenties in a low-cut peasant blouse.

The entertainment at Ed's Grill, Weems thought, disapprovingly.

The barmaid said, "My name's Sharon. What's yours?" in an irritatingly high-pitched nasal voice. She smiled inanely.

Weems showed her badge and introduced herself.

"Do you know a man called Jim Jackson?"

"I told you that was Jim in the paper," one of the trio at the bar said. "That's why he hasn't been in."

"My God. Jim got killed? What happened?" said another, a bald man in a green Hawaiian shirt.

"Sharon, you'd better give us another round," said the third, a tall, thin man with a lantern jaw, whose upper body curved over the bar like a question mark. "And give us three shooters of rye with 'em. I think we're going to need it."

"Three each?" Sharon asked.

"No, of course not. One each," the thin man said.

"So, what happened?" the first man asked. He was

short and wiry, and wore khaki shorts and a T-shirt that read, "I'm with Stupid."

"Somebody killed him," Weems said.

"We know that. It said that in the paper," the thin man said, draining the shot glass. "You'd better give me another, Sharon."

"So, did Mr. Jackson come in often?" Weems asked.

"Just about every night," Sharon offered.

"And sometimes in the afternoon, too," the wiry man put in.

"Did you see him last Thursday?"

"Is that when it happened?" the Hawaiian shirt asked.

Weems nodded.

The Hawaiian shirt turned to the others.

"Thursday night? Do you remember Thursday night? What happened last Thursday night? What date was that?"

"What difference does that make?" the thin one said. "You gotta consult your appointment book, or something?"

"July seventeen," Weems said.

"I'll tell you why I wanted to know the date, smarty. Because July seventeen was my ex-wife's birthday, so I wasn't here. My kids took us to a restaurant, the Mandarin, you know, the Chinese joint."

"You went out to dinner with your ex-wife?" the thin one said. "I think I'd better have another drink."

"You want to go easy on that stuff," the wiry one said. "You're still married."

"That's why I need the drink," the thin one said, and everybody laughed except Weems.

"So you weren't here last Thursday?" Weems asked.

"Nope. Sorry."

"I remember last Thursday," Sharon said.

"You do?" Weems said, doubtful.

"That's the day Gus's kid that works as a bus boy cut his finger on a broken glass behind the bar, and Jim was here, and he said he had his St. John's Ambulance and he'd look at it. He washed it out and stuff and I got the antiseptic and bandages from the kitchen and he fixed him up. He said he wouldn't need stitches. He did a real professional job. Such a nice man."

The thin one spoke up before Weems could get her words out, but he asked the question she was going to ask, anyway. "How do you know that was Thursday?"

"Because the kid, Peter, only works Thursday, Friday and Saturday, and it couldn't have been Friday, could it?"

"Why not?" the Hawaiian shirt asked.

"Because Jim was dead then, you dummy," the wiry one said.

"Oh, right."

"What time was that?" Weems said, hurrying to get her question in.

"Oh, that was in the afternoon."

"The afternoon?" Weems slumped.

"Yes, but," Sharon said, pausing and raising a finger to emphasize the importance of what she was about to say, "Jim came back later, about eight o'clock. He asked how Peter's finger was."

"I don't remember that," the skinny one said. "I guess I wasn't here."

"I know I wasn't here," the wiry one said. "Thursday's my bowling night."

"So, Mr. Jackson was here Thursday night. Now,

please think about this. Was there anyone with him at any time during the evening?"

"No. He was alone, but—"

"What time did he leave?"

"I was going to say—" Sharon frowned at Weems for interrupting her. "— that he got a phone call about nine o'clock. He came in at eight as usual, and about an hour later, he got a phone call."

"Jesus, not his girlfriend again?" the thin one said.

"What a bitch," the wiry one put in.

"You know Mr. Jackson's girlfriend?" Weems asked.

"*Ex*-girlfriend," Sharon corrected.

"I never met her," the Hawaiian shirt said, "but everybody knows she's a bitch, if you'll pardon my French."

Sharon said, "She used to call here for him, and I'd answer the phone and when she asked for him, I'd say his name loud, but as if I was just saying it to her, and I'd look at him, and he'd wave his hands to signal that I was supposed to say he wasn't here. Anyway, it wasn't her who called that night. It was a funny voice."

"A man or a woman?"

"It was like a fake voice, you know. Just said, 'Jim Jackson there?' real quick. After he hung up, Jim paid his bill and left," Sharon said.

"How did he seem? Was he nervous, agitated?"

"Nothing like that. He just said, 'Sorry, boys. Got to run.' Then he took off."

"That was about nine o'clock?"

"About then, yeah."

Weems nodded. "Thank you, Sharon. That was very helpful." Sharon beamed. "And thank you, gentlemen, for your time."

"You didn't tell us what happened," the Hawaiian shirt said.

Chapter Forty-Four

Harris followed Cataldi's Cadillac from the condo that evening to a bar on Steeles, west of Yonge. He saw the goon get out of the car, and watched him go into the bar without opening a door for Cataldi. The light from the entrance to the bar illuminated the inside of the Cadillac. No one else was inside. Harris groaned. He was ready to head back to Cataldi's condo when he saw the goon put his arms around a woman who was waiting for him in the bar, a woman on stilt heels who looked like a hooker.

Harris had a camera in his shoulder bag, a good camera, a Pentax. And he had lenses, including a long one, which he fitted to the camera body, and then he went inside the bar. The goon and his tiny date were dancing. Harris took a seat beside the dance floor and set the camera up on top of the wooden wall separating the seating area from the dancers. The light was bright on the dance floor. He got off a couple of good shots.

Chapter Forty-Five

When Weems got back to Jackson's apartment building, she discovered that one of the uniforms had had some luck. He got out of a scout car as Weems approached.

"Guy in apartment three-eleven saw Jackson leave. He thinks it was about eleven o'clock Thursday night."

"Alone?"

The cop shook his head.

"With a guy. He said Jackson was in bad shape."

"Bad shape?"

"Drunk. The guy was holding him up. He described him as 'white, skinny, tall.'"

"The guy?"

"Well, yeah. Not Jackson."

"Jackson was average height. Did the guy see them from his apartment?"

The cop nodded.

"So, from that angle, and the guy's short—people relate height to their own height—I'm going to guess five-ten to six feet. I take it the guy didn't recognize the person with Jackson?"

The cop shook his head.

"Nope. He said he was wearing a black baseball cap and dark clothing. He didn't see what it said on the baseball cap, and he couldn't be more specific about the clothes. He said they went to the curb and got into a car that was parked there. He doesn't know what kind of car it was, no tag number. It was a 'Canadian car,' he said."

"What the hell are those?"

"American car."

"Did they sit there for a while, or—"

"Drove right off. That way—west."

"Going the wrong direction, but it'd be easier to go around the block, I guess," she said to herself. "Well— that's great. Good work, Officer. Thanks."

Chapter Forty-Six

"Listen to this."

Ken Coulson sat with Stark in Ted Henry's office. The detective-sergeant had called them in for a report. Stark was vague and evasive. Coulson was voluble. He gave Henry chapter and verse. Stark hmmed and nodded. Henry glared at Stark.

"This is Stokes. We got the go-ahead to bug him. I'll just play you the important part. It's a woman. Here."

He switched on a tape-recorder. A female voice said: "Don't fuck around, Howard. You're running scared. You're collapsing. We've got to stick it out. Don't cave in."

"I'm not caving in. It's just—"

"It's just nothing. Get a backbone, for Christ's sake. We've got to meet at the farm. Be there, Howard. Be there."

"She hung up then," Coulson said. He switched off the recorder. Stark had him play the recording twice again.

"It's sort of muffled."

"What, the recording?"

"No, her voice."

"Sounds like she was calling from a cell phone. There's background noise, like she's outside somewhere."

"Anyway, I'll bet you anything, it's Stokes's wife,"

Stark said.

Coulson said, "Why would his wife be—"

"I told you, Ken, she and Cataldi are having it off. You know, I wouldn't even be surprised if Stokes didn't arrange the affair as a kind of part-payment to Cataldi. To keep him off his back, he put Cataldi on hers."

"You've got a sick mind, Stark," Henry said.

"I've come across a lot weirder arrangements. You know something, it wouldn't surprise me if this whole robbery scam wasn't her idea. You should meet this woman."

"What was that about the farm? Do they own a farm?"

Stark shrugged.

"Harry doesn't like women," Henry told Coulson.

Chapter Forty-Seven

Forensics found nothing they thought could help identify the other person who had been in the apartment with Jackson. They were certain he *had* had a visitor and thought it was likely the visitor had done Jackson in.

"The visitor didn't leave anything to identify him or her." The speaker was a man in a white lab coat. His name was Charlie Blain. "He or she didn't smoke. There were plenty of butts, but they're all the same brand, all smoked down almost to the filter and all crushed out in the same way, so that points to them all belonging to Jackson."

"No fingerprints?"

"Millions, all Jackson's. Whoever was with him was wearing gloves."

"In this weather? That'd be sort of hard to explain to somebody you're having a drink with. Maybe his visitor was just careful not to touch anything."

"But he did touch something."

"What's that? How do you know?"

Blain reached a finger under his glasses to rub his eye.

"Because Jackson's prints were on both glasses, so they weren't wiped clean. But on one glass, the prints were all smudged, as if the glass had been handled by somebody after Jackson had held it. Now, unless *you* used the glass to have a drink of Diet Coke—" Blain gave Weems a wry look.

She sneered at him.

"Yeah, well then the person *must* have been wearing gloves."

Weems looked thoughtful.

"Rubber gloves. What if he was wearing rubber gloves? You know, surgical gloves, like we have? They fit snugly, somebody with you might not notice you were wearing them—especially if they had been drinking."

"Could have been."

"Like gloves you could get from a hospital supply house," she said, half to herself. "Anything else?"

"Sure, something I thought you'd ask me about right away."

"What's that?"

"There was enough residue in the booze bottle to test. Pentobarbital."

"Is that right?" Weems said, nodding with satisfaction.

"Yep."

"Well, that's what I thought. It's almost a carbon copy of the Sheltoe killing."

"What's the Sheltoe killing?"

"Happened a couple of years ago. They used the same drug, strangled the victim with a belt. Say, would you have—"

"We sure would. What'd you say the name was?"

"Karen Sheltoe. She was killed in the same area, just a couple of miles away."

"Let's go have a look. You know, of course, that all this, all the relevant stuff, will be duplicated in the squad's file."

She gave him a girlish, do-you-mind look.

"I do, but it'll save me so much time—"

"Yeah, no, don't worry about it. It's no trouble. I'm just telling you."

Blain led Weems into the records room. He slid open the appropriate file drawer and, after a moment's search, drew out a huge folder, carried it to a table and opened it.

"Let's see. Here we are. The Sheltoe belt buckle measured 4.3 centimetres wide by 3.8 centimetres long. Sorry, the Jackson buckle was by 3.8 by 3.3. Not the same buckle. Also, you can see the shape of the bruising on Sheltoe's neck was fairly square. The one on Jackson was wider at one end than the other. Not the same animal, I'm afraid. But what does that mean? People have more than one belt in their cupboard."

"Yes, of course. It's just—if it had been exactly the same—"

"It would strengthen the connection, sure. If you're going to strangle somebody to death, why give him a Mickey Finn first? I suppose because it would make it easier, eh? No struggling."

"Sure, and maybe you're not strong enough to pull it off with physical force alone, or maybe there are psychological reasons."

"Psychological?"

"If you're not going to enjoy the killing, if you're not, you know, a naturally violent person, then if the victim's already unconscious, it becomes more— clinical. There's no writhing and gagging and all that."

"Well, we haven't got the tox screen results yet, but the killer must be somebody who has access to drugs, who knows about drugs, so why not just give the guy enough dope to kill him?"

"Well, in the first killing, the perpetrator wanted it to look as if the victim had been murdered by a rapist. So, in a way, they added the strangling to put us off the scent. But you see, the killer had to be smart enough to know that if the victim wasn't asphyxiated, the autopsy would show that. This time, it could have been the same thing, or it may simply have been that because he's not a trained person, that in the end he wasn't sure how much stuff to give to do the job, or how long it would take. The belt is fast and efficient."

"I see. Makes sense. You know what?"

"What?"

"I think you should be looking for a belt."

Chapter Forty-Eight

A large, weathered sign at the entrance to the farmland declared that an application had been made to change the zoning to permit the construction of single-family dwellings. The York Regional scout car at the roadside told Stark he had the found the place. A York uniformed cop signalled him to stop as he pulled through the open gate. He flashed his badge and the cop waved him on. Along the driveway, he passed the foundation of what had been a farmhouse. The old barn still stood, its big doors hanging open crazily. The light that shone through the many gaps in the barn walls was not from the sun. The sky was overcast. It was a welcome few degrees cooler. The light from the barn was produced by the floodlights of the regional force's Identification Unit. Noel Harris's yellow Volvo was beside the barn, incongruous in a row of shiny white scout cars. A knot of people in casual, summer afternoon clothes, stood talking outside the barn entrance, like a group of friends at a barbecue, York detectives, city Homicide cops, including Ted Henry. The short figure of Ken Coulson leaned against a tree, his expression blank.

Off to the right, a group of Ident officers in coveralls that made them look like technicians in a nuclear power plant were swarming over a black Chevrolet. Its driver's door was open and a body hung out of the car, torso on the ground, legs inside the vehicle.

Stark got out of his car. Henry saw him and came over.

"Where's Noel?" Stark asked.

"In the barn," Henry said, tilting his head in that direction.

Stark started striding quickly toward the building, Henry jogging a couple of steps to catch up with him.

"So, what happened?" Stark said.

"Guy from the next farm found him. He heard shots. He heard a car leave, but didn't see it."

The interior of the barn was lit like an operating room. More men in coveralls were scurrying around. A body lay beside a blue Cadillac behind a grey van. Harris, wearing a soiled T-shirt, was standing beside the body. He came over when he saw Stark.

"This is a hell of a mess," he said.

"How's your head?" Stark asked.

"Just a little sore. I was only out for a few seconds—right out. Then it took me about a minute to get back in focus, and by that time, Bonnie and Clyde had left."

"After this, get to the hospital, get checked out," Henry said.

"So, fill us in." Stark gestured toward the body.

"Last night, I followed the Neanderthal to a club, where he met his girlfriend. I thought I was following Cataldi. When I saw it was just the big guy, I was going to leave, and then when I saw he was with the same woman who came out of the property-management office, I stuck around. I figured it was a lost night as far as Cataldi was concerned, anyway. Then I followed them back to her place, an apartment on Davisville. It was four in the morning by the time I got there, so I slept in the car, and this morning, I followed them here.

"I couldn't drive in after them, but there's a tractor track on the other side of the trees there, so I drove along that, until I got up parallel with the barn. About fifteen minutes later, Stokes arrived. Ten minutes after that, I heard shots. I pulled through a gap in the trees, ran to the barn, came through that side door there with my weapon levelled, saw the woman standing there staring at Stokes's body. I shouted 'police.' Actually, I think I got to 'poli—' when the sledgehammer slammed into the side of my head."

"Sledgehammer?" Henry said.

"Felt like that. I think the big guy just punched me."

"I hate to say this," Stark said, "but why didn't they shoot you, too?"

"I don't know. The only thing I can figure is that Beavis—"

"Who's Beavis?" Stark said.

"The policeman whose body is lying out there," Henry said angrily.

"Sorry," Stark said. "You were saying, Noel?"

"I figure Beavis must have parked on the road and then when he heard the shots, he drove in. If you drive on the gravel road that leads up here, it makes a hell of a racket. They must have heard him, thought there were a lot of us out there, and panicked. They drove straight through the barn doors, smashed them open. Beavis must have been on the radio, calling for backup from the York Regionals—"

"Which you should have done," Henry growled.

"Yeah, I know. Anyway, I guess they came out so fast, they caught him by surprise and as they drove by, they shot him."

"Through the window of the car," Henry said. "And

then they opened the car door, and—poor Beavis fell out."

"So, who owns this property?" Stark asked. "As if I didn't know."

"It's a numbered company," Henry said, "but you're right, Cataldi is the principal."

"So, let's pick him up," Stark said.

"On what charge?"

"What do you mean, on what charge? He—"

"Wait a minute—just cool it. We've got a bulletin out on the bodyguard and his girlfriend. We've gone to her apartment already. She's not there."

"You know who she is?" Stark said. "Who is she?"

"I don't know her name. I mean I haven't got the name with me. Do you remember the name, Harris?"

"No, I didn't—"

"Well anyway, we went to Cataldi's condo, where the goon lives. Nobody's there. We'll find them."

"Did you check his boat? Cataldi's got a boat—"

"Yeah, Coulson told us. The boat's there. We're watching it. In the meantime, we're going to go downtown, and everybody's going to be there, Stark, and you'll tell us everything, no pissing around. We've got a dead policeman. All bets are off. This is going to be a team effort from now on. Harris, you go see a doctor. You're lucky in two ways, you know. You didn't get killed and you didn't shoot anybody, otherwise the goddamned SIU'd be crawling all over us. What a hell of a mess. The press is going to be going nuts."

Stark shook his head.

"You know I don't deal with those jerks—"

Henry waved away Stark's protest.

"Peters wouldn't let you anywhere near them. So,

Stark, what do you think this is? What happened here? What the hell went down?"

Stark sighed. He took out a cigarette and lit it, blew a stream of smoke. He looked at the barn and then turned back and stared at Henry for a time. Finally, he said, "Well, Ted, let's take it from the start—I think it was like this: In the first place, the robbery. That was an inside job. We sort of figured that at the outset. I don't know whether the old man was in on it or not. My guess is he was, but maybe not. In any case, he went to the building on Eglinton for some purpose that had absolutely nothing to do with taking the jewels to the bank. Maybe Stokes sent him there or maybe he even drove him there. I don't know. In the vacant office, something happened that made the old man pull his gun and shoot whoever was there. Now, I imagine it was the goon. Personally, I can't see Cataldi's being anywhere near the place. Okay, Rabinovitch shoots the fellow, but the shot doesn't do much damage to the big guy, and he runs the poor old man through with some kind of weapon, as yet unidentified.

"Moving ahead…Coulson's boys got a tape of a phone call in which Stokes is talking to—well, Cataldi as far as I'm concerned. Okay, we can't prove that, but Stokes did arrange to meet the person, and we subsequently observed Cataldi and Stokes meeting at a restaurant. Anyway, it was obvious on the tape that Stokes was badly shaken up. The old man's being killed wasn't supposed to happen. It was all supposed to be neat and tidy: the jewels get stolen; Cataldi disposes of them and Stokes collects the insurance. He owed Cataldi money for something. And we know he was in big financial trouble, although we don't know exactly why, because the jewellery business seems to be sound. But it looks as if it has something to do with this property we're at now.

"We know Stokes and Cataldi were involved in some kind of deal on property near Stouffville, and this place certainly satisfies that description. Now, it was obvious on the tape that the proceeds from the sale of the stolen jewellery wouldn't be enough to satisfy Stokes's debt to Cataldi, because Stokes talked about not being able to get the insurance money for some time and it was apparent that he was expected to give—the person he was talking to at least, some of that money. Now, we heard him on another tape being told about a meeting at a farm. This is–used to be–a farm. I think that when he got here, expecting to meet Cataldi, he found himself facing the big fellow—"

"Wait a second," Henry said. "I listened to that second tape with you and Coulson. It was a woman. *She* arranged to meet Stokes, right? And at the time, you said you thought it was Stokes's wife. Which, incidentally, I thought afterward was a bit strange. I thought, why would somebody's wife have to make an arrangement to meet her husband like that?"

Stark gave Henry a wry look.

"Okay, I guess it *wasn't* the wife. It must have been the goon's girlfriend. Anyway, we know that Stokes and Cataldi were in the sack together. The girlfriend was probably just making sure Stokes was going to show up. I hardly think Cataldi would trust musclebound and his bimbo to be involved in discussions with Stokes, and Stokes would know this and would be expecting Cataldi to be here. He might well have expected the other two to be here as well, but I'm sure he came here with the idea he was going to talk to Cataldi."

"All this, of course, assumes that Cataldi is involved with Stokes in anything more than the land deal," Henry said.

"Jesus, Ted, Cataldi owns the building where the jewel robbery and the killing went down. Big coincidence, don't you think? Look, I think Cataldi realized that Stokes was going to crack, and he decided to cut his losses. As far as Cataldi knows, the only person who can put him together with Stokes is Stokes himself. I figure the goon was supposed to do away with Stokes and shove him and the Cadillac into a scrapyard crusher. We were then supposed to think that Stokes staged the robbery himself for the insurance, got cold feet and fled the country. When the goon heard Beavis's car, he panicked and took off, killing poor Beavis on the way." Stark folded his arms. "And that, Ted, is what I think happened here."

Chapter Forty-Nine

Jim Jackson's diaries provided the clincher.

Perhaps, as Martha Byers had said, it was her brother's years in the post office that had conditioned him to write things down, keeping meticulous records of every event, every meeting in tiny, but perfectly legible, handwriting. Perhaps it was the experience of having his recollections dismissed as the faulty products of a memory confused by a booze-addled brain. Perhaps it merely added depth and significance to an otherwise empty and pointless existence. Whatever the reason, Jim Jackson had recorded in the monthly Day-Timer books every minute detail in the landscape of his banal life, from incidents of some relative importance to the most inconsequential of occurrences. There were only six books for the current year. Perhaps he had the book for July on his person, and Graeme Adams removed it, Weems thought. There were notations of trivia—"Hopalong Cassidy's horse was Topper. Coca-Cola is spelled with a hyphen. Mt. Everest tallest, 29,030 ft., 8,850 m.; K2 second, 28,250 ft., 8,610 m. Highest mountain in the Americas is Aconcagua in Argentina, 22,830 ft., 6,960 m." There were entries of word definitions and expressions he had encountered. "To beg the question often used incorrectly. It means 'To assume the truth of the very point raised in a question.'"

The diaries' importance to Weems lay in their

complete record of appointments, the tersely rendered commentaries on the happenings of daily life and the occasional notations of Jackson's thoughts and observations. In the book that recorded the events of the month of July, two years earlier, on the day that Karen Sheltoe had been killed, Thursday, July 20, at 6 p.m., it was noted: "Dinner at Jane's." Under the column headed "Diary and Work Record," Jackson had written. "President's Choice lasagna and Caesar salad AGAIN. We argued, but still M.L. She wouldn't let me stay. Left at 9 p.m. Took bus home. Got back at 9:45. Watched TV and a video of *Amadeus*. I thought it was terrific. I wanted to watch it at Jane's, but she said she wouldn't watch it because it would be boring. She said she was going to bed, but she kept looking at her watch as if she was expecting somebody. She almost pushed me out the door and didn't kiss me goodbye. Most of the time, I don't understand her. Saw fellow on the bus with a ring in his eyebrow. What possible reason could he have for that?—"

"Gotcha," Weems said aloud. M.L.? she thought. M.L. What the hell does M.L. mean? Somebody's initials. They argued about M.L. No, it doesn't say "about" M.L., it says "argued but still M.L." She pondered for a time, and it came to her: of course, of course. That must be it. M.L., "made love." They made love. Jesus. Jackson was obsessed with detail, he *had* to make mention of it, but so decorously he wrote it in initials.

In an entry a few days later, Jackson had written, "Jane told police Graeme was with her the night his wife was murdered. That's not true."

"Of course it isn't. Thank you, Jim." Weems

gloated.

She looked through the books at random. In the one for April of the current year, on the page for April 15, Jackson had written, "I am very sad today. I don't know what I'm going to do. Jane has broken off our relationship. I had a couple of drinks before I went to her place. I shouldn't have. She said she never wanted to see me again. She slammed the door in my face. When she says a thing, she means it. She is a very hard person. I know she has been using me these last few years. I can't say I love her, but I don't know what I'll do without her."

A week later, he had written, "Went downtown, bought the chocolates Jane likes from the shop in Hazelton Lanes. Took the bus to her place. She wouldn't let me in."

Chapter Fifty

Stark stood in front of the assembled detectives and delivered his report. He didn't notice Inspector Wallace Peters wince at the mention of Salvatore Cataldi. When Stark had finished, Peters took his place. He gave a pump-up-the-troops speech that sounded more like it was being made by an evangelical minister than a Homicide inspector, reminding Stark that Peters was a lay preacher in some fundamentalist church. At the end of the inspirational part, Peters paused, gazed around the room, lowered his voice and wagged a raised finger in a gesture of caution.

"Now Detective Stark has a theory that Mr. Cataldi is involved in this crime. For the moment—" He paused again. "—we will be very circumspect with Mr. Cataldi. We will *not* approach him. We will search for evidence first. Naturally, if we do discover *hard* evidence to link him with these crimes, then we will, of course, move against him, but not until then. Mr. Cataldi is—a very respected member of the community. Now, mark my words, he is *not* to know, or even to suspect in the *slightest* that *he* is being investigated. For the moment, we are investigating a robbery-homicide and also investigating the murder of a police officer, in which we are pursuing a man who works as Mr. Cataldi's bodyguard. The evidence we do have points to a conspiracy between the bodyguard and his girlfriend and

Stokes—"

"'Among,' you illiterate prick," Stark muttered under his breath.

"Do you all understand that? Okay. Let's get these scumbags—and fast. Stark, I want to see you in my office."

Stark sighed and followed Peters into the office.

"Close the door," Peters said. "Now, listen. I'm going to repeat the same thing I told them out there. Tread lightly with Salvatore Cataldi. You've got him on the brain ever since you tried to pin that murder on him two years ago. I know the man. I've been on committees with him. In my dealings with him, he has always been above board."

Stark raised his hands in disbelief.

"Inspector, come on. I gave my report about the connection between Cataldi and Stokes, about their meeting, about the taped phone call—"

Peters lifted a hand.

"I'm not saying they weren't connected. I'm simply saying we don't have any evidence to link Mr. Cataldi to the crimes. So don't go in roughshod. Of course they were connected. Apparently, they knew each other from Las Vegas, as you said. Gambling's not something I agree with, but in Las Vegas, it's hardly a crime. Now, go see Sergeant Henry and take his instructions—and follow them. And do not go anywhere near Mr. Cataldi, unless you come up with some real evidence. You got that?"

"I don't think there's any worry about that for the moment, sir. He seems to be missing."

****

"What did he say?" Henry asked Stark.

"Peters? Oh, he's had a change of heart. He wants me to arrest Cataldi and charge him with crimes against humanity. He suspects Cataldi led a death squad in Bosnia."

"Okay, okay, knock it off. What are you going to do now?"

"I'm going to go see Barbara Shaw."

"Who the hell's that?"

"Stokes's wife."

"She's been notified already. You want a policewoman to go with you?"

"I'm not going to break the bad news. Is Harris here yet?"

"Yeah. You going to take him?"

"I'm going to put him on her tail. I told you about her and Cataldi. What are you and the boys going to do, Ted?"

"Leg work, Stark, something you know nothing about. The nuts and bolts of good, solid police work. We've got the Hold-up people working with us on this, too. We're doing absolutely complete and thorough forensics. We're putting the fear of God into every fence we know. York Regionals are checking convenience stores, gas stations and so on in the area, checking traffic reports. We'll see if anybody got stopped for speeding or something about the time of the shootings, see which way they were heading."

"Ted, there's something I wanted to ask you."

"What's that?"

"How's Weems doing on the Karen Sheltoe thing?"

"She's very good. You didn't tell me she and you are an item."

"We're friends."

"Oh, I see. Just friends."

"So, she's doing okay?"

"Very good."

"If we get the budget, I'm going to go after her for the squad."

Stark's head jerked. "Oh—I'm not sure that would be a good idea."

"Why the hell not?"

Chapter Fifty-One

There was no answer to Weems's call on the intercom at Jane Adams's apartment. Weems drove to Scarborough North Hospital. The nursing supervisor said Adams worked in the Intensive Care Unit. The supervisor tried to get Weems to say what she wanted to talk to Adams about, but Weems would tell her only that it was a purely routine matter and nothing for her or the hospital to be concerned about. The nursing supervisor called Adams in the ICU and told her Weems wanted to meet her in the lobby.

Weems waited in front of the gift shop. She smiled at a stuffed giraffe in the display window, wondered whether she had time to buy it for her niece, wished she had a child of her own to buy it for. Sighed. She shifted her weight from one foot to the other. Her feet swelled in the hot weather and her shoes were killing her. She watched the candy-stripers go past in their runners and the nurses in their sensible flat soles. That's what she needed: sensible shoes. But she'd look klutzy, she thought. Adams came striding out of the elevator, eyes blazing. She looked, somehow, absurd, in her white uniform, the long slacks making her appear to be all legs.

"How dare you," she said in a loud whisper through clenched teeth. She took Weems by the elbow and led her through the automatic doors into the stifling outside air, and down the walkway halfway to the sidewalk before she stopped. The nursing supervisor, getting a coffee at a stand in the lobby, watched intently. Adams turned to face Weems. "What the hell do you want?" she spit out.

Weems gave her a look that was half amazement, half disgust. She took a deep breath. The sun was behind Adams, making Weems squint.

"You know, I could arrest you right now for obstruction of justice."

"What are you talking about?"

"You lied. Your son wasn't with you on the night his wife was killed. You spent the night with your boyfriend."

"I don't have a boyfriend."

"You did then. Jim Jackson."

"That drunk."

"Do you read the papers?"

"What's that supposed to mean?"

"Do you?"

"Sometimes."

"You didn't see Jim Jackson's picture in the paper yesterday?"

"I didn't read the paper yesterday."

"Jim Jackson is dead."

"What?" It was more a tone suggesting the idea was ridiculous than an exclamation of surprise. There was no shock or sorrow.

"He's dead," Weems said. "He was murdered, in almost exactly the same way your daughter-in-law was killed."

Adams appeared confused. She made some stuttering sounds, then said slowly, "Jim was murdered?"

Weems nodded.

"His body was found in a park near the Bluffs. He'd been drugged with the same barbiturate found in Karen Sheltoe's system and strangled—with a belt, the same way Sheltoe was killed."

"My God." Adams appeared shaken. Her body sagged. She folded her arms across her body as if she had a sudden pain in her gut.

"He threatened you, didn't he?" Weems said.

"What?"

"He wanted you to take him back. He threatened to tell the police that your son wasn't with you on the night Karen Sheltoe was killed, because *he* was with you that night."

Adams regained her composure quickly. She returned to form.

"That's ridiculous. How would you possibly—that's absurd."

"His diaries. We have his diaries."

"Diaries? He was a drunk. He couldn't remember one day from the next. His diaries," she said with dismissive disgust. "I don't know for the life of me why I put up with him for so long. A bloody—postal clerk. Don't you see that anything he might have written about me in his diary would be to get back at me—for throwing him over. He came to my place rolling drunk one too many times. I told him to get the hell out. I haven't seen him since. Sure he called. Tried to get back with me. I hung up on him. He's had plenty of time to doctor those bloody diaries of his to make it look like he wrote them back when it happened. It's just—crap."

Weems shook her head.

"That won't wash. Those diaries will stand up in

court, believe me." She pointed a finger at Adams. "Now, I'm giving you one chance to change your story. You have my card. Call me. You have until tomorrow. If I don't hear from you, I'm going to arrest you and I'm going to charge you with obstruction. You'll be taken away in handcuffs in the back of a scout car in front of all your neighbours or colleagues or whoever you happen to be with at the time. I'm warning you. Call me."

Chapter Fifty-Two

During the week after Stokes was killed, Weems didn't see Stark. She spoke to him on the phone a couple of times, and he asked her how the case was going, but she wouldn't speak about it. The conversations were strained.

With the information she had from the diaries, and after her interview of Jane Adams, Weems called Henry and told him what she'd found and he agreed she had enough to get a search warrant for Graeme Adams's place.

Adams wasn't home. Phillips stood in the doorway, pushed her face close to Weems and burbled about harassment and persecution. Weems finally pushed past her, followed by four uniformed officers. A belt with a buckle that fit the measurements of the one that killed Jim Jackson, a wide black leather one, was hanging in plain sight in Adams's closet.

Adams's massive armoire stood in one corner of the bedroom. It was partitioned, sections for shirts, neatly folded socks, underwear. Some of the sections were empty, as if all the shirts in one section had been removed in one go, all the socks from another section, all the underwear from another.

She found the pentobarbital, three vials of it, behind a box containing a heating pad in a cupboard under the sink in the bathroom off the master bedroom. Weems put the vials into an evidence bag. She studied the shelves above the sink, the medicine cabinet. Something struck her. Phillips had followed her through the house. She stood behind Weems with her arms folded. Weems turned to her.

"Which bathroom does your husband use?"

"This one, of course."

"Then where's his razor? There's only one toothbrush, one deodorant—a woman's deodorant. There are things missing from that glass shelf. There are rings there where things were, shaving cream, or whatever. Where is he? Where's he gone?"

"I don't know what you're talking about. He went out, that's all. He just went to the store." Phillips sat on the bed, her arms folded, her posture so rigid, her expression so fixed that Weems figured she'd be wasting her time trying to shake her with threats. And then something struck Weems, and she ran out of the room, calling to the uniforms as she went down the stairs. Outside the house, she called Ted Henry on her cell phone and told him what she'd found. He said he'd alert the RCMP at Pearson Airport, the railroad cops at Union Station and dispatch a couple of cars to the bus station.

"Maybe you'd better contact the border crossings. He could be driving."

"I'll do that, too."

"Okay. I think I'll head out to the airport."

"All right. I'll keep you informed."

Weems got as far as Keele Street on the 401 when Henry called.

"They got him. He was getting on a flight to England. They're bringing him downtown."

Chapter Fifty-Three

Barbara Shaw seemed almost demure in an ankle-length, cotton dress with a sunflower design. The appearance of modesty was quickly defeated by the fact that the dress was form-fitting and she was wearing little beneath it. Hardly mourning attire, but this time she had a sorrowful expression when she met Stark at the door. There were no tears, but she spoke in a low voice and sighed frequently. She said her husband had been a good man, and asked Stark how anyone could have done this to him.

Stark said nothing. He had thought about confronting her from the outset about Cataldi, but in the end decided to say nothing. He suspected that she might not be as stupid as she looked, but it was still possible she might lead them to Cataldi.

"Do you mind if I look through the place?"

Shaw's sadness vanished.

"What for? The other cops already poked through everything this morning. They took all the papers from Howard's office. Little they cared about somebody's grief. A couple of them looked like they wanted to poke *me*."

"I'd just like to have a look around, if you don't mind."

"What if I do mind? Will that make any difference?"

Stark said nothing. Shaw wheeled and strode into

the front room. Stark went in a direction he assumed would take him to the bedrooms. He had little expectation of finding anything useful, a vague hope of finding some sign of Cataldi's presence. If Shaw had been more vociferous in her protests, he might have been hopeful of discovering Cataldi hiding in a closet. Just to be certain, he did look in the closets and under the beds, and then checked the basement, cracking his shin in the exercise room against a weightlifting bench. He cursed. As she had said, the filing cabinet in Stokes's office had been emptied.

Stark even looked in the garage and the garden shed before he left, not bothering to say goodbye.

****

Harris was parked around the bend. Stark pulled his car up beside the yellow Volvo, rolled down the passenger-side window and slid across the seat.

"It's number two-seventy-three, black roof with a green garage door. There's nowhere to park out of sight, so just stay here. She drives a red Miata. It's got a bumper sticker on it, 'Remember Bill C-68.'"

"The gun-control law. Jesus."

"Here's the licence number." He handed Harris a sheet of notepaper.

"You just want me to tail her."

"Yeah, well, I'm hoping she might go see Cataldi. I don't know. It's a long shot, but let's cover the bases. Keep in touch." He started to slide back to the driver's side and then thought of something. "How's your head?"

"Fine."

"Mmm." Stark nodded.

Chapter Fifty-Four

Weems had just got back to Homicide when she got a phone call from a sobbing woman who didn't identify herself.

"He didn't do it. I know he didn't do it. I can prove it."

Weems shook her head.

"Mrs. Phillips?"

"You're wrong about him. He's not like that. He couldn't—he didn't do it, any of it. You can't keep him in there—"

"Mrs. Phillips. I can't talk to you about this."

"He was going to see her."

"See who?"

"That—Barnes woman."

Weems hesitated. It took her a moment to identify who Phillips was referring to, the wife of the owner of the company Graeme Adams had worked for before he married Brenda Phillips, the woman with whom he was supposed to have had an affair. Was Phillips saying the affair was still going on?

"You knew about their relationship?"

"Of course I knew." The tearful voice had suddenly turned bitter. "That bitch."

"Look, Mrs. Phillips, I can't—"

****

"He's been such a fool. I knew what Graeme was

before I married him. I put up with it because I saw it as a failing—almost as an illness. Quite honestly, I thought that once he had a decent, solid marriage and not some silly, spur-of-the-moment kid thing, he would settle down, that he wouldn't have to pursue every female that came within groping distance. I thought it was something he had inherited from his mother, a sort of desperation to be accepted. Anyway, he did settle down somewhat. I saw to that with some judicious threats. I warned him early on that if there was any more fondling, he was out. He stopped that, but that bloody woman pursued him. Of course, she's besotted with him. He's—he's incredibly charming, you know."

"I'm sorry, are you saying that the affair with Cathy Barnes continued after you were married?"

"It didn't continue. It resumed—more than a year after our marriage, several months ago. In fact, I know exactly when they got back together. It's not important how I know, but I do."

"You said on the phone that your husband was going to see Cathy Barnes," Weems said. "But he had a ticket to England—Manchester."

"That's right. That's where she is—in England. She left three days ago. She went there ostensibly to stay with her mother who is supposed to be ill. The truth is she went to avoid Graeme. She's terrified of destroying her marriage."

"I'm sorry. You've lost me."

"You know, when I suspected they had started up again, I hired a private detective. He did a complete background check. Her parents were reasonably well off. The father's dead. He was a solicitor. They lived in the north of England. Her mother still lives there. Poor silly

Graeme." She sighed. "Now, may I explain why Graeme couldn't have done the killings?"

Weems shrugged.

"Graeme has the same alibi for both the killings. I hate that word. It sounds tawdry. It sounds fake. But, unfortunately, it isn't in this instance. I'm glad he has the alibi, but, God, I wish it wasn't her. He was with *her.*"

"Cathy Barnes."

"Exactly."

"You're saying your husband was with Cathy Barnes when both murders took place and not with his mother?"

"Yes. I imagine his mother didn't know where he was, and perhaps she thought he might have been the killer."

"How can you be sure he was with Barnes?"

"Because both killings took place on a Tuesday night. Tuesdays are when Harold Barnes has his regular monthly lodge meeting. And both murders occurred on the night of the Masons' meeting. Harold Barnes is a Mason. So was Graeme. Graeme was *sponsored* by Harold Barnes. He joined to please the old man. In fact, Graeme insists he's still a Mason. Has to go to meetings every month. But Graeme stopped going to the Masonic meetings a long time ago—because he was meeting her instead."

"And how do you know this?"

The woman was breathing heavily. Finally, she said, "I told you. I hired a private detective."

"And he observed them together, did he?"

"He did. Twice. Both times she went to the Scarborough Town Centre, parked her car and went inside. By the time he got in there, she had disappeared.

He watched her car, and she didn't come back to it until ten o'clock. Obviously, she didn't want her car spotted at the hotel, so she left it there and took a taxi. Graeme arrived home at eleven-fifteen. That was proof enough for me. Anyway, she was seen at the hotel."

"I'm sorry, you just said the detective didn't see her until she got back to her car?"

"No, but *I* did. After the detective followed her to the shopping centre, the next month, the next Tuesday meeting night, I went to the hotel, the Holiday Inn. I knew Graeme had gone there before. I sat in the lobby. I saw her come in the back door. She was wearing sunglasses, dark glasses, can you imagine anything more of a cliché. She went straight to the elevators."

"And you're saying that you believe Graeme was with her on the night both murders occurred?"

Phillips nodded slowly. "Yes," she said resignedly.

"But why would his mother insist he was with her? Why didn't she think he was at a Masons meeting?"

"Because that's the way she would handle it. She would march in and take charge. She probably thought Graeme *had* done it, that he hadn't been at the Masons. So without asking anyone, without any real thought, she'd just say, 'Graeme was with me.' "

After a paus, Weems said, "Listen, Mrs. Phillips, I'm sorry, but none of this is evidence. I suggest you give this information to Graeme's defence counsel. Perhaps Cathy Barnes will testify—"

"She won't," Phillips said, with some desperation.

"Well, it's not my job to collect evidence for the defence—"

"It's your job to find the truth, isn't it?" Phillips said indignantly. "Or are you saying you're not interested in the truth? All you want is a conviction? You don't care whether the person did it, or not?" Her voice had become shrill.

"It's not that at all. Look, if the Barnes woman will testify that Graeme was with her, then—"

"But I told you she won't," Phillips shouted. She lowered her voice. "She won't. That's just it. That's why she went to England in the first place. If she says she was with Graeme, that she's been having a long affair with him, then her marriage is over. That means everything is over for her. Let me tell you about her. It's more than just the marriage she's terrified of losing. You see, Cathy Barnes was never good at anything she did. Her father wanted her to be a lawyer, but academically, she was incapable. She failed in everything except her marriage and her nice little bookkeeping job and her perfectly managed home. They live in a beautiful house in Pickering, down by the lake, and she entertains and goes to his Masonic events, and everything is the way she wants it. And then she gets her little bit of the other on those Tuesdays with Graeme. And other times as well, I don't doubt."

Weems wondered why Phillips had put up with the affair, and then thought she knew the answer to that, but didn't pursue the theory with a question. She said, "Mrs. Phillips, if the woman won't testify, perhaps there's some other evidence—"

"*She's* the evidence. She can clear my husband. But if I send a private detective after her, she'll simply deny everything. She's already laid the groundwork."

"How do you mean?"

"After my husband left Medi-Source and married me, she told Barnes that Graeme had pursued her, harassed her, made suggestive remarks, was obsessed with her. Barnes phoned our house and had a real set-to with Graeme. I listened on the extension. By her saying what she did, she's allayed her husband's suspicions in the event that Graeme says they were together. She would deny it, and say it was another example of his obsession with her, don't you see?"

"Well, Mrs. Phillips, I don't—"

"Look, if you were to find her, confront her, take a statement from her, but promise that it will never be revealed—because it wouldn't have to be revealed, would it? I mean, if you were convinced he was with her—then she will probably tell you the truth. She would believe you because you're a police officer. And if you knew you had the wrong man, you would release Graeme."

Weems shook her head. "Mrs. Phillips—I can't go to England to question a potential defence witness. It's not—"

"I'd pay."

"That's impossible."

"No, it's not. If they won't let you go, tell them you're going on your own, on a holiday, and I'll pay, and no one will know. The fact that I'm paying your expenses won't compromise you in any way, because I can't buy Cathy Barnes' statement. I can't bribe her to say something she doesn't want to say. Please. I'm begging you."

Weems sighed. After a time, she said, "Look, there's no way I'd let you pay. That's out of the question. Impossible. Let me think about it."

"Oh, thank you, thank you."

"No-no. I said, 'I'll *think* about it.' I'll let you know

tomorrow."

Chapter Fifty-Five

The heat was back. When the temperature dropped and the clouds came in, they'd said the back of the thing had been broken, but they'd been wrong, and people had started blaming the weather announcers for the onslaught. One weatherman had been attacked by a prominent lawyer in a Bay Street bar. The lawyer had broken the weatherman's nose. Bus drivers and streetcar operators had been assaulted because their vehicles weren't air-conditioned. Incidents of road rage were epidemic. There wasn't a fan or a room air-conditioner to be had in the city, and installers of central systems were working sixteen-hour days. There were brown-outs nightly from the over-taxing of the power system; the politicians were being blamed for that and were keeping a low profile. Stark had taken to leaving both his air-conditioners on day and night, full blast.

****

There was just one person at Courtland Property Management Inc., the little timid bookkeeper. Her head jerked up when Stark came through the door, bringing with him the stinking breath of the heat dragon. She said something in a tiny, squeaky voice, frightened by his arrival. He wasn't doing anything to ease her nervousness holding his arms out, scarecrow-like, and shaking them as if he were shedding raindrops. It was the heat he was attempting to shake off, while trying to replace it with the air-conditioned atmosphere.

"I'm sorry, what did you say?" Stark said.

She spoke again, no louder.

"I can't hear you. Just a minute." Stark opened the gate in the railing that separated the waiting area from the working area. He went and stood beside the woman's desk. "All right. Now, what did you say?"

"I said, 'Can I help you?'"

Stark smiled, shook his head. "Can you help me? I don't know. We'll see. Do you recognize me?"

She nodded rapidly.

"You're the detective."

He showed her his I.D.

"Stark, Detective Stark. You're alone."

She visibly tensed at the observation.

"I said you're alone. Is that right? Did you want to look more carefully at my identification?"

"No," she said, like a sparrow's chirp. Finally, she looked around the room and nodded.

"You're nodding. What's that mean?"

"I'm alone."

"Okay. Where's whatsisname? Your boss?"

"Mr. Rogers is on vacation."

"When did that happen?" Stark said, interested.

"He's been gone for almost a week. He won't be back for another week."

"What about the secretary, what's her name?"

"Doreen? She's not here."

"I guess you're a bit shaken up with all these policemen coming in today? What's your name?"

"Sheila. What policemen?"

"There haven't been any other officers here?"

She shook her head.

"Jesus. Well, there will be. Can I use your phone?"

She nodded.

Stark took his notebook out and looked up Ken Coulson's cell phone number. The call was answered by Coulson's voice-mail. Stark left a message asking Coulson to have his people search Courtland, looking for anything with Cataldi's or Stokes's name attached. He hung up and smiled at the woman.

She had a quizzical expression.

"Mr. Cataldi owns us," she said, the implication being that his name would appear on many documents.

"I know he does, Sheila. Have you seen him recently?"

She shook her head, and then with obvious reluctance said, "Is this about Doreen?"

"What about Doreen, Sheila?"

She hesitated, then said, "She's been acting funny lately."

"How do you mean?"

"Well—she started acting different after she began going out with Tony."

"Tony?"

"Tony Cataldi."

"Cataldi?"

"He's related to Mr. Cataldi, not close, but like a second cousin or something. He works for Mr. Cataldi."

"He works for him?"

"He's his chauffeur."

"Big guy?"

Sheila nodded.

"And this Doreen and Tony, they're an item?"

"A what?"

"They go out together, they're girlfriend and

boyfriend?"

"For about six months."

"Jesus. What about this acting strange?"

"Doreen's a very private person. She doesn't talk much, hardly at all. Just good morning and goodbye and the rest is business."

"The two of you, you're alone here all day, and you never chat about anything?"

She shook her head.

"Never."

"Okay, go on."

"About how she was acting strange?"

Stark's smile betrayed exasperation.

"Yeah."

"Well, she—started looking different, I mean doing different things to herself whenever Tony picked her up. He used to come and pick her up."

"Used to?"

She hesitated.

"Well, it's just that, I don't know—something. She's—she hasn't been here, and she hasn't phoned. She's never missed a day before and she's never sick, and now you're here. I just have this—feeling."

"About Doreen?"

She nodded.

"You say she's been doing different things to herself. What do you mean?"

"Well, at first just make-up. She never wears make-up, normally, but then—whenever Tony was going to pick her up—she'd wait until Mr. Rogers left. He leaves early. He plays golf."

"Go on."

"Then, after a while, she began to let her hair hang

264

long down her back, and she'd, you know, back-comb it?"

Stark shook his head.

"And then she started bringing in a change of clothes, really weird clothes, I mean—tight clothes and, you know, short?"

"I get what you mean, yes. Anything else she did that was—strange?"

"She drinks."

"She started drinking?"

The woman shook her head.

"No, she always drank. Especially at lunch, but sometimes before work. You could smell it on her breath. She always kept away from Mr. Rogers, and she used that breath spray all the time, but I could tell."

"Okay. She drinks, anything else?"

"I think she started taking drugs."

"Drugs? What kind of drugs?"

"Cocaine."

"Cocaine? Why do you think that?"

"Because she started going to the ladies' room more often than normal, and sometimes I'd go in after her, and on the top of the toilet, the whatdoyoucallit—"

"The cistern?"

"On top of that, sometimes there'd be an empty baggie. And you could see her eyes. They'd get real glassy."

"Mmm. Tell me, Sheila, in the last week or so, has her behaviour become any different?"

"Yes. She—hasn't been here much, and when she has been, since Mr. Rogers has been away, she's been putting on the make-up and the clothes in the morning, and Tony has picked her up and she hasn't come back.

And another thing, you remember the day you came in here?"

Stark nodded.

"Well, that day she came into the office late. She'd said the day before that she had a dentist's appointment in the morning, but when she came in, she was all different, her hair was mussed up and she was all worked up, really nervous. In fact, when you came here, I was sure something had happened—with her, I mean. I didn't know what, but—well, I thought it might have been the drugs. And then after—well—she swears a lot."

"She swears?"

"Oh, yes. She has a terrible mouth on her. She never swore at me or anything, or Mr. Rogers, or really *at* anybody. But if a client called and complained about something, she'd be really polite to them—well, not always polite, but anyway, after she hung up, she'd call them all sorts of names. And then, that day that you were here and after you'd left, she was swearing to herself and calling you terrible names, and she went on like that for the longest time. In fact, when you called her back later, that was the first time I'd heard her actually swear on the phone. But after she hung up, oh, my gosh—"

"What about yesterday? Was she here yesterday?"

Sheila shook her head. "Not all day, and she never called."

"Okay. Well, listen, there'll be some policemen coming in here later. Don't worry, they won't bother you."

"What is it about? Is it the drugs?"

Stark shook his head.

"Look, here's my card. If she calls, or if you hear from Cataldi, or if you see them, or Tony, you call me right away. All right?"

The little woman studied his card and nodded.

Chapter Fifty-Six

The notation in Jim Jackson's diary that Adams was lying about being with his mother on the night of the Sheltoe murder wasn't enough to hold him. Less than an hour after his arrest, his lawyer had him released on a writ of habeas corpus. In fact, Weems was given a dressing-down by an assistant Crown attorney for having arrested Adams based on scanty evidence and without consulting the Crown's office. She took the rap and didn't say she had the approval of her superior, Henry.

Adams was immediately allowed to resume his trip to England. He'd arrived at the airport hours before his flight, so he was able to get back to Pearson with ample time to board.

Adams must have been in contact with his wife, because Adams's lawyer called Weems and said Adams vehemently denied resuming the affair with Barnes, although he admitted they had had a relationship before he married Phillips. He continued to insist that he had been with his mother on the night his wife was killed and that he had been by himself at the Greek restaurant on the night of Jackson's slaying.

"Let me read you this statement from my client," the lawyer said. "I quote: 'I demand that no one should approach Cathy Barnes about this matter. She is not involved in any way, and she is not to be brought into this. It would be unconscionable to put her in a completely unwarranted embarrassing situation. There is no reason to contact her, and no communication with her must be engaged in. These are my express wishes and I implore you to respect them and her privacy.' It's signed by Mr. Adams. I'll fax you a copy."

Weems then called Phillips and told her what her husband's lawyer had said. She read her the statement.

"Yes, I was mistaken," Phillips said.

"I'm sorry?"

"I was wrong about the Barnes woman. You don't need to talk to her. It's not necessary."

"I don't believe this. What about the private detective—why are you changing your mind like this? Did your husband threaten you?"

"Of course not. I made all that up about the detective. I was just—I was worried when you arrested him. I knew he hadn't done anything wrong, but I panicked. I have to make things right now."

She hung up.

****

After wrestling with the idea for some time, Weems decided she would go to England to speak to Barnes. What finally persuaded her was the vehemence of Adams's denial. He had been adamant that she shouldn't speak to Barnes, and it was obvious that he had gotten to his wife and pressured her to rescind her account of her husband's affair and his being with Barnes on the night of both murders. Weems also knew she needed some time away from Stark to consider where their relationship was going—if anywhere. And this was Weems's first murder case. She wanted it to be perfect, no loose ends. She wanted to be promoted to the Homicide squad permanently. If she didn't speak to

Barnes, it would always bother her. She didn't tell Henry what she was going to do. He would have ordered her not to go. She knew the department wouldn't let her take a vacation in the middle of a case, even though, with the latest developments, it was obvious the case was going nowhere, and the investigation was hardly pressing. She told Henry she was having problems with Stark, and could she take a long weekend, a Friday and a Monday, to chill out.

"Of course, you can," Henry said. "No problem."

Chapter Fifty-Seven

Stark drank himself close to a stupor at Carbo's. Morty tried to get him to go home. He told Morty to go fuck himself and petulantly went and sat at the bar beside another regular, Roberta Berkowski. She worked for an ad agency. Stark couldn't stand her. She had a big mouth and an empty head. They drank tequila, sucking a slice of lime and licking salt off their hands, getting the process out of order and laughing at each other. They went back to Stark's place and engaged in a rough imitation of love-making that fell far short of the real thing. Both of them passed out on the floor in front of the couch. In the morning, Stark awoke to Powder's rough tongue licking his eyelids. Roberta wasn't there, and he had no recollection of anything after the tequila. He turned the bathtub tap on to a drizzle and Powder sucked at it. The phone rang as Stark was urinating. He sprayed the lid and the floor.

"Hello."

"You sound awful."

"Ted?"

"Durham Regionals have found Cataldi's car at Frenchman's Bay, beside the yacht club."

Chapter Fifty-Eight

The travel agent had booked Weems into the Bankfield Hotel in Cottingley, a district in the northwest corner of Bradford, West Yorkshire. Weems's experience as a traveller was limited and had frequently been painful. She'd been to Florida as a child with her parents so many times she finally came to regard it as a penitential pilgrimage. Among other voyaging lowlights, she'd endured a hiking holiday in Algonquin Park with a detective-sergeant on the Arson Squad, an outdoorsy type who kept calling her a "softy" until the week of nature hell was mercifully cut short when he fell into a rock-strewn gully and broke his arm. She'd fallen in lust with a sweet-faced gigolo in Spain who had stolen her credit cards. She'd spent the best vacation in a week at the Sol Palmeras Hotel on Veradero Beach in Cuba, where she passed the time lying on a chaise longue dragged into the shade of the trees fringing the beach, drinking daiquiris and speaking to no one. She had divided most of the rest of her holidays between enduring weeks at a friend's parents' cottage in Muskoka, on Lake Joseph—the friend's marriage finally relieving her of that duty—and staying home. She had never been to England. She had never driven on the left-hand side of the road, and had never in her wildest imagination expected to find herself in a city called Bradford, which she had never heard of, except in the guise of a vegetable market town north of Toronto near the Holland Marsh. The travel agent, who had clearly never been to Bradford, either, had enthused about it, assured her that it was close to her final destination, Ilkley; that it was, she read from a brochure, "a central location within easy driving distance of the moors, close to Haworth, the home of the Brontës, and Leeds—which has excellent shopping." Besides, it being midsummer, most of the good hotels were booked. That made her nervous about what her accommodations were going to turn out to be, and her nervousness increased on the trip from the Bradford Interchange, as the train station was called, to the hotel.

Bradford had a dark and dismal aspect, gloomy, tired, worn at the edges. Everything stone, everything old. There was something else about it that made it feel pleasant, something Weems couldn't identify at first, and then she realized: the temperature was cool. She had the cab driver—who, incongruously, had the face of a south Asian, but a broad Yorkshire accent—take her for a spin around the downtown. The city centre was dominated by the town hall, a massive, gothic-looking stone building that loomed over a central square. She wondered apprehensively what sort of a place this Bankfield would be, but was pleasantly surprised to find a dramatic contrast with the city—a spacious, modern hotel, with bright, clean rooms and all the amenities.

The desk clerk helped her arrange for a rental car.

"Would you prefer a small car, luv?"

"I think I'd better, yes. These streets are so narrow."

"Yes, you'll be used to open spaces in America, won't you?"

"Canada."

"Oh, I'm sorry. I know you Canadians don't like to be confused with Americans. But I have to apologize. I'm afraid your accents sound the same to me."

"You people all sound like you're on *Coronation Street,*" Weems said, smiling.

"Oh, that's Lancashire, luv, the other side of the Pennines. This is Yorkshire, but the accent *is* similar. Do you get *Coronation Street* in Canada?"

"Mmm."

"Well I never."

"Lancashire? That's Manchester, isn't it? I landed there."

"It is, yes."

"That's only about thirty miles away, so I suppose that's why the accent is the same."

The clerk, a woman in her fifties with dimpled cheeks and the raw, ruddy complexion Weems identified as typically English, laughed.

"Oh, it might sound the same to you, luv, but it doesn't to us. In this country, the accent can change in five miles."

"I see. Tell me, where are all the refugees from? They look like they're from Afghanistan or somewhere like that."

"Refugees?"

"I noticed downtown a lot of dark-skinned people and many of them were in native dress." She leaned conspiratorially closer. "They look like they're wearing pyjamas."

"Oh, they're Moslems, luv. They live here. It's the way they dress. It's their religion, you know. Many don't, of course, but lots do. Most of them were born here, luv. Some people don't like the Asians." She lowered her voice. "They call them Pakis." She nodded. "Me, I say live and let live. They're not the ones involved in the crime, you know. That's against their religion. Well, I mean, there's a bad lot in every group, isn't there? But I say it's nearly always the whites that are causing trouble." She took on a shamefaced look. "You must have heard of our football hooligans. Louts, the lot of them. Course it's played up in the press. It's not a bit as bad as they make it out to be. England's a pretty fine place to live, if you ask me. And you're in one of the finest places in the country, right here. Oh, some people find Bradford a bit dreary. But all around the city is moorland, you know. The Dales are to the north, and there's York. It's magnificent. And Harrogate and Ripon and Bolton Abbey and on and on. And on the coast, there's Scarborough—"

"There's a Scarborough where I come from."

"Is that so—and Whitby and Robin Hood's Bay, and oh, well, you'll see. There's loads of pamphlets here on all the sights, Harewood House and Ripley Castle and everything. But you know—and I was born and bred in Bradford, on Toller Lane, so I am prejudiced—but the city itself is full of sights, too, the Cartwright Hall and Saltaire. Oh, I'm going on too much. You'll want to get this car business settled."

Chapter Fifty-Nine

The forensic people found nothing of a great deal of value in or around Cataldi's Cadillac, beyond two sets of footprints, one large and one tiny, on either side of the car, ending at a walkway that led toward the docking area. Stark met Henry there. All the relevant interviews had been completed. An inventory of the docked boats had been taken. None was missing.

"Of course not," Stark said. "They didn't need a boat. Cataldi picked them up in his."

"His yacht hasn't moved from its berth, Stark."

"But he knows how to run one, doesn't he?"

"What's your point?"

"He's borrowed somebody else's boat, some friend's, and picked up his two associates here, as arranged."

Henry shrugged.

"Well, what else?" Stark said, spreading his hands. "What else would they come here for? Somewhere you can pull a boat in in the middle of the night and take on a couple of passengers. Unless you think they're out there right now, swimming to Rochester?"

Stark's cell phone rang. It was Harris. Henry heard Stark say, "Waste of time, or not, stay with her, at least for today. If she doesn't move, we'll see if we can get a bug on her phone tomorrow." Stark then told Harris about the discovery of Cataldi's car. Before he disconnected, he gave a final admonition to continue the surveillance of Barbara Shaw. "And start that goddamned car of yours every once in a while. Otherwise, when you need it, it won't go—They what?—Oh, yeah? So what happened?—That's nice of them." His tone became sneering: "Yeah, okay, okay. So complain to your shop steward." He pressed the "end" button. "Jeez."

"What was that about?" Henry asked.

"I've got Harris watching the Shaw woman—"

"You told me that."

"He was beefing about it. Apparently the York Regionals got a complaint about this old beat-up yellow Volvo parked on this fancy residential street in Aurora, and they sent a scout car. In the end, they had an unmarked car come around and spell him, so he could go take a pee." Stark chuckled. "I guess it is kind of out in the open there, no bushes for him to duck behind. He was just complaining about what an inconsiderate bastard I am to leave him like that."

"What else is new?" Henry said and laughed.

Chapter Sixty

Weems spent the first hour with the car, a tiny Nissan Micra, driving around residential streets near the hotel, getting used to shifting with her left hand. Fortunately, her own car had a standard transmission, and an old boyfriend had taught her the technique of using the emergency brake to hold the car on hills. That proved invaluable here, since it was all hills. Weems discovered that, in stark contrast with the grid system in Ontario, the roads here suggested that the ancient English roadbuilders had had an aversion to straight lines. Streets would go one way only as long as they had to and at the first opportunity would veer off in another direction. The car-rental man had explained to her another of the adventures of the English road system, the roundabout. But nothing he'd said prepared her for her first encounter with one, on the way to Ilkley, and the horn-beeping and fist-shaking her hesitation had elicited.

The map the desk clerk had highlighted for her would take her on a route, the woman had said, that would pass the Cow and Calf.

"The what?"

"You've heard of *On Ilkley Moor Baht 'at*?"

"No, I'm afraid I haven't."

The desk clerk started to sing: "Wheear 'as ta bin sin ah saw thee, On Ilkla Moor baht 'at? Wheear 'as ta bin sin ah saw thee? Wheear 'as ta bin sin ah saw thee? On

Ilkla Moor baht 'at? On Ilkla Moor baht 'at? On Ilkla Moor baht 'at?

"I see," Weems said with a chuckle. "And what language is that?"

"Language? It's English—well, it's Yorkshire."

"What does it mean?"

"On Ilka Moor baht 'at? It means on Ilkley Moor without a hat. It's quite famous. Anyway, the Cow and Calf are on the edge of Ilkley Moor, overlooking the town of Ilkley. Not the pub. There's a pub there—serves nice meals, by the way. It's *called* the Cow and Calf. But across the road from it are two huge rocks, one's larger than the other, that's the Cow. The Calf is the smaller one. They're real landmarks."

"I'll keep an eye out for them."

"You'd better keep the other eye on the road. There'll be lots of traffic and the road is a bit narrow— by your standards. I've been to Canada. Oh, it's thirty years ago now, to Edmonton in Alberta. Do you know it? I have a cousin there."

"No, I've never been. Anyway, I'll be on the lookout for the Cow and Calf."

Weems did pull into the parking lot at the Cow and Calf pub, partly to take a longer look at the rocks, partly to scan the broad panorama of the valley below that the high moor afforded, but mostly to catch her breath from the terror-filled drive that getting there had been. The road *was* narrow and winding and crowded with cars, all of which wanted to go a great deal faster than she was willing to risk.

Finally, she ventured down into Ilkley, a quaint little town lined with expensive boutiques and trendy restaurants. She parked in a lot off the main street and inquired in a bookstore where she might find the address Brenda Phillips had given her. The house, on a steep street running up from the main avenue, which Weems had learned the English call the high street, was within walking distance. Her trek up the hill was to no avail. The house consisted of an upper and lower flat, what Weems would call a duplex, but there was no answer at the lower flat, in which Phillip's instructions had told her she'd find Cathy Barnes.

"They're away, luv," an elderly woman called down from atop the flight of stairs leading to the upper flat. "They've gone to Scarborough. They'll be back Saturday."

"Damn it," Weems muttered, then called out a *thank you* to the woman.

"May I tell them who called?" the woman asked.

"No, that's all right. I'll drop back."

"Very good."

Chapter Sixty-One

The morning after they found Cataldi's car, Stark was awakened by someone shaking him.

"Jesus Christ. What the hell?"

"It's a phone call for you."

Stark didn't recognize the voice of the female who had awakened him. As he climbed out of bed, he gave her a look of puzzlement through the fog of waking. It turned immediately into a stare of icy shock. The girl was wearing one of his shirts and little else, couldn't have weighed much more than eighty pounds and might have been as young as sixteen. Stark felt a sudden, sickened emptiness, as if someone had pulled a plug and everything had drained out of him. The girl handed him the phone. He could hear a voice on the other end shouting something. He put the phone to his ear slowly, watching the girl as she left the bedroom.

"I—I'm here," he said absently.

"Stark?" It was Ted Henry.

"What?"

"Is that you?"

"Yeah."

"It doesn't sound like you. Listen, get down here right away. Cataldi's here."

The name animated Stark.

"Cataldi? He's there? Where?"

"Here. Homicide."

"You're kidding. Where'd they find him?"

"Nobody found him. His lawyer called Peters. Just put your pants on and get down here, and who the hell was that who answered the phone? Tell me it was your niece."

"I'll be right there." Stark hung up. For a moment, he avoided thought. Finally, he slipped on a robe and went into the kitchen. The girl was sitting at the table, eating toast and jam. Beside her, slurping a bowl of Weems's Shreddies was a bare-chested boy. "What the hell," Stark said. "What the—what's going on here? Who the hell are you?"

"Take it easy, Mr. Stark," the girl said. "We found you outside last night, on the sidewalk. You must have fallen."

Stark realized for the first time that his right knee and right shoulder were sore.

"We brought you in here," the boy said. "We wanted to take you to the hospital, but you wouldn't let us. We were afraid you'd hit your head, so we stayed here. We took turns watching you for a while, but you seemed to be sleeping okay, so we went to bed in the other room. Oh, listen, I hope you don't mind us having the toast and cereal?"

"The—no—that's okay." Stark sighed. "Well, thank God for *that.*"

"Well, we couldn't leave you lying there, Mr. Stark," the girl said.

"How do know my name?"

"You don't recognize me?" The girl smiled.

Stark shook his head.

"Marie Kitto, from the fruit store across the road?"

Stark had a sudden light of recognition. He pointed

at the girl.

"Your father's the owner, Mike."

"That's right, and this is my husband, Kevin Murphy. We live over the store. My parents bought a house around the corner."

Stark thanked both of them. He realized that they were older than he'd thought, in their early twenties. He apologized for putting them to the trouble, said he must have tripped and hit his head, that he'd been working long hours lately, asked them whether they would mind not telling anyone about finding him like that, and they said they wouldn't, that it was Marie's father's turn to open the store that day, and when they went in, they'd say they spent the night at a friend's.

"Great. So—that's not my shirt, then?"

"It's Kevin's."

Stark nodded. He noticed that the big air-conditioner in the front window was going full blast and went over and put it on low.

"Look, I have to go," Stark said, coming back into the kitchen. He took a key from the top of the fridge. "Here's a spare key. I'll pick it up from you—some time. It's a dead-bolt lock. You have to lock it with the key. If you don't mind, would you turn the air-conditioner off before you leave? And thanks again."

Stark looked at the couple at his kitchen table. There was something odd about the scene, something he couldn't put his finger on. And then he realized: Powder was sitting on one of the kitchen chairs.

Chapter Sixty-Two

Weems spent the next two days sightseeing, mostly wandering through the filigree of roads around and over the thickly muscled landscape of the moors, captivated with the paradox of their bleakness and delicate intricacy, their grandeur and their intimacy. She was fascinated that within a few turns of a valley road, she felt as isolated as if she was in the middle of a vast wilderness, and yet in a straight line, if there had been any straight lines in Yorkshire, a few kilometres away she'd have passed through a crowded market town. She had read in a guidebook that in the mere 2,039 square kilometres or 787 square miles of West Yorkshire, lived 2,093,500 people. That's 1,027 persons per square kilometre, she had calculated—most of them, she had determined, and which she thought was an ideal situation, in the cities of Bradford and its adjacent larger sister, Leeds.

She had discovered that the desk clerk had been right. Bradford, despite its brooding face, was an interesting city, a living monument to the industrial revolution, built by and for the production of wool from the backs of the thousands of sheep that roamed over a landscape separated into large rectangles described by thousands of miles of dry stone walls that ran like grey stitching over the rippled fabric of the moors.

On the Saturday, she returned to Ilkley.

Cathy Barnes's greeting confused Weems. Barnes was puzzled to see her, but displayed no fear. And where Weems thought she would have to try both threats and pleading even to be able to put the questions to the woman, there was no resistance at all, no reluctance to answer, no attempt to keep her from entering the flat. In fact, Barnes greeted her warmly.

"This is a surprise. You're the detective, aren't you? I'm good at faces. You wonder how I know who you are. I saw you at the warehouse. The receptionist told me."

Weems was impressed.

"Yes, that's right. I'm Carol Weems."

"To what do we owe this honour? You must be the woman Mrs. Hancock said had called the other day when we were away in Scarborough."

"Who is it, Catherine?" A voice was heard through an open door. "Is it Mrs. Hobley from the church?"

"No, Mother, it's not. Come in, Carol." Barnes led her into a lounge at the front of the house, a very elderly feminine room in shades of mint green and pale yellow, with chintz-covered couches and chairs, embroidered footstools and every flat surface crowded with china and glass. One tall wood-and-glass case was filled with Royal Doulton figurines, while a massive Lladro arrangement of a woman and a dog occupied most of the top of a wider china cabinet against one wall. There were crocheted doilies everywhere, and each piece of furniture was draped with intricate white antimacassars. A thick, Persian carpet completed the effect. A frail-looking woman with thinning white hair sat in an armchair. In one hand, she had a book. The free hand, resting on the arm of the chair, trembled slightly. The woman's smile was as warm as her daughter's. Barnes introduced them:

"Mother, this is Carol Weems. She's from Canada."

"Oh, isn't that nice. How do you do, my dear."

"Carol, this is my mother, Margaret Hoggarth."

Weems took the woman's proffered hand. "Pleased to meet you, Mrs. Hoggarth. Lovely day today."

"It is, yes. I was just saying to Catherine that it looked like it was going to be nice, wasn't I, dear?"

"Yes, you were, Mother." Barnes raised her voice a notch when she spoke to the old woman.

The three exchanged small talk for a while, in which Weems, tactfully, said she was visiting in Bradford and had decided to call on Catherine, whom she knew in Toronto. Barnes said she would make some tea, and Weems said she would help her, but the old woman said they would never allow a guest to do such a thing. So Weems made the excuse that she needed to visit the washroom, which puzzled the woman until Barnes translated, "The toilet, Mother."

"Oh, I see. It's just at the end of the hall, my dear."

In the kitchen, Weems said to Barnes, "Of course, you know why I'm here?"

Barnes looked at her with her head tilted to one side. Finally, she said, "You mean you're not visiting someone in Bradford? No, of course you're not. Someone must have told you where I was. I must admit, I am rather puzzled. Why are you here?" She stopped smiling.

Weems sighed. "Let's go at it this way: why did *you* come here?"

Barnes shook her head. "Because my mother had a bad turn last week. I came as soon as I could. We have to sort out someone full time to stay with her. Mrs. Hancock, upstairs, looks in throughout the day, but she's seventy-seven herself. And now mother needs someone with her all the time."

"You're not here is to avoid answering questions about Graeme Adams?"

"I don't know what you're talking about."

The mother's voice called out.

"Catherine."

"Coming, Mother. Listen, it's time she had a lie-down, anyway. I'll get her into her room and then you can explain."

They returned to the lounge. The old woman was struggling to get out of the armchair.

"What are you doing?" Barnes said angrily.

"I have to use the toilet. I'm perfectly capable. I'm not an invalid."

"Mother, the woman from the agency is coming this afternoon. You remember?" She turned to Weems. "We thought you were she when you knocked."

"Of course I remember," the old woman said. "I'm not addle-brained, you know."

"Well, she's supposed to be here in half an hour. I suggest you have a lie-down, so you'll be fresh when she gets here. You'll be able to judge better then whether she's up to your standards."

"I *am* a bit tired. I'm sorry to leave you like this, Mrs. Bean. Perhaps we'll see you again before you go back to Canada."

"That would be nice," Weems said.

After a few moments, Barnes came back into the lounge, pushing a trolley with a silver tea service and a plate of petit fours and biscuits. She poured two cups of tea.

"Milk and sugar?"

"Just milk."

"All right, then. What is this about?"

Weems gave a long-suffering sigh.

"Okay. I have reason to believe you were with Graeme Adams on the night the two killings of which he is accused occurred. I have reason to believe that you can provide him with an alibi, but that you are reluctant to do that because it will endanger your marriage—"

"What?" Barnes appeared stunned.

Weems held up her hand to halt the interruption.

"But I want to assure you that if you sign an affidavit stating that you were, in fact, with Adams, it will never be made public, because the case against him simply won't be proceeded with—provided you can convince me that you are telling the truth."

"My God, what a mouthful!" Barnes sighed deeply. She leaned forward and cradled her face in her hands, her elbows on her knees. Finally she sat up straight and looked hard at Weems.

"What are these two murders you're talking about? I know he was questioned about his wife's killing. But what is this other murder?"

"His mother's boyfriend—ex-boyfriend. Adams has been charged with both killings."

"What? That's insane—Graeme? He couldn't kill a fly. And you say I'm supposed to have been with him? Where in the name of all that's holy did you get that ridiculous idea?"

Weems said nothing.

"I haven't seen Graeme for more than a year, not since he announced he was getting married."

"Mrs. Barnes, I can assure you, your husband will not be told anything about this. There's no reason to fear for your marriage."

"What are you talking about? I know there's no reason to fear for my marriage. It's perfectly sound."

"So, you never had an affair with Graeme Adams?"

Barnes shook her head.

"That was—I hadn't been married long, and I discovered something about Harold—I don't want to go into it. Anyway, Graeme came along. It was a particularly vulnerable time for me, and he is—Graeme can charm the skin off a snake. And he was—very adventurous. It happened. We had a fling, but then he announced he was getting married, and that was the end of it."

"Somebody told me the news he was getting married left you devastated."

Barnes glared at Weems.

"Devastated? Who told you that? It was that little tart in shipping, wasn't it? I saw you go outside with her." Barnes glanced toward the bedroom her mother was in, realizing she was almost shouting. She lowered her voice to a whispering hiss. "That's who you've been talking to, isn't it?"

Weems studied Cathy Barnes for a time. She shook one finger in the air. Barnes watched the wagging finger with a puzzled expression.

Weems said, "You've implied you have no more interest in Adams, and yet this outburst suggests otherwise."

Barnes made a face.

"Don't be ridiculous. I just don't like being gossiped about, especially not by my own employees."

"But they're not *your* employees, are they?" Weems leaned forward. "They're your husband's employees.

And the only way you have any authority over them is through him, isn't it? So if your marriage collapses, everything in your life collapses, too?"

"What *are* you talking about?"

"You weren't very successful in your life, were you? Failed in your education and so on. It wasn't until you met and married Harold Barnes that your life changed. He wasn't a very good lover, but you made up for that by having Graeme Adams on the side. Now, you have a rather perfect little lifestyle, but Graeme Adams is suddenly a threat to that. You could be asked to testify that he was with you on the night of both the murders. Adams was going to meet you over here. We arrested him at the airport with a ticket to Manchester."

"You're mad. He doesn't even know I'm here."

"Am I mad?"

"Completely insane. Look—" She breathed deeply, stared at the ceiling for a time, and finally said, "All right. I don't see it would make any difference now anyway. God, I hope I'm not going to be charged with hiding evidence or something. I *was* with Graeme on the night his wife was killed. Naturally, I didn't want my husband to know. As it turned out, I didn't have to say anything. His mother saw to that by saying that he was with her. If she wanted to protect him, so be it. I knew he hadn't killed her. He was with me all night. My husband was out of town. But I haven't been anywhere near him since he got married, except for necessary business contacts."

She looked defiantly at Weems, who returned a hard stare. Their eyes remained locked for some time.

Weems said: "Are you saying it's just a coincidence that you're here and Adams was on his way here, not just to England, but to this part of England? It was clear to us that he had decided to run, that he was trying to escape capture."

"I don't know anything about that, but I can tell you that Graeme comes to England several times a year. His firm are Canadian agents for a drugs firm in Manchester. So, he could have been coming over on legitimate business, but even if he were trying to escape—though God knows what from: he couldn't kill *anyone*—but *if* he were, then it's perfectly natural he would go somewhere where he had many contacts, isn't it?"

Weems was trying to look past the woman's confidently righteous expression, trying to detect a twitch or flutter, seeking some sign of dissimulation. But the woman's appearance was implacable. There wasn't even a display of the outrage guilty people often adopt to deflect accusations.

"The person who told me about you and Adams was his wife, Brenda Phillips," Weems said. Barnes's jaw dropped. She started to say something, but Weems cut her off. "She hired a private detective, who followed Graeme Adams to a hotel once a month, on a Tuesday night, when Adams was supposed to have been attending a meeting of the Masonic Lodge, of which, I understand, your husband is a member. Both murders were on nights that coincided with Masonic meetings. She said the detective followed you on two of those nights, and that you left your car at the Scarborough Town Centre and didn't return to it until several hours later. He didn't, as it turned out, see you at the hotel, but Brenda Phillips says that she went to the hotel on one occasion herself, and did see you there. So—what's your response to those allegations?"

291

Barnes gave a dry laugh.

"I'm flabbergasted."

"Do you deny seeing Adams once a month, on the nights he was supposed to be at a Masons meeting?"

"Yes, of course I do. He was *at* the bloody Mason's meetings. My husband is the Worshipful Master, whatever the hell that is—I think it's all mumbo-jumbo. We don't speak about it. It's rather a bone of contention between us. But Graeme *does* go to those meetings, quite regularly, in fact. Now, for all I know, and knowing Graeme, I wouldn't be the least bit surprised, he might well arrive late, after having spent a short, but energetic, stay in a hotel room. I'd be surprised if he restricted himself to once a month, but perhaps that's his regular piece. Might well be that Brenda was partly right, that it is one of the Masonic wives, but it certainly wasn't I."

"You told your husband that Adams had sexually harassed you—"

"Did she tell you that? Brenda?"

Weems nodded.

"My God. Listen—please. The story you have been telling me is Brenda Phillips' story. The story she told you about me is the story of *her* life. She came from a well-off background. It was *she* who failed at everything she tried. *She* dropped out of law school. *She* was a great disappointment to her family, who let her know it loudly and often. *Her* only success came in marrying Jack Phillips. She was working as a clerk in the office and he took a shine to her. God knows why. You've seen her. You have to admit, she's not exactly attractive. And she still works as a glorified clerk, despite her title. Graeme runs the company. She's not capable of it. Listen—I have a degree in business from the London School of

Economics. Do you hear what I'm saying? I *do* run the business. In fact, I turned it from a struggling local company into a national concern. We have branches across the country. When Graeme met Brenda, he knew he'd found his meal ticket, the bastard. Do you know why I scowled when he announced he was going to marry Brenda? Because the son of a bitch had told me he was marrying her for her money, but he said that that didn't have to change anything between us.

"When I told him to go to hell, he continued to phone me, even wrote me letters, love letters. After the second one, I wrote 'return to sender' on the envelope. No doubt poor Brenda opened it. Graeme really spun her a line. He was the first man who wasn't a troglodyte, or a desperate old crone, like Jack, who had ever shown any interest in her, and that can't be surprising to you. Graeme and Brenda were having an affair at the same time he and I were together. I'm convinced that mother of his encouraged it. Of course, both Graeme and Brenda had spouses that stood in the way of their eternal bliss, until they both conveniently shuffled off their mortal coils. Jack died of heart failure. Poor what's her name, Karen Sheltoe, was raped and murdered.

"Funny thing about Graeme," Barnes went on. "Even though he's the next thing to a gigolo, he's ordered around by women. All the women in his life control him. I'm sure it comes from being brought up by a dominant mother. Even in his first marriage, it was like that. Karen was some kind of amateur prostitute in Australia, but he was still smitten by her, and when she told him she was pregnant and that he had to marry her, he did. He—he obeyed her. You know what he told me? He told me that if he hadn't married her, his mother would never have forgiven him, that he had been brought up always to do the right thing. Isn't that something? And he obeys Brenda the same way. He's about the only one in the company who does. Otherwise, the place would collapse around them. Of course, he's terrified she'll kick him out."

"But not so terrified he wouldn't try to continue his affair with you?"

"You still don't believe me? Okay. First of all, you have to realize that Brenda is paranoid. All right? Now, this detective, you say, followed me to the Scarborough Town Centre on nights that my husband was at his Masonic meetings. Well, that's true. I do leave my car there. In fact, if he'd followed me *every* Tuesday night, he'd have seen me go through the same routine. I leave my car there and take the LRT to the Lawrence East station where a friend who's very timid—it all has to do with underground parking lots—anyway, she picks me up in her car and we drive to our garden club meeting. If I had to prove this, I could, of course. So, as you see, I can't offer Graeme an alibi for the murder of—who did you say it was? His mother's boyfriend?"

"Ex-boyfriend."

"Why would he want to—"

"I can't say—"

"No, I suppose not, but I can't believe Graeme is capable of such a thing. And you've certainly made a mistake charging him with the murder of his wife. What made you suddenly discount the alibi his mother provided him?"

"I can't tell you that."

"No. Well—and Brenda told you Graeme and I were having an affair? She must have told you where I was, did she?"

Weems nodded.

"It's paranoid delusion. The poor woman is not quite right. On the other hand, Graeme is bizarre. He's got a sexual appetite like—well, to be crude about it, he's led around by two things, is Graeme: women and his penis. Yes, he does what the women in his life tell him to do. The funny thing is, he and Brenda got together when *I* sent him to Hermes because they kept screwing up our deliveries."

"Your deliveries?"

"Yes. They're one of the shipping companies we use. Anyway, I sent him over there to straighten out their record-keeping, *her* record-keeping. After Jack died, the place went to pieces. That woman is an idiot."

"Let me ask you this," Weems said. "If what you say *is* true, do you think Brenda Phillips asked me to come here because she truly believed you and Graeme were having an affair, and that you'd be able to alibi him and that she was willing to put up with the humiliation of that being confirmed because she loves him so much, or needs him so much, or do you think she might have had some other reason?"

"I can't imagine what that would be. Paranoiacs love it, you know, when they can find confirmation of their delusions, when they can increase the intensity of their self-punishment. It may sound strange, but if I had agreed that I had been having a relationship with Graeme, and that had saved him, she would have been punishing herself by saving him. It's all part of the self-hatred and bitterness, do you see?"

"You know, Graeme Adams denied the two of you were having an affair, and *demanded* that no one should question you about it. And now—I believe I know why he didn't want me to."

"Why is that?"

"I'd rather not say."

Chapter Sixty-Three

Cataldi was sitting in Peters's office, leaning with relaxed confidence on one elbow, his leg crossed over the opposite knee, a dark green boat shoe swinging pendulously, as if keeping time to some unheard beat. He was wearing a tapered, dark-chocolate shirt and baggy, pleated, cream-coloured slacks with large cuffs. He had changed his hairstyle: the part was in the middle, and the hair slicked back. He looked like a playboy from a bygone era, and his casual elegance gave him a certain psychological advantage over Peters's proper pinstripe, Henry's yellowish-green double-breasted and Stark's rumpled, tan Buffalo-bought linen. Only Cataldi's lawyer's forest-green, perfectly fitting Italian silk suit and flowered Versace tie offered Cataldi competition, and since they were both on the same side, the effect was to give their team a positional advantage before the game had even begun.

Peters addressed Stark.

"Sal—Mr. Cataldi has been explaining that he returned home this morning from a friend's place to discover his car was missing. He immediately called nine-one-one and reported it stolen."

Stark opened his mouth to say something, but Peters silenced him with a raised hand.

"His cousin wasn't at home, but he wasn't surprised by that, because the young man had said he was going off on a trip with a friend—to Las Vegas." Peters paused deliberately, raising his eyebrows, to indicate his disapproval of the destination. "Of course, we've told Mr. Cataldi what has happened, and how we suspect his young cousin, Tony, and his employee, Doreen, are involved in the jewel robbery and the killings of Constable Beavis and Howard Stokes."

"A terrible shock," Cataldi said, turning to look at Stark with an expression of scandalized disbelief that Stark saw as mocking defiance.

"And you had nothing to do with it?" Stark said, eliciting a murderous glare from Peters.

"Detective Stark!"

Stark raised his hand as Peters had done, met by a look of increased outrage from the inspector. When Stark had arrived, the lawyer had been introduced to him by Peters as "Mr. Cataldi's esteemed legal counsel, Jeffrey Marcus."

The lawyer spoke: "Mr. Cataldi has no knowledge of and certainly no involvement in the alleged crimes." He sounded bored.

"The crimes alleged," Stark muttered under his breath.

"I'm sorry?" the lawyer said.

Stark shook his head. He said, "Let me ask you this, Cataldi, why would you come here with your lawyer if you're not involved in a crime, but are merely reporting one? It's a pretty expensive way to do things, wouldn't you say, to hire a lawyer just to say you've been robbed?" He looked at Peters and then quickly away from his disapproving glare.

The lawyer started to respond, but Peters spoke over him: "A person in Mr. Cataldi's position is used to dealing in legal matters with the presence of his counsel. I should have thought that a man with your liberal track record, Stark, would appreciate that."

This time, it was Henry who gave Stark a loaded look.

"So, where have you been?" Stark asked Cataldi.

"At a friend's."

"Where's that? And who's that?"

"Bronte. And his name is Calvin James. I can, of course, give you his address and phone number. He will tell you I went there the night before last. And I remained in his abode, a most delightfully situated condominium overlooking the lake, until early this a.m."

"This Mr.—uh, James, did you say?—does he have a boat, Mr. Cataldi?"

The lawyer leaned forward to speak, but Cataldi pushed him back.

"He may. It's entirely possible. Why do you ask?"

"Because it looks very much like your cousin Tony and his Faye Dunaway friend, Laureen—"

"Doreen," Henry corrected.

"—Doreen, were picked up by a boat at the Frenchman's Bay Yacht Club. That's why I ask."

"Now, wait a minute. My car was found at the yacht club. Okay. You think Tony and Doreen drove it there. Okay. Why would they have to have been picked up in a boat? Did you ever think they might have stolen one? After their previous escapades, I don't think they'd have the least compunction about sailing off in somebody else's water craft, do you?"

Ted Henry spoke: "They checked, the yacht club people checked. All the boats were accounted for."

"What kind of boats? You're talking about power

boats, big boats, sailing boats?"

Henry shrugged.

"I suppose so. What are you saying?"

"What about a rowboat? Tony doesn't know *how* to run a power boat, and certainly not a sailing vessel. But he's clearly physically equipped to use a rowboat."

"Christ," said Stark with a dry chuckle. "What do you think, he's going to row to Lewiston?"

"Of course not, but it would be a good way to put you off his track, wouldn't it? He takes a rowboat out, and you think he must be rowing to a larger vessel, but he merely lands farther along the coast."

As if at a signal, Peters picked up his phone and pressed a button on the keypad. "Marilyn, call the Frenchman's Bay Yacht Club, and ask them whether they're missing any rowboats." He hung up the phone and smiled at Peters and his lawyer.

"All right," Peters said, "I imagine everyone could use a coffee, eh? And some doughnuts?" He called Marilyn again and ordered the coffee and doughnuts. "Nothing yet? Oh, you haven't got through to them yet. Okay. Keep trying." He hung up. "She hasn't got through to the yacht club people yet."

They sat there awkwardly while Peters and Cataldi talked about golf. Stark stared at the ceiling. He desperately wanted to get Cataldi alone in an interview room, and yet he doubted that that would produce any results. The fact was he had no direct evidence to link Cataldi to the robbery and the murders and he was beginning to doubt he ever would. The lawyer was making notes, and Henry leafed through a copy of the *Christian Digest* he had found on the corner of Peters's desk. Finally, Marilyn came in with the coffee and doughnuts and word from the yacht club.

"A dinghy is missing from one of the sailing boats," she said, and Peters gave Cataldi a beaming look of support.

Chapter Sixty-Four

"Did you have a nice long weekend?" Ted Henry asked Weems.

"Very productive, thanks, Ted."

"Well I have some news for you."

"And I have some news for you. Can I go first?"

Henry shrugged.

"Yeah, sure. Go ahead. What's your news?"

"Well, as I said, it was productive. I went to England to see a woman called Cathy Barnes. You probably don't remember the name, but you'll see it in the reports on the case."

"You what? You went to England? Over the weekend?"

"I went to see this woman because Brenda Phillips, Graeme Adams' wife, told me that this Barnes woman was having an affair with her husband and that Barnes could provide him with an alibi for the night of the murders."

"Listen—"

"This Barnes woman—well, it turns out she *can* give him one for the night his wife was killed, but she *can't* give him one for the night of the Jackson murder."

"Explain."

"It seems, he was with Cathy Barnes, and not with his mother—we knew that he wasn't with the mother from Jackson's diary—but Barnes said Adams was with

302

her all night when Karen Sheltoe was killed."

"And you believe this?"

"Yes, I do believe it. He didn't kill his wife, but he could have killed Jackson. Except—"

"Except what?"

Weems gave a little shake of her head.

"I'll tell you that in a minute. First, though, you realize what this means about the Sheltoe murder?"

Henry sighed. "What?"

"Well, the mother gave Adams the alibi. He was the obvious suspect. The rape thing was such a phoney. But if you know the background of the case, of the people involved, and keeping in mind the way the Sheltoe woman was killed, that she was drugged before she was strangled. Okay? And if you know that Jane Adams, the mother, is a nurse, and therefore, has access to the kind of dope the killer used, you see, then you come to the conclusion that it was the *mother* who was providing an alibi for *herself.* And the reason Graeme Adams didn't want me to go to England to talk with Barnes—he didn't, by the way: he had his lawyer read me a statement in which he practically ordered me not to go interview Barnes. The reason was that he knew that she wouldn't blow his alibi, but rather his mother's alibi. *She* killed Karen Sheltoe. *She* had the motive; *she* had the opportunity; and *she* had the means."

"Jesus," Henry said. He took a deep breath and let it out. "Okay, so you don't like him for the Sheltoe killing, but the Jackson murder—"

"I think the wife did it."

"What?" Henry shook his head as if a bug had just landed on his nose.

"No kidding. I think the whole thing revolves

around Graeme Adams, from one side and another. You have the mother who was ambitious for him, and you have the wife, the very, very ugly wife, who wanted to keep him. Okay, now—"

"Carol—"

"Let me finish. It was Brenda Phillips who asked me to go to England to interview the Barnes woman. She told me about the alleged affair. She wanted me to talk to the woman. She insisted on it. Why? Incidentally, she changed her mind after her husband was released. I think he threatened her. He probably told her he'd dump her for Barnes if she didn't change her story. I'm sure she's pretty desperate to hang on to him."

Henry sighed in an expression of confusion.

"Okay, so why was she insistent that I talk to Barnes? Well, of course, she knew the Barnes woman wouldn't give her husband an alibi for the Jackson murder, but by asking me to go there, it took attention away from her, see what I mean? The evidence that we found against Adams, the belt and the dope, was in the house where Brenda Phillips lived, too. All that evidence could equally point to her. I think she did it."

"Are you finished now?"

"Mmm."

"Okay. Nice theory, but—while you were traipsing around England, we did a little police work over here, a little nuts-and-bolts police work, and we found a couple of things."

"Like what?"

"Like Adams' phone records. It seems that—well, you remember that Jackson got a phone call at that bar on Kingston Road and that that's what led him to leave and—" Henry waved a hand in circles indicating the progress of events "— that's what led him to meet somebody and that somebody did him in, right?"

Weems nodded impatiently.

"Okay—so, we discovered that a phone call was made from the Adams residence at the relevant time to that self-same bar on Kingston Road. Now, unless Adams was making a reservation for a Greek meal—he did say he was in a Greek joint—but anyway, there you are. Adams called Jackson and arranged to see him."

"My God, Ted: the barmaid said she couldn't tell whether it was a man or a woman on the phone. It could just as easily have been—Brenda Phillips."

"Wait. I haven't finished. All this is academic, and I will tell you why."

"Please do."

"You know the diaries, the daily diaries that Jackson kept?"

"Of course."

"Well, there was one missing from the bunch that were gathered up in his apartment. We found it when I sent the boys and girls to take the place apart. Under Jackson's mattress was the latest diary. I have a copy here of everything that was in it. There's a lot of nonsense, but then, here's the relevant part—on the day he was killed, and I quote: '9:20 p.m. I got a call at 9 p.m., twenty minutes ago, at Ed's. I let the lads think it was a woman. Why not keep them guessing? It was Graeme Adams. He said he wants to speak to me about something important. It has to be about Jane. I'm sure it's good news. I could tell from his voice. We arranged to meet at my apartment. I'm here waiting for him now. I have my fingers crossed.'"

Chapter Sixty-Five

"Ken Coulson is going to have his people watch both Cataldi and Shaw. He has a personal axe to grind." Stark and Harris were sitting at the counter in Holtzman's. Stark had forgone the pleasures of the smoking room, Harris having refused to sit in there.

"Beavis?"

Stark nodded. "Nobody in our squad will play tag with that sonofabitch Cataldi after what Peters said. Unbelievable."

"He really threatened suspension?"

"That's right. He issued a directive stating that Cataldi is no longer a suspect and should no longer be subject to surveillance or questioning or any form of investigation, even indirect. And he could make it stick, since anybody going after Cataldi in any way would be ignoring a direct order. He warned Hold-up as well, and since Homicide is leading the case, Hold-up is under the same constraint. However, because it was their guy that got offed, Coulson said the hell with Peters. They're going to ignore his order. So, we'll work with them."

"Beavis's funeral's tomorrow. Are you going?"

"Yeah, if only to keep Coulson on side. I hate those things."

"Do you know the statistics on cop deaths in this country? Relative to firemen or industrial accidents, for example—"

Stark held his hand a few inches in front of Harris's mouth.

"What?"

"Don't go on, Noel. I'm not in the mood for one of your liberal diatribes."

"Well, you're not one of *them.*"

"No, I'm not. But I'm not one of you liberals, either." Stark and Harris looked over their shoulders in response to the blast of traffic sounds from Queen Street that meant the door had been opened. Sid was in the smoking room, deciding what horses to bet that day, and enjoying a Cuban cigar, a gift from his cousin. He'd asked Stark and Harris to let him know if a customer came in. "And don't serve them yourself," he admonished Stark. "The last time you did that, I was twenty bucks short when I went to balance. Cops, you can't trust them," he had said to Harris, who had nodded.

Two uniformed officers came into the deli, a boyish-looking male, Homer Wingate, and a tall Chinese-Canadian female, Joyce Lee, whose broad shoulders and swagger had had Stark once suspecting she was what he called, rustically, "one of them there funny girls," until she'd borrowed his apartment for an afternoon romp with a trucker called Sergio, who eventually skipped town owing Joyce a good deal of money.

"Well, well, here they are, the dynamic duo. Why the long faces, folks?"

"The officer who got killed, Sarge," Homer said. "It's hit us both very hard."

Harris looked away.

Stark said, "Yeah, well, it hit us all pretty hard, too, didn't it, Noel? Do you know Noel? This is Noel Harris, from 32 Division. He's helping me with my enquiries."

They shook hands with Harris. "Would you two like a coffee? I'd get it for you myself, only Sid won't let me go behind the counter. He doesn't trust me."

"No, thanks, we don't want anything," Joyce Lee said. "We saw your car, and we wondered how you were doing with the Beavis killing? You're on that, aren't you?"

"Actually, we're investigating more than just the officer's death," Noel put in. "Saul Rabinovitch and Howard Stokes are dead as well."

"Thanks, Noel," Stark said. "Yeah, we're on it. In fact, we know who did it. All we have to do is find them. Unfortunately, I don't think we're going to do that. We also know who *the brains* is behind the killings, but I think our chances of nailing him are slim to none."

"Why's that?" Homer asked.

"Because he takes care of business," Stark said. "The two people who could link him to the thing are, without doubt, stomping about on the bottom of Lake Ontario in pairs of Mafia, i.e., concrete, overshoes."

"You think Cataldi *killed* them?" Harris said.

"Of course he did. That Doreen woman is clearly a lunatic. She's suffering from the Bonnie syndrome."

"The what?" said Joyce.

"As in Bonnie and Clyde. Funny, isn't it, Clyde used to be a hipster's name, could be either a hip guy or a dork, depending on how you used it—"

"You're digressing," Harris said.

"Eh? Well, anyway, this latter-day Bonnie and Clyde lost it, began shooting everybody in sight." He nodded at Homer, "Including poor Beavis. None of this could have been part of the plan, and I don't think our pal Cataldi—"

"Cataldi?" Lee said. "Wasn't that the guy in that murder of yours a couple of years ago?"

"It's the same guy. He keeps coming up like a bad penny."

"You're kidding?" Homer said.

"No, I'm not kidding, and believe me, he is not going to have taken too kindly to these two becoming Murder Incorporated, particularly not when it involved killing a cop, which would normally mean all stops being pulled out in the search for the killers."

Homer and Joyce looked at each other. "What do you mean, 'normally'?" Lee asked.

"I mean, a certain inspector in the Homicide Unit has put Salvatore Cataldi off limits."

"Why?" Lee asked.

"Yeah, that's what I want to know," Harris added. "Are these two lovers or something?"

"That, I doubt very much. Although they do appear to be very close. No, I have no idea why."

"They've issued us pictures of the two killers," Homer said. "We've got the unofficial-official word to roust everybody we know. All leaves have been cancelled."

"Yeah, well, I'm afraid all that's going to be a waste of time."

"There's a jewel robbery involved, eh?" Joyce said. "They've told us to shake up every antique store, jewellery shop, every fence that we know."

"You're not going to find that stuff around here, believe me," Stark said.

Homer looked thoughtful.

"If your inspector is hampering the investigation into a cop killer, don't you think you should go over his head?"

"Well, I could go to Nuttall, but—"

"Who's that?" Harris asked. "Deputy-Chief Nuttall?"

"It doesn't matter," Stark said. "The fact is we could wale Cataldi with rubber hoses and we'd be no farther ahead. Anyway, we have our ways," he said to Wingate and Lee. "Cataldi is in hand, but keep that to yourselves, all right?"

The two nodded. Joyce said, "Listen, what about this link between him and your inspector, what's his name?"

"Peters."

"Would you like us to do a little research on that?"

Stark gave Harris a look.

"Well—sure, as long as you're extremely discreet."

"Of course." Lee nodded.

"Go ahead. See what you can find out."

"Good," Lee said. "Okay, Homer, let's go. We've got work to do."

After they'd gone, Stark's phone rang. It was Bernie Hardcastle from the Pawn Squad.

"Stark?"

"Guilty."

"Somebody may be, after I've told you what I've found."

"Found about what?"

"About some estate jewellery?"

"You've found it?"

"Well—not exactly. Let's get together."

"Okay. Where we met before?"

"The place with the smoking room, sure."

"I'll wait for you here. Is that all right?"

"I'll be there in fifteen minutes."

Chapter Sixty-Six

"Well, it goes along with what everybody has said about Adams and his relationship with his mother. My God, it's sad. You realize what it means? You see how sick this is?"

Henry had begun looking through Cathy Barnes's statement. Weems had taken it down longhand, the letters large and rounded, the lines straight, spacing even, easy to read, while Barnes's signature at the bottom was indecipherable. "You really believe this woman, do you?"

"Yes. I didn't tell her about Jackson's diary. And if she was lying, then why wouldn't she say he was with her on the night of Jackson's murder? By the way, Sarge, I gave my word to Cathy Barnes that what she told me was only to be used to persuade the Crown—to persuade you, really, to drop the Sheltoe case against Adams. If you're going to proceed with it anyway, you won't be interested in her statement, but you'll have to let the defence know that they should talk to Barnes."

"Mmm. The thing that bothers me is—I mean, it all fits together neatly if Graeme Adams is the killer in both cases—but if he didn't kill his wife, then why was the M.O. in the second killing almost a carbon copy of the first one? It only drew our attention to the connection and pointed the finger at Adams. Why would he do that? If he'd just bashed Jackson over the head or something, taken his wallet, made it look like a mugging, whatever, we might never have linked Jackson to the Adams—" Henry gave a short laugh. "Hey, I just realized, it's the Adams Family."

"Yeah, right. I think we should bring a forensic shrink in on this one."

"You know what they charge?"

"Look. This is how sick this is. Adams *wanted* to get caught, he wanted to get blamed for the first killing, too. I told you how adamant he was that I shouldn't interview Cathy Barnes. I was thinking afterwards that that was because his alibi that he was with his mother was also *her* alibi, and he didn't want us to suspect her, but now I realize it was because he knew Barnes could give him a *real* alibi. He doesn't want an alibi. He wants to sacrifice himself to protect his mother. That's why he killed Jackson, because he wasn't sure just how much the old boyfriend knew about his mother's involvement in Sheltoe's murder. And he left every clue he could without making it too obvious, the pentobarbital in the bathroom, the belt hanging in plain view in his closet. Trying to leave the country. You know, Jane Adams must hate men so much they're nothing but tools to her, even her own son."

Chapter Sixty-Seven

Stark and Hardcastle commandeered the smoking room once again, and once again Sid Holtzman went away with a long-suffering sigh. Stark lit a Gauloises and waited while Hardcastle fiddled and faddled with his pipe, an enormous, rich-orange meerschaum.

"That's quite an instrument."

"Meerschaum," Hardcastle said. "It's one of my favourites. My wife bought it for me in Syria. She's in the travel business, so she can bring me back good English tobacco and pipes from all over the world."

"That's nice, Bernie. So tell me, what have you got?"

"Provenance."

"I'm sorry?"

"Well, one of the big things we try to check in cases of stolen property is provenance. We want to find out where the stuff came from, discover its history, see whether it's genuine, that sort of thing."

"And, you found what?"

"The names Stokes gave—sad thing about that Officer Beavis, wasn't it?—"

"Very sad."

"—the names he gave us, where he bought the estate jewellery?"

"What about them?"

"Well, they didn't really jive."

"Jibe."

Hardcastle tamped his pipe bowl with a blackened thumb and relit it. Stark rolled his eyes.

"So, as I was saying, there were three parties involved, okay?"

"Three, yes."

"Right. One was a lawyer in Forest Hill, the other was a doctor on Teddington Park. They're both old money, old families. But the third one, he's an accountant in North York, nice big house and all, but new money. No background. Grew up in the Junction." He puffed on his pipe and looked at Stark.

"I'm sorry, is this supposed to mean something to me?"

"Where do you get estate jewellery from?"

Stark raised his hands. "Bernie, I don't want to play a quiz here."

"Well, you can buy estate jewellery, a piece at a time, no problem. But to have a whole collection of it, you either lay out a lot of money because you're a collector, or because you want to speculate on it—you're going to buy and sell it—or you inherit it."

"Bernie, do you want another coffee?"

"That would be nice, sure."

Stark slid open the door and shouted, "More coffee, Sid."

Holtzman brought a carafe. He had an unlit cigar clenched in his teeth. "Here," he said, putting the carafe on the table, "enjoy yourselves." He slid the door shut.

"Okay, you inherit and so on."

"This one fellow, the accountant, he had nobody to inherit from, so he couldn't have got it that way, could he?"

"I guess not, no."

"No, he couldn't. Now, the other two could have. But because all three were given as the source of the pieces, I checked into all of them."

"And?"

"The first thing I did was check with some contacts of mine in the insurance business, investigators. We work together quite closely, as you can imagine."

"I can, yes."

"Now, if you have, say, a million dollars' worth of estate jewellery, you're going to have it insured, are you not?"

"I imagine you are."

"They didn't. None of them did. But, interestingly enough, they did have riders on their policies, two of them, anyway, the lawyer and the doctor, for specific items of jewellery. I've got the information here somewhere." He fished into his jacket pocket.

"Bernie. That's okay."

"The point is, why would they insure certain pieces, none of which were included in the list Stokes gave us, incidentally, and not the stuff they sold to him, mmm?"

Stark shook his head. "I don't know."

"Because the stuff didn't exist, that's why."

"What?"

"There was no estate jewellery. There was no jewel robbery. It didn't happen. It was a scam."

"Jesus. But why would these three—"

"Yeah, I know what you're going to ask. Here's what I did. I looked for something in common that they might have had, something that tied them together."

Stark nodded impatiently.

"Now, that took a little while. I put a couple of

people on it. We asked discreet questions here and there, talked to some people we know, that sort of thing, and what we found out was that all three of these yobos like to gamble. In fact, they like it a little too much, a lot too much. And then we got a lucky break."

"Which was?"

"The lawyer takes his car into a neighbourhood garage for repairs. One of our people took his car in right after he'd been in there, chatted up the garage guy. The lawyer drives a Jag; our guy admired the car, asked this and that, and one thing led to another. The garage guy said the lawyer once took him to a weekly card game that the lawyer goes to, every Wednesday. The garage guy said it was too rich for his blood. On the Wednesday night, we followed the lawyer to a restaurant in Etobicoke. The guy goes up the back stairs, the fire escape, goes through a whole knick-knock, knick-knock, secret knock sort of thing and in he goes, and then, bingo, don't the other two come along, the accountant and the doctor and up they go and go through the same routine." Hardcastle gave a self-satisfied grin.

"Okay," Stark said. "They play cards together."

"Remember that guy you told me about, the one who owns the building where the robbery went down?"

"Cataldi."

"Guess who owns the restaurant?"

"Cataldi?"

"Bingo."

Chapter Sixty-Eight

At Rabinovitch's apartment building, the caretaker greeted Stark like an old friend.

"How's it going, buddy? I see you brought a pal with you this time. How are you, buddy? Is he treatin' you all right?" he said to Harris. "So, what can I do for you?"

"I want to have another look in Mr. Rabinovitch's apartment," Stark said.

"Well, yer welcome to it, buddy." The caretaker chuckled. "But yer not going to find much."

"What do you mean?"

"Jeeziz, b'y, I thought the Royal Newfoundland Constabulary was bad enough fer gettin' things muddled, but you fellas is no better, it appears."

"What are you talking about?"

"I'm talkin' about the fact that the apartment is cleaned right out. There's nuthin' left but the furniture—and the dirty dishes, and I imagine—" He put his hand up to his mouth conspiratorially and whispered, "a few critters." He laughed. "Yer fellas came over here the other day and took everythin'."

****

Stark called Ted Henry, who told him that he'd sent Ident to the apartment, and they'd removed all the papers and photographs.

"What the hell for?"

"A policeman has been killed, Stark—and you'd

317

better be at the funeral."

****

Stark and Harris sorted through the boxes of material from the apartment for two hours.

"I don't think we're going to find anything," Harris said. "The old man was hardly the organized type. He didn't exactly have much need for a daily agenda. There's not even a notebook in here. Anything he wrote down is in the margins of the *Racing Form.*"

"Keep looking."

Harris groaned. Twenty minutes later, he said, "Hey."

"What?"

"What are the names of those three guys?"

Stark looked in his notebook.

"George Witherspoon, Tim Quinn and Hal O'Connor."

"That's it."

"That's it, what?"

"The last name, Hal O'Connor, on a scrap of paper. It was tucked in the back of his Israeli passport. I went through it once already, but I didn't see it."

"Does it have his phone number?"

"No, not a phone number. It just says, 'Hal O'Connor, seven hundred dollars.'"

"Well, what do you know." Stark smiled. "It's a marker from a card game. I thought so. Quite a chummy a little group. Let's go pick up this trio."

"Do you think we should?"

"Why not?"

"Well, with people like this, the threat of embarrassment might be more effective than anything else. Maybe we should be discreet, but ominous."

"You know, Noel, I think you might just be right. Come on."

Weems brought Jane Adams in for questioning. It proved to be the waste of time Weems had imagined it would be. The woman was even colder than Weems had already seen her to be. The only emotions she displayed were indignation, bitterness and resentment. The clincher was what she said when Weems told her that they wouldn't be prosecuting her son for the murder of Karen Sheltoe because they knew that *she* was the killer. There wasn't a flicker of change in the woman's expression.

"You have absolutely no evidence against me, or you would have charged me." She gave a small sigh of resignation, a sigh ending a chapter in her life, a sigh that drew a line and turned a page. "My son is a fool."

****

Weems delayed writing her final report in the hope that something would emerge that would allow them to charge Jane Adams with the murder of her daughter-in-law. In fact, Weems didn't give up trying to come up with a theory that would point to the woman's having been the killer of poor Jim Jackson, too, despite the evidence against Graeme Adams—especially his belt's being a perfect match with the marks on the slain man's throat. Weems clung to the hope that Graeme eventually would face the fact that his mother had abandoned him and that then he would retract his story of having been with her on the night of Sheltoe's killing. But the detective, in time, came to realize that without physical evidence to link Jane Adams to the murder, the shattering of the woman's alibi would mean nothing. The final piece of the picture that would convict Graeme was provided by the witness who had seen Jim Jackson leave with someone on the night Jackson was killed. The man unhesitatingly picked Graeme Adams out of a lineup.

The background notes for the Crown attorney that Weems included with her report left no doubt that she saw Graeme Adams as a victim:

"Graeme Adams was the creation of his mother in more than the biological sense. While this writer had little opportunity to observe Jane Adams and her son at any length, comments made by others who knew them strongly suggested that Jane Adams had controlled and manipulated Graeme throughout his life. Remarks the woman made to me indicated a resentment and bitterness that may have sprung from her having been abandoned by her husband and left to raise Graeme.

"The biggest act of rebellion he displayed was in going to Australia where he met and married a prostitute, Karen Sheltoe. He returned to Canada and was once again subject to the control of his mother, who, it appears, pushed him into an affair with Brenda Phillips, whom she saw as providing an opportunity for Graeme to gain financial security and position. Phillips's husband's death made her an attractive prospect in Jane Adams's eyes.

"It is this writer's belief that Jane Adams murdered Karen Sheltoe, because Sheltoe stood in the way of Graeme's potential marriage to Brenda Phillips, not only because she was his wife, but also because she could implicate Graeme in a sex charge involving a young male prostitute in Sydney, Australia, and because she could reveal that she herself had been a prostitute when Graeme had married her. Such revelations might well have led Brenda Phillips to reject Graeme. It has not been possible to gather hard evidence that would enable a charge to be laid against Jane Adams in Sheltoe's death. The alibi she provided for her son on the night of Sheltoe's killing also gave her an alibi, and even though I determined that Graeme was in the company of one Cathy Barnes on the night of the murder, I could find no other evidence to connect Jane Adams with the crime.

"Graeme Adams' relationship with Cathy Barnes appears to have been just one of a series of sexual affairs in which he was involved. Brenda Phillips seems to have been aware of these encounters. She believes her husband had resumed the affair with Cathy Barnes, and she hired a private investigator to follow them, and even had an investigation carried out in England concerning Cathy Barnes' links there. Cathy Barnes denies the resumption of the affair and provided a credible account of her actions as they pertained to Brenda Phillips' suspicions. This writer, acting on her own and during the course of a leave, travelled to England after Brenda Phillips had insisted that Cathy Barnes could provide Graeme Adams with an alibi for the time of Jim Jackson's murder. I am now of the opinion that Brenda Phillips had reason to believe that her husband had killed Jackson, and that her insistence that Barnes could alibi Graeme was an act of desperation. I think she honestly believed that they had been together on the night of the murder, although that belief may well have been based on an irrational assessment of the circumstances.

"The Karen Sheltoe murder investigation was reopened as a result of a series of anonymous phone calls alleging that Graeme Adams was the killer. Adams was informed that new information had come to light, but the nature of that information was never disclosed. I believe

Graeme Adams knew that Jim Jackson was aware that Adams and his mother were not together on the night of the Sheltoe killing and could throw suspicion on Jane Adams. He probably knew that Jackson had tried to resume his relationship with Jane Adams and had been rebuffed, and he may have feared that, in the course of his involvement with Jane Adams, Jackson had acquired other evidence implicating his mother. I believe Graeme Adams killed Jim Jackson to protect his mother because he knew, or strongly suspected, that his mother had murdered Karen Sheltoe. It is my view that it is not beyond the realm of possibility that Jane Adams either directly ordered her son to kill Jackson or planted the seed that led to the murder.

"Jim Jackson's phone records show no calls made to police headquarters. He could, of course, have made the calls from a pay phone, but I now believe that Jim Jackson was not the person who made the calls. An interview I conducted at Graeme Adams' former place of employment led me to believe that employees there were of the opinion that he was responsible for Karen Sheltoe's death. It's possible one of those employees made the calls to headquarters. I don't believe that if Jim Jackson had made the calls, which would have indicated that he suspected Adams, he would have been eager to have a private meeting with Adams, as his diary suggested he was. In light of those conclusions, it appears Jim Jackson's killing was pointless."

****

Weems picked up the phone to call Stark. Her hand hesitated over the number pad. She punched in the first three digits, paused, and hung up.

Chapter Sixty-Nine

Hal O'Connor, the doctor, turned out to be a dermatologist with an office in a tower at St. Clair and Yonge. The waiting room contained nothing that suggested the function of the enterprise. There were no before-and-after posters of blemished faces; there was no rack of medical literature, no sign warning that anyone without a valid health card would have to pay. The walls were arrayed with art, various prints and original drawings, whose creators Stark didn't know, and one large painting he recognized as a Christopher Pratt. The furniture was all Italian provincial, and looked uncomfortable. In the lobby of the building, Stark had said to Harris, "You'd better do the talking. You look more like you're liable to get acne than I."

"I don't know. Isn't there something called 'senile acne'?"

There was nothing utilitarian about the waiting room: the receptionist's desk, an ornate table, matched the décor. The receptionist didn't. There was nothing Italian and certainly nothing provincial about her. Her hair was blonde and trailed down her back. She had a build like a Victoria's Secret model, squeezed into a short, tight dress, and her complexion was, appropriately, perfect. Stark had written a note in the lobby. He handed it to her.

"If you take this in to Dr. O'Connor, I believe he

will see us. It's confidential, and quite urgent." He smiled. The young woman gave him a supercilious look, but did as he had asked, and he was pleased that when she returned, she asked them to take a seat. Stark sat directly opposite her. Harris shook his head and sat by the door. It was Harris who saw the phone-pad light go on.

"Does he have anybody with him?" he asked quickly.

"No, but—"

Harris moved first, but Stark was right behind him. The receptionist's mouth opened, but they were through the door before she could protest.

"Put the phone down now," Harris said. Without waiting for the doctor to comply, he took the receiver from his hand and replaced it on its base.

"What are you doing?" the doctor said. His tone was frightened rather than indignant. The receptionist had followed them into the room.

"I'll call security," she said.

The doctor sighed, shook his head.

"Never mind, Sherry. It's all right. Just—I'll call you if I need you."

Stark waited for her to close the door behind her, and then turned to face O'Connor.

"You'd better sit down," the doctor said.

"You know why we're here?" Stark said.

O'Connor looked from one to the other, transparently trying to decide whether to play dumb. His choice became apparent when his expression changed to a poor attempt at puzzlement.

"I have no idea," he said finally, defiantly folding his arms, as if suddenly realizing that this was *his* office, after all, that his family had influence, that he was a doctor and these were merely stupid cops.

Stark smiled sardonically. He was enjoying himself. He was tempted to light a cigarette and blow smoke in the doctor's haughty face.

"Of course you do," Stark said, in a caricature of a patronizing tone. "You must have been shitting yourself for the past few days, doctor."

"Pardon me?"

"Look, let's cut the crap, shall we? We know you agreed to say you sold the jewellery to Howard Stokes. We also know there was no jewellery: it didn't exist. Okay? And now you can relax, because we have no interest in charging you, Dr. O'Connor. On the other hand, if you don't co-operate, we could change our mind and get a conviction without a problem on a charge of conspiracy to commit fraud. Do you understand?"

The doctor opened his mouth to utter a denial, and then closed it again, and nodded in resignation.

"Good. Okay, let's hear it."

There *was* a weekly card game above the restaurant, the doctor told them. Yes, O'Connor said, in answer to Stark's question, Tim Quinn and George Witherspoon and he were regulars. They didn't always play together; there were a couple of tables, occasionally even three, and, of course, they weren't *always* there. But Howard Stokes and Saul Rabinovitch *were* always there, at least they had been there whenever he was there.

All five of them were in serious financial difficulty, he confided, entirely as a result of their affection for games of chance. They all had drawing rights at the house, and all had stretched those rights to the limit and sometimes beyond. The house encouraged this practice, since it took a healthy percentage of every pot, and, as with all skilled gamblers, the fortunes of the five at the table would wax and wane over time, and the house collected on their winnings and their losings, as well as levying an exorbitant rate of interest on their draws.

Occasionally, when losing streaks became prolonged, each of them would have to dispose of assets to pay down his draw.

"That Pratt in the waiting room, for instance, the painting?" O'Connor said. He had become matter-of-fact in his dissertation now, relaxed with the relief of confession, a phenomenon Stark had witnessed many times before. "It's now the property of one Martin Tammer. I sold it to him and leased it back. And Stokes—" He paused in reflection and sighed. "Poor bastard. He, uh—" He gave a weak chuckle. "He replaced all the diamonds in one of his wife's necklaces with fakes. The only one of us who didn't have anything to sell was old Rabinovitch." He shook his head. "They didn't let him draw much, and he was a canny player, so he didn't often lose a bundle. When he did, Stokes would bail him out. Anyway, what happened was we, all five, got really, really stretched at the same time, and then Stokes came up with this proposal. What he said was, 'I'll give each of you a hundred grand, and all you have to do is put a list of jewellery pieces I'll give you in a safe place, and if anybody asks you about them, you say you sold me the pieces for the prices I'll quote you. I'll give you receipts. You don't have to worry about a thing. It's just for tax reasons, that's all.'" O'Connor sighed. "We knew it was stupid, but we were pretty desperate, and Tim Quinn, he's a lawyer—he said, 'Yeah, but if Revenue Canada comes calling on us, we'll be nailed.'

'No-no,' Stokes said, 'not if you lost money on the sale. I'll provide you with an appraisal, not by me, but by a colleague, who fortunately died six years ago, and the amount you sell the pieces to me for will be less than the appraised value.' 'That's fine,' Quinn said, 'but when we acquired the jewellery, presumably we're supposed to have inherited it—' 'No,' Stokes said, 'you bought it from the guy who did the appraisal. You see, happily for us, he had some legal problems and right after he sold you the pieces, he departed for Argentina, where, God rest his soul, he died two months later, I'm told with a smile on his face in the arms of a very lovely senorita.' Yeah, I know," O'Connor said, "how do I remember every detail of what he said? It's as clear in my mind as if it just happened." He raised his palms. "Anyway, that's it, that's the whole thing. And the killings and the robbery and all that—we had *nothing* to do with that, *nothing.* I swear."

Stark and Harris looked at each other.

"That's it?" Stark said, gritting his teeth. O'Connor gave a puzzled nod. "What about Salvatore Cataldi?"

"Who?"

"Cataldi, the guy who runs the card room?"

O'Connor pursed his lips.

"The guy who runs the card room is Owen Nicholls. I don't think that's his real name. He's Slavic-looking. He owns the restaurant. I suppose you're going to raid the place, or something."

"Jesus."

"You never had any dealings with anybody else?" Harris said. "Stokes was the only one you talked to about the jewellery scam?"

"Well, it wasn't really a scam as far as we were

told—"

"Never mind that," Stark said. "You're absolutely sure that Stokes was the only one involved in this thing?"

"Absolutely. Look, my neck's on the line here. If there was anybody else, I'd tell you. I swear."

Chapter Seventy

"What about the other two?" Homer Wingate asked Stark. Stark, Harris, Homer and Joyce Lee were sitting on a bench in Kew Beach Park, having come from the funeral of Constable Beavis. Stark was smoking, watching the young mothers in their shorts pushing strollers. Harris was intent on an ant dragging a leaf many times its size.

"Same story with them," Stark said, "And I asked them some loaded questions. I suggested that O'Connor had told me certain things that he hadn't, but they still didn't bite. I told them O'Connor had fingered Cataldi, but their reactions to that were so puzzled they had to be telling the truth."

"How do you know O'Connor didn't call them as soon as you left him?" Joyce Lee asked.

Stark smiled.

"Because we took O'Connor with us, and Noel stayed with him in the car. And then we took Quinn along as well. No, there's no question in my mind that they've never met nor heard of Cataldi. Stokes made the proposal and all the arrangements. Of course, I'm just as positive that the whole scam was Cataldi's idea. It's not something a guy like Stokes would come up with on his own. I think he owed Cataldi a lot of money, and on top of that, guys like Cataldi are always looking for an angle, a way to suck more out of a situation. It's like the way

329

the Indians would kill an animal for the meat, but then would use every single part of it, skin, bones and guts, for something. Anyway, I think he's beaten us again. The only people who could have testified against him are dead."

"At least he won't be making any money on the deal," Lee said.

"You know something. I'll bet you he does. In fact, I'm telling you he will."

"How could he?" Harris asked. "That guy from the Pawn Squad called the insurance company. They won't pay off now."

"You're forgetting Cataldi's girlfriend, Barbara."

"She can't collect the insurance, either. What are you talking about?"

"She'll get Howard's life insurance, which will be a bundle. She's got the house, her furs and jewellery. She might even collect on her uncle's insurance."

Lee said, "Do you think she's going to share that with Cataldi?"

"You just don't know the way these guys work. A debt's a debt. He's going to collect from her and he's going to get a hell of a lot more, too. He won't come out of this without making a profit. She'll be very sorry that she got involved with him, believe me. When Cataldi's finished with her, Barbara Shaw will be lucky if she's not walking a beat on Wellesley Street."

"Well, we have something to tell you about Mr. Cataldi," Homer said.

"What?" Stark asked.

Homer opened his mouth to answer, but it was Joyce Lee who spoke: "We found out why your Inspector Peters is chummy with him."

"Oh, yeah?"

"Yeah. It appears that the inspector is some sort of religious fundamentalist."

"Yeah, Peters is a holy roller, all right. What about it?"

"Strange bedfellows," Lee said. "There's some sort of inter-faith council of right-to-life types, and guess who else is part of this group, along with Peters?"

"You're not telling me Cataldi is—"

"That's exactly what we're telling you," Lee said smugly. "What do you think about that?"

"I think it's disgusting," Harris said. "That son of a bitch."

"Jeez, don't be equivocal, Noel," Stark said.

"When I was a little boy, my Aunt Grace—oh she was such a lovely person. My father's sister. The family were Baptists and very strict. She got pregnant. She wasn't married. In those days, there was no abortion on demand. Anyway, she went to some quack who butchered her. She went home and bled to death. And now here's this—I can't imagine anything more hypocritical."

"That's a lesson in life, Noel," Stark said. "But, you know, it's not good for a cop to have a personal axe to grind when it comes to catching villains."

"You're one to talk. You've got a personal crusade against Cataldi yourself."

"No, no, you're mistaken. The only thing personal about it is I don't like to be beaten. It bugs me that this bastard has got away with it again. I don't care whether he's an anti-abortionist or not. But he killed people on my turf—"

"Please," Noel said, "with all due respect, spare us,

will you."

Chapter Seventy-One

Ted Henry told Stark about Weems's success. When he didn't get the response he'd expected, Henry asked Stark whether there was some problem between him and Weems.

"Everything's fine, Ted, back the way it's meant to be."

Stark spent the evening in Carbo's.

"You look good tonight, Harold, not so uptight," Morty said. "You resolve your romantic difficulties?"

"Oh yes. All resolved. All straightened out, Morty."

"Ah, so when's the big day?"

"The big day is now, Morty." Stark slid off his stool and went and sat beside the piano player.

"What's this? You're not my type."

"Yeah, that's too bad. Let's sing some songs."

"What do you want to sing?"

"How about my theme song?"

"'One More for the Road'?"

"'Here's that Rainy Day'."

****

Later, Stark chatted up a statuesque redhead in a yellow, flowered, off-the-shoulder sundress. He was intrigued with the freckles on her back. Morty called him over with a finger wag.

"What?"

"I thought you and Carol—"

333

"You thought wrong. What did you want?"

"The roller-coaster life of Harry Stark."

"You mind if I—"

"You're wasting your time with that one."

"Why?"

"She only plays with girls."

****

Stark was glad it had turned out to be an early night at Carbo's when the phone woke him at six-thirty the next morning. It was Noel Harris. What he said in response to Stark's groggy hello hit Stark like a jolt of electricity and shocked him into wakefulness.

"I'll be right there."

****

Salvatore Cataldi was slumped in a heap on the floor of the entrance hall of his condominium suite like a marionette with its strings gone slack.

"How'd he do it?" Stark asked Harris. The apartment was filled with the usual assortment of crime-scene people, most of whose presence in this instance was unnecessary.

"The coroner hasn't arrived yet, but it looks like Cataldi was strangled, and I think his neck is broken."

Harris inclined his head down the hall to his left. Stark took another look at the body, shook his head, and he and Harris went in the direction Harris had indicated.

"Who's that crying?" Stark asked.

"Barbara Shaw."

"God."

"She was hysterical. The paramedics are with her. They're going to take her to Sunnybrook."

They went down a short hallway and entered a vast room that was more like a hall in a museum than the living space in a private home. It was crammed with antiques, the walls crowded with fine art, lush Persian carpets scattered over a coral-coloured ceramic tile floor. Sitting erect and incongruous on a chintz-covered, straight-backed, ornately scrolled chair was Tony Cataldi.

Chapter Seventy-Two

Transcript of an interview with Antonio Carlo Guiseppe Cataldi, taped at Toronto Police Service headquarters, Homicide Unit.

Date of birth: May 13, 1970. Age: 27. Place of birth: Toronto, Ontario.

Present at the interview: Detective-Sergeant Ted Henry, Homicide; Detective Harry Stark, Homicide; Police Constable Noel Harris, 32 Division.

Stark—I've read you your rights, and you understand them? Don't nod, Tony. You have to speak for the tape recorder?

Cataldi—Okay.

Stark—And you understand that you have the right to consult with a lawyer and have one present at this interview?

Cataldi—I'm going to tell you everything. I don't need no lawyer for that. I want to get this over with.

Stark—Tell us about it.

Cataldi—The whole idea was Uncle Sal's.

Stark—What's Uncle Sal's full name?

Cataldi—Salvatore Cataldi.

Stark—You live with him?

Cataldi—Yes.

Stark—Go ahead, Tony.

Cataldi—Well, like I say, it was Uncle Sal's idea. Howard Stokes owed Uncle Sal a lot of money. They knew each other from the card game.

Stark—What card game is that?

Cataldi—The card game above Uncle Sal's restaurant.

Stark—Your Uncle Sal owns the restaurant?

Cataldi—Yeah.

Stark—Okay, go on.

Cataldi—Well, Uncle Sal owed money, too.

Stark—Let me ask you something, Tony. Do you always call him Uncle Sal? I mean, he's your cousin, isn't he, and he's, what, maybe ten years older than you?

Cataldi—He's not that much older, but I've always called him Uncle Sal.

Stark—Sal owed money?

Cataldi—Yeah, he has a company that manages buildings, and I guess a lot of them aren't doing too good, so the people that own them are way behind on paying Uncle Sal, and he owns a big piece of land.

Stark—Is that the land where Constable Beavis was killed, and Howard Stokes?

Cataldi—Yeah, that's it. Him and Stokes owned that land. There's some problem with the zoning, or whatever it is. Uncle Sal was supposed to sell the land to builders to put up houses, but there's something wrong with it, something to do with a river. There's all this water underneath it, or something. Anyways, it's going to cost a lot of money to fix it right so he can sell it. So about a year ago, Uncle Sal and Howard and the old guy, Saul Rabinovitch, they went to Las Vegas and Howard hit a lucky streak and won a lot of money, so Uncle Sal made him buy some of the property, you know, like made him come in with him on the deal.

Stark—Made him?

Cataldi—Uncle Sal don't look tough, but when he says you gotta do something, you'd better do it.

Henry—To your personal knowledge, can you say that Uncle Sal, Salvatore Cataldi, is involved in organized crime?

Cataldi—You mean the Outfit?

Henry—Yeah.

Cataldi—Uncle Sal's not a made guy or anything.

Henry—But is he involved in organized crime?

Cataldi—I don't know anything about that.

Stark—So he made Stokes come in with him on the property. What else?

Cataldi—Well, they owed taxes on the land, and Uncle Sal was making Howard pay the taxes, but meantime, Howard kept losing money at cards and on the horses and stuff, and he didn't have the money to pay, so Uncle Sal got this idea about faking a jewel robbery, because he said Howard's family had been in the jewellery business for a long time, and they had never tried to pull a fast one, so the insurance companies wouldn't say 'boo' if he reported a robbery.

Harris—This was all Salvatore Cataldi's idea?

Cataldi—Oh, yeah. But Howard said he couldn't pretend to have jewels that he just didn't have. He said the insurance companies would never believe that he had them. so Uncle Sal said, yeah, but if you pretend you bought the jewels from somebody, then they'd believe it. Uncle Sal said they wouldn't just make it up out of the air. He said Howard would be able to show that he bought the jewels. 'How am I going to do that?' Howard said. Well, Uncle Sal had it all figured out already, because there were these three guys that played cards regular that owed a lot of money to Uncle Sal, and he said they would pretend that they bought the jewels from them. I don't know everything about it. Uncle Sal didn't exactly tell me everything. I just heard because I was always around, you know? So then they were going to pay the old man.

Stark—Saul Rabinovitch?

Cataldi—Yeah. They were going to pay him ten thousand, because he owed Uncle Sal, too. So they were going to pay him ten grand to pretend he'd been robbed. Like, he was a whatever-you-call-it for Howard.

Stark—A courier.

Cataldi—Right. So I stole this car, and I parked it behind the bank, and then I stole these licence plates to put on the van.

Stark—Why would you do that?

Cataldi—That was Doreen's idea.

Stark—Doreen Holmes?

Cataldi—Yeah, poor Doreen. That bastard.

Stark—Do you want to stop for a while, Tony?

Cataldi—No, I'll be okay.

Harris—How's your head? You okay?

Cataldi—I'm fine.

Stark—It was Doreen's idea to steal the licence plates.

Cataldi—Yeah, because we parked the van behind the building on Eglinton that Uncle Sal's company manages. And Doreen said, if we leave the van in the lane, somebody's going to see it and the licence plate and then they would know that we had been in the building, and they'd want to know why Saul was in there. I drove around for a while until I found a car I could get at without being seen and I lifted the plates and put them on the van. We were supposed to go up to the vacant office. It was just supposed to be me. Uncle Sal didn't know nothing about Doreen. I didn't think there was any reason she shouldn't come along. She wanted to, and it wasn't going to be dangerous or anything. I mean it wasn't like there was going to be a real robbery or anything.

Henry—You want a drink of water, or anything?

Cataldi—No, thanks.

Stark—So you were going to go upstairs in the office building, to the empty office. Why? What were you going to do there?

Cataldi—Well, it was different things. First, the old man said he wouldn't do it unless he got his money up front. We had the ten grand with us to pay him. But he was supposed to be—well, let me do this in order, 'cause I don't want to get mixed up. I was supposed to bop him a couple of times so he'd look roughed up. And then we'd go behind the bank and Saul was supposed to lie down on the ground until somebody found him. Sal figured we couldn't do that, like bashing him and stuff, because we were just faking it. he figured we couldn't do it out behind the bank because somebody might see us, so we went to the office where we could do it and nobody would see, you understand? But, okay, here's the money bit. Because Saul said he wouldn't do it without getting the money up front, so Sal says, 'What happens if they find this ten grand on him? Where's he goin' to put ten thousand dollars? In his shorts?' he got the idea we could go to the empty office and stash the money behind the cold air register. I brought along this screwdriver to do that, and I unfastened the screws and everything, and then the old fart says ten grand ain't enough. He wants more. He wants fifty grand for the job. And I says we ain't got no fifty grand, and he says, call Sal and have him come down here right now and bring me fifty grand, or I ain't goin' through with it. Then Doreen—Shit, I should never have let her come along.

Stark—But you did. What happened with Doreen?

Harris—The subject has paused with his head in his hands.

Stark—You all right?

Cataldi—Yeah.

Stark—Okay. Doreen what?

Cataldi—Doreen goes nuts. She says, 'You fucking old bastard, you're lucky to be getting anything. You owe all this fucking money and Sal's giving you the chance to get clear and now you want more. Fuck you. Then Rabinovitch pulls out this gun and points it at Doreen, and she says, 'The fucking old prick brought a gun. Go ahead, shoot, you cocksucker.' And he did, and she fell down. And I had the screwdriver in my hand, and I drove it right into his chest. I'm sorry. I didn't mean to do it. I mean, I didn't mean to kill him. I had to, I mean I did have to. He had the gun. I mean, he shot Doreen. I thought he'd killed her, what else could I do? The stupid bastard.

Stark—You stabbed him in the chest with the screwdriver?

Cataldi—What else could I do? He had a gun. He shot Doreen.

Stark—How long had you and Doreen been going together?

Cataldi—About four months, I guess.

Stark—You met her because she worked for your uncle, and you saw her at the, whatever the name of that place is on Main Street?

Cataldi—Courtland, yeah. She was different, you know. We hit it off right away. Usually I have trouble with chicks, I mean girls. Doreen was no chick. I mean I got lots of experience with chicks. Christ, most of them are whores, you know. But Doreen was different. She was a real person. Goddamn, goddamn. Poor Doreen.

Stark—Yeah, poor Doreen. Can we get back to what happened?

Cataldi—Well, that was it, pretty well. Doreen wasn't badly hurt. I ripped the sleeve of her blouse open and I could see that he had just winged her. I mean, it hadn't even, you know, gone into the arm or anything, just barely touched the outside. I knew we could fix it up ourselves. She wouldn't have to go to the hospital or nothing.

Stark—So you left Rabinovitch there and you took off?

Cataldi—Yeah, I ran down to the van ahead of Doreen and got it started, and then she came down right behind me and jumped in and we drove away, and then we didn't know what to do, and Doreen said, 'What about that property your uncle owns? There's a big barn there. We can hide the van in there.' So we went there."

Stark—And then what?

Cataldi—And then nothing. It was over. We just went out about our business. Uncle Sal told us to act like everything was normal.

Stark—Okay, let's jump to the barn. What happened when the shooting went down?

Cataldi—It was Doreen.

Stark—What do you mean?

Cataldi—Well, she went sort of crazy, you know, after she got shot and that, and she called Howard. It was after Uncle Sal said he was afraid Howard was starting to chicken out, and Doreen called Howard and told him he should straighten out and all that, and then she told Uncle Sal that she thought Howard was going to tell the cops. Uncle Sal said we should get our asses up to the barn and he'd bring Howard there. So we went there, and Uncle Sal came and we waited for Howard, and he came and he was really scared, and he said he wanted to get out because we had killed Saul and that, and that it wasn't supposed to be like that and everything, and he said the insurance company was starting to make trouble and asking questions, and he figured they wouldn't pay up,and then Uncle Sal just pulled out this gun. I didn't know he had it. I didn't know he was going to do it. I swear I didn't. And he shot Howard. He didn't say nothing. He just shot him. I was over in the corner taking a leak, but I was looking over my shoulder, and I saw him shoot. And then this guy suddenly came through the side door with a gun and started yelling, 'Police.' He was kind of crouched over and he didn't see me and I just kicked him in the head and he went down. And then we heard this car on the gravel coming in, and Uncle Sal ran outside and the next thing I hear these shots and I go outside and Uncle Sal is standing beside this car and he opens the door, and this guy falls out.

Stark—Constable Beavis.

Cataldi—I didn't know his name then, but yeah, that's who it was.

Henry—Christ.

Cataldi—Uncle Sal told us to go to the yacht club at Frenchman's Bay. He told us how to get there, and he said he'd pick us up in a boat later. He said we should wait until it was dark and then steal a boat. He said we'd be able to find one hanging from the back of a big boat and we should take it and row out into the lake and hold up a light. I went to a Canadian Tire and got a big flashlight. And he said he'd pick us up and take us over to the States and give us some money and we should stay there until he told us to come back.

Stark—What happened then?

Cataldi—We did what he said, and we found this rubber boat on the back of a big sailing boat, and I got it off and we rowed out into the lake. We sat out there for hours, but finally he came along and we got on to this boat and Uncle Sal told me to tie the rubber boat to the back of the big boat, and we went out into the lake for a while and Uncle Sal was all smiles and pleasant and everything, and then all of a sudden, he pointed the gun at us and he said, 'Okay, this is far enough.' And he made us get into the little boat, and then he unfastened the rope and then he shot Doreen.

Stark—We can stop.

Cataldi—No. I want to finish. Doreen just flew into the water. I mean, I knew she was dead. He hit her right in the forehead. I could see the hole. God.

Stark—He didn't shoot you?

Cataldi—He didn't get a chance because I jumped back into the boat, but I couldn't get a good grip on the railing and he smashed me on the head with the gun, and I fell into the water. He didn't knock me out or nothing, but I knew he'd shoot me if I came back up, so I ducked under the water and swam over to the other side of the boat, and then I pulled myself along right to the back where I could hide under this part that came out like over my head. I had to watch it because it was near the propellor. Uncle Sal waited for a long time and then I guess he figured I'd drowned because then he pumped a bunch of shots into the rubber boat, and it sank, and then he started up the motor and drove away. But there was some life jackets in the rubber boat, and they floated, of course. I grabbed on to about three of them and held on to them and then I put one on me and kept the other two, and I floated in the water for a while, and then I took the other two and I strapped them around my legs, so it was like a raft or something. I could see it bright where the shore was, and I started to swim toward it. I couldn't go fast because of the lifejackets, and I'm not a very good swimmer, so it took me pretty well all night to get to the shore. And then I got behind some bushes and took my clothes off to dry, and then I slept. And I knew the cops would be looking for me, so I had to keep out of sight. Mostly I walked through fields and ravines and stuff. I went behind factories and along railroad tracks. I wasn't sure where I was a lot of the time, but I knew what direction to go in, and I knew what I was going to do when I got there. And when I got to Uncle Sal's place, I opened the door with the key I had, and sneaked in. I could hear him in the bedroom with that Shaw broad, and I waited, and when Uncle Sal came out, I, grabbed him in a hold and lifted him up off the floor. He ain't very big, and I shook him a couple of times, and I held him there until he stopped kicking and went limp, and then I listened for his heart, but there was nothing, so I knew he was dead. The Shaw broad came out and started screaming, and I told her to shut the fuck up, and pushed her back into the bedroom and closed the door, and then I called 911 because—I figured it was over.

Chapter Seventy-Three

The day had begun on a high for Stark, but the elation had faded with surprising quickness. And he felt empty. He fought to stifle the thought that what was missing was someone to share his success with, that solitary pleasure is thin gruel. He didn't even have colleagues to celebrate with. No one in the squad liked him, and in any case, he wouldn't have wanted to spend the evening trading ribald insults. He suggested a drink to Henry and Harris, but Henry had a family barbecue to go to. "Sorry, Stark," he said, with a quick wave as he hurried out of the office, almost as if he found the suggestion frightening. And while Noel held a grudging admiration for Stark, spending the night in a bar with him while Stark drank himself into oblivion didn't hold much attraction. He said, "love to, but a friend has tickets to a play I've been wanting to see for a long time."

"Oh. Say hello to Ernie for me, will you, and, do me a favour, ask him who was right and who was wrong about Salvatore Cataldi."

Harris was stunned.

"You know about—"

"You and Ernie? Yeah, Morty let it slip."

"Morty?"

"Morty Greenwood at Carbo's."

"Carbo's? Oh, the piano player." Harris nodded. He had a slight frown of concern. "That's right, you took me in there the time I was working with you on that other case. But how did he know?"

"Ernie told him, I guess."

"Ernie? What was he doing in there? He only likes country and western."

"He likes only country and western, or country and western only."

"Jesus. What was Ernie—"

"They know each other. Uh, don't worry about it. Ernie drops in when he's in the neighbourhood in case I'm in there. And, believe me, you don't have to worry about Ernie and me."

"No—"

"Noel, don't worry about it. I've got my own problems. Go see your play. And by the way, I guess Henry told you, eh? You're on the squad. You're still a constable, though, of course."

"Sorry. I did mean to thank you. He told me what you said."

"Forget it. Maybe I'll see you tomorrow."

"Not before Monday, I hope."

"What's today?"

"Friday."

****

Stark had made a deliberate effort not to think about Carol Weems. He'd had lots of practice with such things in the past, so he had been mostly successful in shutting out any top-of-the-mind thoughts of her. But her image remained stubbornly just below the surface, and it would be some time before his unconscious mind would be able to lose it, to bury it among the other scattered dusty clutter of his memories. Her image rose to the surface now, and he told himself he should call her, tried to persuade himself that it was likely that being away from him had made Weems realize she belonged with him. But Stark's unconscious, fettered as it was with his ego, was less able to accept the possibility of rejection than was his conscious mind, with its ability to rationalize. so he didn't call.

When he got back to his apartment, Stark found a key on the kitchen table. Weems's key.

"Carol?" he called out. There was no answer. He went into the bedroom. The closet door was open. Powder was curled in the middle of the bed. Several hangers in the closet hung empty.

Stark slumped on the bed. Powder got up and rubbed her head against his arm.

"Bitch," Stark said through his tears.

A word about the author…

John Worsley Simpson was a journalist--reporter and editor—for many years with major-market newspapers in Canada and the U.K. and with Bloomberg News. He has several published novels, including Undercut, which was runner-up to Kathy Reichs' Deja Dead as best first novel for 1997 in the Crime Writers of Canada Arthur Ellis Awards. Other traditionally published novels include Counterpoint, Shadowmen and A Debt of Death. Another novel, Death Never Says Goodbye, was published through Amazon and Create Space. He is married and lives in Barrie, Ontario, Canada with his wife, Colleen, and dog Measha.

http://www.johnworsleysimpson.info

Thank you for purchasing
this publication of The Wild Rose Press, Inc.

For questions or more information
contact us at
info@thewildrosepress.com.

The Wild Rose Press, Inc.
www.thewildrosepress.com